Acclaim for Robert Ferrigno's

THE WAKE-UP

"An ultra-hip comic caper. . . . The dialogue crackles and the plot moves briskly. . . . Ferrigno keeps the plot sharp and taut as *The Wake-Up* moves to its unpredictable ending."
—*Ft. Lauderdale Sun-Sentinel*

"Fast-moving, hard-driving. . . . Ferrigno's punchy prose will hold you through the night." —*Los Angeles Times*

"Devilishly delightful. . . . *The Wake-Up* is relentless, brutal and scary. . . . [Ferrigno] delivers his usual gut-punches, electroshocks and sweaty palms." —*Seattle Post-Intelligencer*

"*The Wake-Up* is a white-knuckled roller-coaster ride . . . a morality tale where the good and bad guys die in equal numbers. . . . Ferrigno can limn a character in a few sentences." —*The Oregonian*

"Ferrigno has not only transcended the crime novel, he's blown it up. . . . *The Wake-Up* is . . . a streamlined package of dynamite with a compelling plot, a strong moral sense and genuine affection for all of his characters. A rare combination in any type of fiction these days."
—*Las Vegas Review-Journal*

"*The Wake-Up* has it all. Death, drugs, destruction, surfing and pretty girls. *The Wake-Up* is guaranteed to be a pleasant afternoon."
—*Contra Costa Times*

"Ferrigno packs plenty of action into his story, taking the reader on a roller-coaster ride through the high income and lowlife of Southern California, with enough twists and turns and sudden drops to demand Dramamine." —*Seattle Weekly*

Robert Ferrigno

THE WAKE-UP

Robert Ferrigno is the author of seven previous novels, including *Scavenger Hunt*, *Flinch*, and the bestselling *The Horse Latitudes*. He lives with his family in the Pacific Northwest. His Web site is www.robertferrigno.com.

THE WAKE-UP

THE WAKE-UP

A Novel

Robert Ferrigno

VINTAGE CRIME / BLACK LIZARD
Vintage Books
A Division of Random House, Inc.
New York

FIRST VINTAGE CRIME/BLACK LIZARD EDITION, AUGUST 2005

The Library of Congress has cataloged the Pantheon edition as follows:
Ferrigno, Robert.
The wake-up / Robert Ferrigno
p. cm.
1. Swindlers and swindling—Fiction. 2. Forgery of antiquities—Fiction. 3. Los Angeles
(Calif.)—Fiction. 4. Drug traffic—Fiction. 5. Revenge—Fiction. I. Title.
PS3556.E7259W35 2004   813'.54—dc22 2003070765

Vintage ISBN: 1-4000-3387-X

Book design by M. Kristen Bearse

www.vintagebooks.com

Printed in the United States of America
10 9 8 7 6 5 4 3 2 1

FOR

MY BROTHER, JAMES

ACKNOWLEDGMENTS

Thanks to my editor, Sonny Mehta, and to my agent, Mary Evans, for their assistance and encouragement.

There is only one basic plot:
things aren't what they seem.

— JIM THOMPSON

THE WAKE-UP

PROLOGUE

The Engineer's bodyguard gave Frank Thorpe the jitters. The man wasn't doing anything that should have given him cause for concern— he leaned against a black 850 BMW sedan, lost in the pages of a porn magazine, while the Engineer stretched nearby. Same as usual. Thorpe bent down, pretended to retie his running shoes, heart pounding. The bodyguard had to be three hundred pounds at least, with a head like a hammer, and Cyrillic tattoos ringing his squatty neck, busy now staring at *Tits and Clits Annual.* Thorpe smiled at his own nervousness, strung out on adrenaline, imagining the worst. You'd think he'd learn. The moment of truth . . . it applied to Thorpe even more than to the target.

The Engineer took off down the path that circled the park, a soft intellectual in a bright red jogging suit, arms pumping twice as fast as his legs. He sprinted about thirty yards, just far enough to be out of sight of his bodyguard, then pulled a cell phone out of his jacket, walking now as he punched in the number.

Thorpe stood up, a tall, gangly forty-year-old in shorts and a hooded sweatshirt, loose-limbed and agile. No need to hurry. The Engineer's call to Kimberly would be brief, only long enough to confirm their rendezvous at the Four Seasons tonight. The big date, almost three weeks in the making. The Engineer had started running laps the day after he first met Kimberly, ordering the fruit plate at lunch, to the guffaws of the rest of Lazurus's crew, mostly suety, barrel-chested Ukrainians forking in meat and cheese. Any day now, Thorpe expected the Engineer to begin touching up the gray in his hair.

The park was quiet midweek, filled with new moms in color-

3

coordinated workout clothes, pushing high-tech running strollers, their hair in braids and pigtails. Thorpe must be getting old; mothers didn't use to look so good. In a grassy field, a couple of college guys tossed a football back and forth. One of them had an arm, too, a real cannon, arcing tight spirals forty and fifty yards. Under other circumstances, Thorpe might have asked if he could play, too, give them a surprise; instead, he trotted onto the dirt running path.

The Engineer sat on a wooden bench, his call finished, staring into space. He was in his mid-thirties, with sensual, thickly lidded eyes, and thin, ascetic lips. A face at war with itself. Right now he would be thinking of Kimberly, imagining how the evening might go, deciding on what to order from room service. There had been no bodyguard with him the day he had bumped into her at the mall. Some men might wonder how they had gotten so lucky, this chance meeting with Kimberly, a shy, pretty college girl who had commented on his cute Italian accent. Not the Engineer. He and Kimberly ordered lunch in the food court, exchanging lies over tacos and soft drinks, and when she said she had to go, the Engineer had asked for her phone number, apologizing for his boldness. Thorpe had watched from the second balcony, sipping an Orange Julius.

The Engineer got up from the bench, took off at a slow canter.

Thorpe gave him a lead, then started after him. It was a perfect Southern California morning, ripe with the smell of fresh-mowed grass and carbon monoxide. A great day to squeeze the Engineer. Squeeze him until he bled all his secrets.

People liked Thorpe when they met him, thinking afterward how easy he was to talk to. A Gypsy in Seattle had known better. She was a bejeweled matron operating out of a concrete rambler on Route 99, a garish place with brightly colored pebbles in the driveway and a neon sign in the window advertising ADVICE LOVE MONEY. She started to read his palm, then dropped it as though it were molten. She said his heart had more twists than a snake, and that his future was beyond all reckoning. She almost looked sad for him. The Gypsy was a rip-off, but that didn't mean she wasn't right once in a while.

The Engineer disappeared around a bend, the path winding through dense trees.

Thorpe ran faster now, his footfalls barely making a sound. He waited until the Engineer approached a cutoff, then raced abreast and tripped him, sent him tumbling. The Engineer scrambled up, running suit streaked with dirt, but Thorpe was on him, pushing him backward down the cutoff until they were out of sight of the running path.

"You want money?" panted the Engineer, eyes wide.

"I'd rather have some thermal lenses," said Thorpe. "I'm putting together an over-the-horizon radar receiver, and Wal-Mart is out of stock."

The Engineer stiffened, braver now that he knew he wasn't being mugged. "There is a fellow waiting for me. You should try your joke on him. He likes to laugh."

"Gregor?" Thorpe loved the look on the Engineer's face when he used the bodyguard's name. "I don't think that tub of shit has a funny bone in his body."

The Engineer's hooded eyes made him look sleepy, but Thorpe knew better.

"Lazurus should have stuck with dope and tax-free cigarettes; you start exporting microswitches to Belarus, people wonder what you're up to."

A thin film of sweat gleamed over the Engineer's upper lip. "You are FBI?"

Thorpe shook his head. "The Bureau still has a dress code. You believe that?"

The Engineer pulled out a pack of cigarettes. Tapped out an unfiltered Marlboro, hands shaking slightly. He watched Thorpe as his gold Zippo flared. "CIA?"

"Too macho. My shop, we're more like Boy Scouts with a really sick sense of humor."

Smoke trickled from the Engineer's mouth. "You do not look like a Boy Scout."

"Kimberly isn't going to make it tonight, so you can save yourself a trip to the hotel. *See,* there's my good deed for the day." Thorpe saw the Engineer's eyes harden. "It must be disappointing, all that foreplay and no payoff. The roses were beautiful, by the way. I dropped some of the petals in my bubble bath, kind of a sensual experience after a long day." Thorpe could feel the rage and the electricity in the air. He *loved* moments like this. Billy said the best operators had a cruel streak, and Thorpe was as good as he had seen. "I hate to tell you, but those calls you made to Kimberly didn't go to her directly; they rang first in an office downtown and were rerouted to her cell phone. The number that appears on your billing records is a cubicle in the federal building." He let it sink in. "Could be a problem for you with Lazurus."

The cigarette dropped from the Engineer's open mouth.

"Later today"—Thorpe checked his watch—"Lazurus is going to get word that someone is talking to the feds. Someone *close.* How long you think it will take him to pull the phone records of everyone in his crew?"

"I told Kimberly nothing. This is not legal, what you are doing. There are rules—"

"Actually, there aren't. The FBI has rules, even the CIA has rules, but my shop, we make it up as we go along. It's part of the fun of working there." Thorpe saw the Engineer hesitate. "Hey, you want to leave, be my guest. I won't stop you. I'm sure you can convince Lazurus that you're a team player. I bet he's a good listener."

The Engineer was rigid, hands clenched, trying to decide what to do.

Thorpe watched him but didn't interfere. The Engineer was smart; he would make the right move. A successful squeeze only worked with someone intelligent enough to realize that cooperation was their only option, *full* cooperation. "I have a car parked nearby, and a safe house waiting. We want to know what merchandise you've bought for Lazurus, who sold it, and what he's got you looking for next. Or you can finish your run, and tell Lazurus all about the bad man who tried to turn you."

"Kimberly . . ." The Engineer's voice cracked. "She will be at the safe house, too?"

Thorpe nodded. The Engineer smiled, grateful at the news, and

Thorpe almost felt sorry for him. Then he remembered what the Engineer did for a living. Death row was filled with men who sent valentines to their mothers, and drew pictures of kitty cats playing with balls of twine. Thorpe would gladly throw the switch on all of them.

"This thing you are doing . . . it is clever," said the Engineer. "Lazurus will not know how long I have been working with you. He will not know how deep the betrayal goes. He will suspect everyone—" He stepped back into the trees as his bodyguard lumbered past on the main path. "This is *trouble.*"

Thorpe was equally surprised at the bodyguard's abrupt appearance.

"You said Lazurus would find out *later.* What else are you wrong about?"

Somebody at the shop had screwed up; the place hadn't run smoothly since Billy quit. Thorpe led the Engineer through the trees, the man right behind him, huffing and puffing. They stopped in the brush at the edge of a second parking lot. His rented Jeep was still there. While they watched, three men got out of an idling black Mercedes.

The men looked around, scowling; then the driver got out, too, stood beside the car. The other three headed for the trees, their route taking them forty or fifty feet from where Thorpe and the Engineer crouched. The park was small—both parking lots would be staked out now, Lazurus's men fanning out along the running path.

Thorpe flipped open his phone.

"Yes, call for help," the Engineer whispered, clinging to him. "Say 'Come *now.*' "

"There *is* no help. No reinforcements. No black helicopters. There's just you and me."

The Engineer released his grip. "Then we are dead."

Thorpe called the safe house.

"I saw Lazurus kill a man once," the Engineer mumbled. "A broker who sold us industrial milling equipment. We had used him before, but this time he substituted an inferior grade of ball bearings." He stared straight ahead. "Lazurus brought him to a warehouse filled with old bicycles, rusted bicycles with flattened tires. The broker knew something bad was happening even before Lazurus lit the blowtorch. The blowtorch . . . it lights with a popping sound. The broker jumped when he heard it. I jumped, too."

Kimberly answered on the first ring. "Trouble," said Thorpe. He watched the driver pace beside the Mercedes, a sturdy young guy in jeans and a leather jacket, hair slicked straight back. "The Engineer and I are still at the park. We have company."

"How did that happen?"

"You tell me." Thorpe heard voices behind them. "We're playing hide-and-seek."

"Call the cops. Tell them to come with their sirens full on. Maybe you'll scare off—"

"Too late."

"The broker tried to explain that it had been a mistake," said the Engineer, plucking leaves off the bushes. "He took out his wallet, showed Lazurus photographs of his family, his wife and children. Lazurus looked at the photos for a long time, with no expression on his face, just looking. Then he took the blowtorch and burned them up."

"Ditch the Engineer," said Kimberly. "Tell him you'll be right back, and stroll away. Lazurus's men won't stop you. They don't know you."

The Mercedes driver kept one hand on the car as he bent forward, checking first one shoe, then the other. Thorpe slipped his 9-mm out of the front pocket of his sweatshirt, dropped the safety.

"Leave him, Thorpe. We won't get to debrief him, and that's a loss, but Lazurus won't know that. He'll still have to retool his whole operation."

"First Lazurus burned the photographs. . . . Then . . . then, he burned the broker."

Thorpe closed his phone. "That's a sad story, and when this is over, we'll sit down with some herb tea and have a good cry. Right now, I want you to take off your clothes."

"You are serious?"

"They'll be looking for a red jogging suit. If you're buck naked underneath, you'll *still* be less noticeable." Thorpe waited as the Engineer undressed, raising an eyebrow at the man's polka-dot bikini briefs. "Those may buy us an extra couple of seconds while your pals try to stop laughing." He tucked the Engineer's cell phone into his sweatshirt.

The driver of the Mercedes was still scraping the bottom of his shoes on the pavement when Thorpe reached the edge of the parking lot. Thorpe heard shouts from the woods, then gunshots. The driver looked up, reached for the pistol in his waistband, and Thorpe shot him twice in the chest, the man flopping backward as though jerked by a string. Thorpe was running now, the Engineer right behind.

Bullets dinged the nearby cars, popping out windshields. Thorpe returned fire, hit another one of Lazurus's men, sent the others diving for cover. Thorpe emptied the magazine as the Engineer ducked into the Jeep. Thorpe threw open his door, when something knocked the wind out of him. He straightened up, got behind the wheel. A bullet shattered his side-view mirror as he peeled out of the lot. Thorpe watched his rearview as they sped away. He thought of the Mercedes driver tumbling to the pavement, and how strange it was to die with dog shit on your shoes.

"Alexi . . . the driver," said the Engineer, "I was playing chess with him last night."

Thorpe raced onto the I-5 freeway. No one had followed them. He took out his phone again. There was blood on the keypad.

"Are you all right?" Kimberly asked before he even spoke.

"We're on our way. He's fine. I got shot in the side."

"Do I need to find you an ER?" Kimberly's voice was even.

"No." Thorpe pulled a pair of white socks from under his seat, pressed them against the wound. "See you soon." He broke the connection. The white socks were turning pink. He pressed them harder against his belly, driving with one hand.

The safe house was in an upscale development, a house like every other in the neighborhood, except for the tiny video cameras covering the front and back. Kimberly and Weeks were standing in the doorway as Thorpe drove up. Kimberly had her dark blond hair pulled back and was wearing jeans, cowboy boots, and a clingy blue silk T-shirt, looking not at all like the innocent girl who had bumped into the Engineer at the mall. She would handle the initial interrogation. She looked eager to get to work, striding toward the car while Weeks stayed put, big arms crossed.

"It's not as bad as it looks," said Thorpe as Kimberly leaned in the open window.

The Engineer got out of the Jeep, stood there in his polka-dot briefs, shifting from one foot to the other, waiting for Kimberly to notice him. Weeks smirked.

"I called that plastic surgeon we've used before," Kimberly told Thorpe, her mouth tense, their faces so close that Thorpe wanted to kiss her, but he hurt too much. "He only had consultations scheduled. He sent his staff home. You want me to drive you?"

Thorpe shook his head.

Kimberly checked his eyes. "You're not getting all heroic on me, are you, Thorpe?"

He looked back at her, lingering. "Not a chance."

I

Out of the corner of his eye, Thorpe saw Kimberly heading toward the escalator. He ignored her. It took everything he had, but he managed it, jaw tightening as he concentrated on the revolving luggage carousel at LAX. He had been standing there for the last ten minutes, matching up travelers with the bags sliding down the chute. He had nailed a computer jock and his yellow plastic Hello Kitty knapsack, even paired the dreadlocked skateboarder with an incongruous brushed-chrome footlocker—the peeling Reggae rainbow sticker on the case had been the tell. Nice catch, but it didn't mean anything now.

Vacation was a bitch, and permanent vacation was even worse. He didn't expect much from this trip to Miami; he was just tired of sitting around his apartment. Miami was as frantic as L.A., overcrowded with tourists and drunks and geezers doing fifty-five in the fast lane, but there was Cuban food and Cuban music, airboating through the Glades by moonlight, and conch chowder at Shirttail Charlie's. There were still parts of the Keys where you could slip through the mangrove trees, stand knee-deep in the warm Atlantic, and it was so quiet that you could hear mermaids singing sad songs under the sea. "A lapse in judgment," that's how the shop described the Lazurus fiasco—they might as well be accusing him of forgetting to take his vitamins or failing to rotate his tires.

Near the exit, a thin Hispanic kid was selling confections, holding out a wooden tray filled with candy and nuts, small oranges, and chunks of fresh coconut. A sweet-faced kid no older than nine or ten, standing there in hemmed cutoffs and a Mickey Mouse T-shirt. Most people hurried past, not making eye contact, but the kid's smile never

faltered. Thorpe liked the kid's hustle, the way he positioned himself
to get maximum foot traffic, head high. No matter what the need that
brought him here on a school day, he was no beggar. Thorpe had seen
him refuse money from an old woman who wasn't interested in his
goods, accepting her handful of loose change only when she took a
pack of Chiclets and a single chocolate Kiss.

A chunky teenage girl with chopped black hair stood by the
carousel, the four gold rings through her lower lip making her look
like a hooked tuna. Thorpe pegged her for the gray rubberized suitcase, but she grabbed a Louis Vuitton overnighter instead. Daddy's
girl, and he had missed it. Thorpe turned, saw Kimberly riding the up
escalator to the main concourse, a pale green sundress clinging to her.
He was sweating now, but he stayed where he was.

The sign over the carousel blinked. Luggage from American Airlines
flight 223 would be unloaded next. About time. Thorpe's 7:00 a.m.
flight to Miami had turned back barely a half hour out of L.A. with engine trouble—if the luggage didn't arrive soon, he was going to miss
the alternate flight. At least a dozen nervous passengers had decided
not to reschedule. Flames shooting out of the port engine could do that
to you, particularly with the pilot's calling for calm over the intercom,
his voice crackling. Thorpe was as superstitious as anyone, seeing por-
tents in soap slivers and broken shoelaces, but he never let that stop
him. If God really wanted to communicate with him, he could fire off
a certified letter.

Thorpe glanced again toward the escalator, glimpsed Kimberly's
bare legs, the green dress swirling around her knees as she disappeared
from view. Unable to stop himself, Thorpe gave chase, taking the escalator three steps at a time.

Halfway down the concourse, he spotted her, deep in a crowd of travelers. He lost sight of her for a few moments; then the crowd parted and
there she was, wearing the same green dress she had worn the first time
she made contact with Lazurus, a demure dress of some silky synthetic,
which only hinted at her lithe figure. Frantic now, Thorpe bumped his
way through the swarm of people separating them, lightly touched her
shoulder.

"Yes?" The woman stared at him. Lovely woman . . . but she wasn't Kimberly.

"Sorry." Thorpe backed off, embarrassed, beelined over to a coffee stand, and ordered a Mexican-style espresso.

The heavyset woman behind the counter levered out the inky brew from a stainless-steel manual machine, using two hands. She added a dash of cocoa and three sugar cubes to the cardboard cup, then took his three singles for the coffee. She rang up the sale, tore off the register receipt, showed it to him. "You got a red star. Coffee's on the house. You're a lucky man."

"You're a lucky man," said the plastic surgeon for the fifth or sixth time.

"If I was lucky, I wouldn't have been shot," gasped Thorpe.

"You're lucky that someone of my skill is working on you," said the surgeon as he examined Thorpe's gunshot wound. "Working solo, too, no anesthesiologist or surgical nurse in attendance. . . . Let those ER butchers try doing that." He shook his head. "You tell Billy we're even now."

Thorpe closed his eyes. Stretched out on the table, an IV in his arm, he wasn't about to tell the surgeon that Billy was retired. He could feel the man's fingers probing his flesh.

"That hurt?" asked the surgeon. "I had to be cautious with the anesthetic; it's not my area of expertise." He chuckled. "I can promise you a beautiful scar, however."

"I'm a lucky man."

"Told you."

The lights were bright, even through his closed eyelids, but something nagged at Thorpe. It had been bothering him the whole drive over, but he just couldn't remember what it was. The surgeon chattered away, but Thorpe was drifting, hearing bullets whizzing past him in the parking lot, and car doors slamming. He remembered racing through traffic, and the Engineer turning around to see if they were being followed. He must have groaned out loud with the memory.

"Hang on," said the surgeon.

Thorpe could still see Kimberly leaning against the Jeep, and lying there in the operating room, he got a whiff of her perfume. He fought to stay awake. Her fragrance was fainter now, and he tried to hang on to her, but she was walking away, walking back to the safe house with the Engineer. Thorpe sat up. The surgeon tried to push him down, but Thorpe shook him off, grabbed his cell phone from the counter.

"Are you trying to kill yourself?" asked the surgeon.

Thorpe listened to the phone ring. The Engineer's gait had changed slightly as he and Kimberly approached the house, become almost jaunty, and at the top of the steps, he had looked back at Thorpe. It had lasted only a moment, and Thorpe was bleeding and desperate to leave, but there was something wrong with his expression.

The surgeon fiddled with the anesthetic drip that ran into Thorpe's arm.

The phone clicked. "Kimberly!" Thorpe's tongue felt thick. "The Engineer. He's not . . . he's not right."

"None of us are," said the Engineer. He had lost all trace of his Italian accent. "Look at Kimberly. A little liar, that's all she was. And you, Frank, so cocky before, all that razzle-dazzle. You don't sound so fearless now."

"Let me . . . speak to Kimberly."

"Say 'Please.' "

"Please, don't hurt her." Thorpe dragged the surgeon closer. "The safe house . . . 911."

"Where are you, Frank?" asked the Engineer.

Thorpe licked his lips. "The Fuck You Hilton."

"That's the spirit."

Thorpe floated on a vast black lake. He felt the surgeon take the phone from him. Someone was sobbing, the sound sending ripples across the water.

"Mister?" The woman at the coffee stand was holding out his three dollars. "I told you—your coffee is free."

Thorpe shoved the money into his pocket, walked away without a word, still hearing the Engineer's last words. He sat down at one of the nearby tables, more convinced than ever that this vacation was a mistake, a retreat, not a respite. Kimberly was dead and the Engineer was alive, and no vacation was going to change that. Not that staying home presented much hope. He had laid out the bait for the Engineer, offered himself up without success, and Thorpe had grown tired of waiting.

Thorpe sipped the thick sweetened coffee and watched the people

streaming past. Commuters double-timing it, laptops swinging with
every step. Grandmothers with too many carry-on plastic bags, tissues
tucked into their sleeves. College girls in Stanford sweatshirts, sorority
tattoos discreetly stitched onto their ankles, easily hidden when they
joined the PTA in a few years. A woman caught his attention, a middle-
aged woman sitting at a nearby table, her cup of frozen yogurt melting
while she tracked the line waiting at the security checkpoint. An ear-
piece was almost hidden by her hair. Ten demerits for the *almost*. She
looked over, but he didn't react, his expression of practiced boredom
deflecting any further interest in him.

Practiced boredom was a specialty of the shop. They had even used
it on him, sending some weary desk jockey with fine gray hair to sit on
his bed in the plastic surgeon's recovery room, the man plucking at the
bedsheet while he told Thorpe that his services were no longer required. *All that surveillance, and you didn't ID the main player, Frank.
How do you think that makes us look?* The desk jockey yawned. *I won't
even mention the mess at the safe house.* Thorpe had beckoned the man
closer, said he couldn't hear him, but the desk jockey kept his distance,
tossed Thorpe an envelope stuffed with cash.

The woman whom Thorpe had mistaken for Kimberly walked
slowly past, checking her flight ticket, looking lost. It wasn't the first
time Thorpe had seen Kimberly since she had been killed. He saw her
running along the beach, he saw her waiting in line at the new John
Woo movie, and once, in the produce department at Ralph's, he had
seen her trying to select a ripe cantaloupe. He knew it wasn't really
her. The photos taken at the safe house were proof enough. He knew it
wasn't her, but he always made sure anyway.

Thorpe still didn't know how the Engineer had pulled it off. He had
observed Lazurus and his crew for months. Lazurus was a thug, violent
and obscene and heavily guarded; the few phone intercepts had caught
him raging, giving orders to subordinates who were desperate to
please, fearful of his wrath. Lazurus might have thought he was the
boss, but the man running the operation was the Engineer; that soft,
pink technocrat, the faintly ridiculous Engineer with his puppy love
and awkward manners. Lazurus was just an unwitting stand-in, another

patsy who never knew what hit him. If it hadn't been for the carnage at the safe house, Thorpe would have applauded the charade.

Some poor bastard pushed a baby stroller down the concourse, one kid in the stroller crying, another one slung against his chest, sleeping. Dear old Dad was sweating in droopy jeans and a stained polo shirt, thinning hair plastered across his scalp, and looking happier than he had any right to. It always amazed Thorpe. Where did that happiness come from?

No kids for Thorpe. No friends or family, either. He didn't even have an ex-wife to bitch about, to call in the middle of the night, drunk and lonely, talking about the good times that neither of them remembered. He didn't have anyone. Kimberly was the closest he had come, and she was dead. Fourteen years in uniform, the last ten in Delta Force, sent on missions he couldn't talk about, and then came the shop, with its secret mental compartments. Thorpe was the neighbor you called at 4:00 a.m. when your car broke down in the middle of nowhere, the one who would come and get you, and not tell you to check your oil once in awhile. Then one day his apartment would be empty and he would be gone, with no forwarding address. Sudden departures and no emotional entanglements were part of the appeal of the job, an essential part of the pay package. The shop gave him an excuse to be who he really was. It was a lousy trade-off.

Angry at himself, angry at the Engineer, angry at the sun and moon and stars, Thorpe finished the coffee in a quick swallow, then headed toward the escalator. Maybe the kid by the luggage carousel had mango slices for sale. Thorpe jiggled the empty cardboard cup as he walked, listening to the sugar cubes rattle around like blind dice.

A businessman in a blue suit walked rapidly down the escalator, elbowed Thorpe aside without a word, and kept moving. Thorpe forced himself to stay put. In his present mood, once he started, he might not be able to stop. He watched the businessman's crocodile briefcase swinging as the man plowed down the escalator, a real hard charger.

The kid was still by the door, at his post. He held out the tray, called to the businessman. Without breaking stride, the businessman smacked away the kid's tray with his briefcase, a solid roundhouse blow, scattering gum and candy, the kid stumbling backward onto the floor, blood streaming down his face. The businessman stalked out through the sliding glass doors.

Thorpe chased after the businessman, double-timing it, but a skycap cut him off with a line of carts, the skycap oblivious, talking on a cell phone. By the time Thorpe got outside, the hard charger had stepped into a waiting red Porsche convertible, a beautiful blonde behind the wheel. Thorpe watched them roar off, the blonde's hair floating behind her in the sunshine. She kissed the man as she accelerated into traffic, kissed him hard and deep, horns blaring around them, the blonde not caring. The hard charger didn't kiss her back, just lolled against the headrest and let her do all the work.

Inside, the kid was on his knees, picking up his goods. "You okay?" asked Thorpe, bending down beside him, helping gather the breath mints and scattered sticks of gum, piling them into the tray. *"¿Está bien, niño?"*

The kid didn't answer; he was busy organizing the gum and candy in his tray, stacking them up, his hands shaking. The edge of the tray, or maybe the briefcase, had split his upper lip, and blood was leaking from his nose, too. His T-shirt was spattered, Mickey Mouse's innocent grin stained with red. The kid kept blinking, cheeks flushed, as humiliated as he was hurt, and Thorpe knew that look. The kid didn't cry, though. Not one tear. Thorpe had a few medals in a safety-deposit box. He would have given them all to the kid if it could have done any good.

Thorpe dabbed at the blood with a tissue. *"¿Está bien, vato?"*

The kid still didn't answer, and Thorpe could see anger in his eyes now, recognized it, too, seeing not a sudden fury that faded as rapidly as it came, but something colder and more dangerous. All those so-called experts, Ph.D. numbnuts who thought personality changes were the result of a slow accretion of experience, were wrong. It just took one false move to fuck you forever.

"*¿Cómo se llama?*" Thorpe said gently. "*Me llamo Frank.*" He kept himself at eye level with the kid, nodded to the door the hard charger had gone through. "*Este hombre es un estupida. Un porque.*"

The kid got to his feet, holding on to the tray, his gaze unwavering now. Tiger, tiger, burning bright, thought Thorpe. He and Thorpe were two of a kind now, and it was the saddest thing Thorpe had ever seen in a child. "*Me llamo Paulo Rodriguez,*" the kid said, edging away.

Thorpe watched Paulo go, watched him until he disappeared deeper into the airport. The hard charger had stolen something from the boy, something only the hard charger could give back. Thorpe turned toward the luggage carousel, saw his bag going round and round, and knew he wasn't going on vacation. Not today. He had glimpsed only the license plate of the red Porsche as it sped off, just caught a flash of numbers, but it had been enough. Old habits, the good, the bad, and the ugly. Thorpe grabbed his bag, then went outside and hailed a cab. Time to go home and give the hard charger a wake-up.

2

"What are you doing back here?" Claire wiggled her toes at Thorpe as she reclined in a blue wading pool set onto the grass at the center of the courtyard. Her yellow leopard-print tank suit contrasted with her deep tan, her short dark hair sprouting in all directions. "I thought you were on your way to Miami."

"Poor boy couldn't *bear* to leave us," chirped Pam, her roommate, a slim hennaed redhead in a string bikini. She toasted Thorpe with a can of light beer, water sloshing over the edge of the pool and onto the grass. "Welcome home, lonesome."

Thorpe closed the gate to the apartment complex, walked toward them. Claire watched him approach from under her sun visor, one leg cocked.

"Come on in and take a dip," invited Pam, tugging on her top. Eleven a.m. and her eyes were already bloodshot.

"There's not room in there for an anchovy," said Thorpe.

"She didn't get a callback," explained Claire, and Thorpe wondered if she had spotted some telltale sign of his disapproval.

"It was just a stupid suntan oil commercial," said Pam. "Not even one line."

"Everything okay, Frank?" asked Claire.

Thorpe idly touched his side, felt the scar, the two of them making eye contact. "Fine. I just needed to postpone the vacation for a few days . . . a week at the most." He walked into his apartment. He could still hear the music from poolside. He took his laptop out of the suitcase, set up on the kitchen table, and logged on to the Net, the connection made with a prepaid cell phone. Thorpe didn't believe in landlines or phone numbers with his name on the bill. His fingers clicked over the keys. The only e-mail was from Billy.

"Still no sign of the Engineer. Come see me, Frank. You have to be getting bored," it read.

Thorpe wasn't surprised at the message, but he was still disappointed. Billy had run the shop since its creation. He had been Thorpe's recruiter, his rabbi, his protector—Billy tolerated Thorpe's insubordination, his disdain for proper channels, his failure to ask permission. All Billy cared about were results, and Thorpe got results. A year ago, Billy had quit without a word to anyone. There had just been a memo from Hendricks, the new boss, saying Billy had left to spend more time with his wife and children. A joke typical of Hendricks. Billy was gay. He had as much of a family as Thorpe did.

Billy might have left the shop, but he was still connected. The day Thorpe came home from the plastic surgeon's office, Billy had sent him an e-mail, advised him to stay away from fried foods, and offered him a job. Thorpe turned down the job, but he had sent an e-mail back with a request. It was a major request, but Billy had made it sound like a very small favor. Typical Billy: dismiss the hook, and thereby sink it deeper.

"Still no sign of the Engineer. Come see me, Frank. You have to be getting bored."

Thorpe spiked the message, sent it into the void with all the other invitations from Billy. Invitations to breakfast or golf, Vegas jaunts and sailing cruises, all with invisible strings, all declined. Thorpe missed the work, but he didn't miss Billy. Thorpe had never made the mistake of thinking they were friends.

Through the sheer curtains, Thorpe had a clear view of the iron gate to the courtyard of his apartment complex, Los Castillos—six detached mission-style bungalows with white stucco walls and red barrel-tile roofs. Los Castillos was just off Redondo Boulevard in Belmont Shore, a kick-back beach town just south of Long Beach, a first-names-only place, where bartenders dreamed of selling screenplays and temp workers were convinced they were at least as talented as Julia Roberts. Everyone was waiting to be discovered, but not working too hard at it. It was an easy place to get lost in, and Thorpe felt right at home.

His apartment and utilities were billed to one of his fake identities, Frank Deleone, an infant who had died in a car accident outside Bakersfield almost forty years ago. The shop didn't know his fake name or where he lived. Neither did Billy. He didn't think so anyway. You could drive yourself nuts trying to achieve perfect security.

Thorpe wandered over to the window, watched Claire and Pam lounge in the pool, the boom box pounding out the latest Marshall Mathers, Claire's toe ring moving to the beat. He went back to the laptop. He missed the shop, the ease with which he could call up information on anyone, and, even more than that, the ability to put that information to good use, to make things *happen*. "To take arms against a sea of troubles" . . . fuckin' A. It was all gone now, access denied, his pass codes invalid.

Good thing Thorpe had a backup. A man without a backup was a man who overestimated God and underestimated the devil; that's what his father used to say. Frank Thorpe was just a spectator now, but Frank Deleone had a valid California life- and casualty-insurance license. Thorpe had actually taken the state exam, which was dull beyond belief, but insurance companies had more complete databases than most police departments, the computation of premiums and risk requiring more rigorous cross-checking than crime and punishment.

Thorpe entered his password into an industry search engine, plugged in the license number of the red Porsche. The computer cursor flashed while he waited, and he wondered again why he was here, instead of on a plane to Miami. Strange the things our fates turned on: a kid selling gum and candy, a hard charger in a hurry, and a beached spook with a bad attitude. There wasn't an astrologer on the planet that could have predicted the confluence of events that had put him back in business, but here he was.

Not that Thorpe had any intention of doing the hard charger any permanent damage. No reason to go full court. Thorpe was just going to give him a wake-up. That's what they called it in the shop when you wanted to send a message, a love tap to prod a source, to remind a restless contact of his vulnerability. A hotel receipt placed under a married man's pillow or an "insufficient funds" hold placed on a Cayman Islands bank account worked wonders. Thorpe just wanted to get the hard charger's attention, to show him how quickly the storm clouds could roll in on his sunny world. Just a little wake-up.

The computer screen blinked. Halley Jean Anderson was the registered owner of the Porsche. Twenty-four years old, unmarried. Three speeding tickets in the last two years flagged her in the high-risk category. A year of community college, no degree. Resided in Corona del Mar for the last three months. Swanky address. Employment: consultant at Meachum Fine Arts, Newport Beach, for that same last three months. Thorpe felt the familiar tingle in his fingertips, like playing draw poker and knowing you had caught the inside straight without even checking. You just *knew.* Maybe Halley Anderson had a trust fund, but he didn't think so. Girls with a trust fund didn't go to community college.

Someone was knocking on the door. It had to be Pam and Claire. The outer gate was always locked, but Thorpe had made sure it was squeaky, too, regularly wetting down the hinges so it stayed rusty. He checked the peephole anyway.

"Hey, Frank!" Pam grinned. "Got any lemons we could borrow?"

The two of them followed him into his kitchen, dripping water with every step. When he opened the refrigerator, Pam hip-checked him, plucked three lemons off the rack, started juggling them, her breasts going peekaboo.

Claire, older and quieter than her roommate, sat on the counter, long legs swinging as she watched Thorpe. A part-time college psychology instructor, she had probably already factored in the effect her position on the countertop would have on him, had precisely calibrated the proper speed with which to swing her legs.

"How about some tequila to go with the lemons?" asked Pam. She opened a cabinet, pulled out a bottle of Cuervo Gold. "I'm taking the day off, and Claire doesn't have a class until— Whoopsie!" Lemons rolled across the floor. "Come out and play, Frank."

"Maybe later."

Claire placed a cool hand on his forehead. "You sure you're okay?"

"Depends on the meaning of the word *okay.*"

After the plastic surgeon had cleared him to go home, Thorpe had grabbed a cab to Santa Monica, then taken another cab, from another company, to Long Beach. He took a bus to the Shore and slept. For a couple of days, he stayed in his apartment, too sore and too tired to do more than watch TV. Claire and Pam had come by every day with a six-pack of Carta Blanca, making him canned soup and scrambled eggs, keeping him company. They burned the soup, left bits of shell in the eggs, and didn't clean up. The beer was always cold, though. Not that he could have more than a couple of sips, what with all the anti-biotics he was taking.

Thorpe's cover story was that his gunshot wound was the result of a botched carjacking outside San Francisco. Claire asked to see his scar, then actually teared up when he showed her. The two of them brought him copies of *Maxim, Stuff,* and *FHM,* and she and Pam would argue with each other over the women in the magazines, disagreeing over which starlet had had surgery, which one was showing incipient droop-age, and which sexual advice to the frat boys was worse than useless.

Claire whiled away his recovery by giving him psychological tests, Rorschach and Iowa Integrated and Dynamic Assessment. The tests were supposed to be unbeatable, but Thorpe fudged his answers so that the results were contradictory. She kept rechecking her findings, curs-ing softly, and giving him more tests. Claire and Pam talked too much and teased him without mercy, but on the days when they failed to come by, he kept listening for their footsteps, hoping they would show.

Now Thorpe walked them to the door, then sat back at the computer. He logged off the insurance database and on to the California Division of Corporations. The president and sole proprietor of Meachum Fine Arts was Douglas Meachum, Laguna Beach.

Thorpe tried the *L.A. Times* site, but the paper's archives drew a blank on Meachum Fine Arts or Douglas Meachum. The *Orange County*

Register had done a bare-bones business story three years ago, when the company opened, "offering artwork tailored to the client's own unique aesthetic profile." Right. The *Register* story contained a couple of quotes from Douglas Meachum on the "esoteric and proprietary" methods used to align the art with the client, but there was no photo of him. The *Gold Coast Pilot,* however . . . bingo. Thorpe should have started there. The *Pilot* was a local weekly targeted at the yacht and tennis club set, the oceanfront nouveau riche crowd. Two years ago, they had done a full-page color feature on Meachum Fine Arts. He double-clicked on the accompanying photo, got a good look at Douglas Meachum posed in front of an ugly-ass Dalí watercolor, a look of blithe condescension on his lean, handsome face. Meachum was the hard charger.

He went back to the insurance Web site. Douglas Meachum was forty-five, lived in Laguna Beach, had a new Jaguar and three-year-old Ford Explorer on his policy. Pristine driving record. No tickets, no accidents. He did, however, have a wife. Thorpe wasn't surprised that Meachum was a player—it went with the arrogance and sense of entitlement that Thorpe had seen in the man's walk, the tilt of his head.

A woman answered the phone at Meachum's gallery, identified herself as Nell Cooper, chief sales consultant. She said Mr. Meachum was on a business trip but would be back tomorrow, and perhaps there was something *she* could help him with? Thorpe said no, then asked if Halley Anderson was working today. Nell Cooper said there was no one with that name employed there. Thorpe thanked her and hung up. Then he called Halley Anderson. She picked up on the fourth ring.

"Hello."

"Hi, Halley. Is Doug there?"

Hesitation on the other end, one hand muffling the receiver as she said something.

"Who is this?" demanded Meachum, on the line now.

"I saw you at LAX this morning. You were in such a rush, you knocked a kid down. You bloodied his nose and didn't even stop to say you were sorry. Bad manners, Doug."

"How did you get this number?"

"I wanted to give you a chance to apologize to the boy."

"Are you an attorney?" asked Meachum. "Some ambulance chaser who thinks I'm going to admit to hitting this little wetback?"

"I didn't say he was Latino, but don't worry, I'm not a lawyer. The boy's name is Paulo. You just have to tell Paulo you're sorry, and that will be the end of it."

Silence on the phone.

"What's there to think about, Doug? You draw blood, you apologize. It's common courtesy, but it will make a big difference to Paulo."

"Did my wife put you up to this?"

"I'm just trying to give you a chance to make things right," said Thorpe. "Remember all those fairy tales about the old woman who knocks on the castle door late one night, asking for a meal? An old woman who turns out to be a witch, or an angel? The lesson is always the same, Doug. When in doubt, be kind."

"I'm not feeling very kind at the moment, Mr. . . . . Ah well, I don't really care who you are. Suffice it to say, if you bother me again, I'll contact the police."

Thorpe listened to the dial tone. No apology. Well, a guy who took the easy way out wasn't the type who decked a kid and kept walking. Thorpe wasn't surprised at Meachum's response. He smiled. Truth be told, he wasn't disappointed, either. He got up, stretched, and went outside.

"Frank!" Pam toasted him with the tequila bottle as Claire waved.

Frank sat down on the grass beside the blue wading pool, admiring the way the water glistened on their skin. Rainbows everywhere and no pot of gold. Pam passed him the bottle. He took a swallow, felt the fire, and bit into a lemon wedge, the taste sharp and clean on his tongue. Bees buzzed in the flowers nearby. He took another swallow, then passed the bottle back.

"Hey, you." Claire rested her head on the edge of the pool. "Something happen today? You hit the lottery or fall in love?"

The tequila hit him hard and fast on an empty stomach. "Something like that. I've got all these possibilities . . . and no consequences."

"What's he talking about?" asked Pam.

Claire stretched in the sun. "It's like when we walk into a club and there's hotties everywhere, and we just have to decide which one to smile back at." She scooped water out of the pool and let it run off her fingers and onto her throat. "Most of the time, that's the best part of the evening, *before* we decide, when they're all spread out there before us, eager to please, and we haven't had to listen to their career plans."

Pam took a swallow of tequila. "Speak for yourself, girl."

Claire looked at Thorpe, her short hair beaded with water. "Did I get it right, Frank?"

"Yeah, you stuck the dismount." Thorpe lay on the warm grass, feeling the glow of the tequila, enjoying the sun and the music. He hadn't felt this good since he was fired.

3

Meachum's house in Laguna was a piece of cake. Thorpe had seen Pokémon lunch boxes with better security. Located in a quiet neighborhood five blocks inland from the Pacific Coast Highway, the house was a modest stucco rambler dating from the 1960s, with large windows and a front walkway of worn paving stones. The yard was overgrown with shade trees, dry leaves drifting down. On the front porch, Thorpe could see two white wicker rocking chairs. No armed-response stickers on the windows, no motion-sensitive lights in back, no sign of a dog. The place was a walk-in, open and easy and inviting. Hard to imagine the hard charger living there.

Even late in the afternoon, people were still parking on the narrow streets and making the trek to the beach, towels slung over their shoulders, sandals flip-flopping on the cracked sidewalk. Thorpe, in shorts and a Santa Barbara 10-K T-shirt, had made a circuit of the block, checked out the alley behind the rambler. Half the homes had their back doors wide open, hoping to catch some breeze. If anyone asked what he was doing, he carried a flyer from a nearby open house as cover—a three-bedroom, one-and-a-half-bath fixer-upper offered at $799,500. No one had asked him what he was doing, though. Laguna was a live-and-let-live town.

Thorpe started down the alley toward his car, which was parked a few blocks away. He had accomplished what he'd come for. A casually dressed stranger in the neighborhood would draw no attention. He could bide his time, then slip inside while the Meachums were sleeping, and leave something for the hard charger—a torn copy of the state of California's community property statutes maybe, or the section of the tax code that detailed the penalties for putting a phantom employee on the books. Tuck it into Meachum's briefcase, or the pocket of his suit jacket.

In a few days, Thorpe would show up at the gallery, check out the artwork, and when Meachum came over, he would ask him if he wanted to apologize to Paulo now. The hard charger would tighten a little around the mouth, demand to know what Thorpe *really* wanted, but he would do it. Even if he wasn't afraid of his infidelity being exposed, even if he and his wife had an "understanding" and his business accounts were straight, the thing that would make Meachum go woozy, the absolute nuts guarantee, was realizing that Thorpe had traipsed into his life. Once you cracked the Fortress of Solitude, there were no more hard chargers. Meachum would make the apology, and then wait for Thorpe to make the next move. A move that would never come. Thorpe had other priorities: He had decided not to go on vacation; he was going to stay around here until he found the Engineer. He could go to Florida after he killed the Engineer.

Thorpe kicked a soda can down the alley, feeling good. A couple of old hippies approached, passing a joint back and forth. The woman's doughy flesh pushed out of her cutoff jeans, her breasts pendulous in a macramé bikini top, the man a scarecrow in tie-dyed trunks, a floppy hat atop his head. Hair everywhere, truck-tire huaraches on their feet, the two of them smelling of pot and patchouli. He watched them stagger away, holding hands now, fingers entwined, and the sight filled him with wonder and a longing that made his chest hurt. He hurried out of the alley and onto a side street, stumbling in his haste, as though being chased.

Up ahead, a woman strode up the steep hill from downtown, a bag of groceries clutched in each arm. Her face was shiny with sweat, a handsome olive-skinned woman with dark hair curling past her shoulders. She wore a white embroidered peasant blouse, white pants cuffed at the ankle. She shifted the bags slightly as she reached the top of the hill, blew her hair out of her face, and grinned at him as she caught him watching.

Thorpe smiled back.

The woman gasped as the paper bag in her right hand broke, sending a cascade of groceries onto the sidewalk, a rain of fruits and vegetables and shattered glass jars. A bottle of Perrier foamed over her sandals. She held the other bag with both hands, surrounded by shards of glass, as Thorpe ran to help.

Thorpe bent down, pulled a sliver of green glass from her foot, and wiped away the spot of blood with a fingertip. Her white cuffs were spotted with mayonnaise.

"Be careful," she said as Thorpe gathered up the broken glass.

"I'll be careful. . . . Son of a *bitch*." He stood up. A piece of clear glass was embedded in his knee. He hadn't even seen it on the sidewalk.

"You're hurt." She shifted her groceries again, concerned.

"I'm fine. Stupid, but fine." Thorpe pulled the piece of glass out of his knee.

She didn't move her feet, but scooped up loose fruit, then gave them a quick check and put them in the other bag. Her hands were nimble as she selected the groceries, the thick nails trimmed and unpolished, utterly feminine. He bent to help her, and the two of them worked together until the sidewalk was clean. Thorpe carefully folded up a paper bag they had put the pieces of glass in, and walked it over to a garbage can. He turned and found her standing beside him.

"You're bleeding. Follow me. I live just a block away."

"It's okay."

"Don't be so male."

"Do I have a choice?"

"You got hurt helping me. Let me return the favor. Come on, tough guy." She beckoned, and he followed her, the two of them walking side by side. "I'm Gina."

"Frank. Can I carry that bag?"

"We're almost there. Are you house shopping? I saw you had a brochure."

"Just looking."

"It's a nice neighborhood." She slowed a few minutes later. "Here we are. Come up on the porch. I'll get some bandages and antiseptic."

Thorpe stared. It was the Meachum house. Stunned, he watched her climb the steps.

Gina must have misunderstood his hesitation. She nodded at one of the rattan rockers on the porch. "Make yourself comfortable. I'd invite you in, but the house is a mess." It was a nice lie, and he appreciated her making the effort. She took her groceries inside, the screen door banging behind her.

Thorpe climbed onto the porch, still unsettled by the fact that Gina was Meachum's wife. He sat down, rocked gently as he looked out at the neighborhood, feeling as though any sudden movement would upset some fragile cosmic equilibrium. He felt the same way sometimes when he was on assignment, closing in on a subject, making conversation, his senses so acute that he worried his own elevated heartbeat would give him away. He kept rocking. The houses all had tiny front lawns, but most of the neighbors let their shrubs run rampant, growing high, vines blooming over the windows, giving more privacy. He liked the feel of it, the tropical excess. Sometimes it was just best to give in to nature.

"What are you thinking about?" Gina stood in the doorway.

"I like your place."

"Thanks. I grew up in this house. My husband keeps wanting to remodel, but I can't do it." Gina came onto the porch with a first-aid kit, sat down across from him. "You don't have anything catching, do you?"

"No. I'd tell you if I did."

She propped Thorpe's leg up, used a gauze pad to wipe off the blood with those strong hands, no hesitation in her touch. Her black hair was thick and a little coarse—she pushed it back with her wrists as she worked—and her sweat was fragrant. He wondered how Douglas Meachum could cheat on her. He saw Meachum and the blonde driving away from LAX, and Thorpe wondered what kind of lies Meachum told himself when he was alone with the blonde, what lies he told the blonde about Gina. He watched her bent over his knee, and he realized that he couldn't involve her in the wake-up. He was going to teach Meachum a lesson, but the house was off-limits. He would have to squeeze Meachum through his business.

"*Ouch.*"

"Don't be a baby." Gina cleaned the edges of the wound with a Q-tip now. Bits of color were speckled at the base of her cuticles: red, yellow, blue.

"Are you a painter?"

She rubbed her cuticles, pleased. "You're very observant." She checked the cut, put a fresh gauze pad on the wound. Her cell phone was beeping. "Hello." She looked at Thorpe. "I'm on the porch. Where are you?"

Thorpe could hear Meachum's voice through the receiver, saying, "I'm still in New York. Where'd you think I'd be?"

Gina averted her eyes, turned toward the street so that Thorpe couldn't see her face as she listened. "No, I haven't been by the gallery."

"Why the hell not?"

"Don't talk to me like that." Gina checked the gauze pad. "I'm busy, that's why." She looked away. "I had an accident walking home from the grocery store. A man helped me." She glanced at Thorpe. "I don't know; I just met him. He cut himself on some glass helping me, so at this moment I'm taking care of him." She pulled the phone away from her ear, disgusted, and snapped it shut. It started beeping again, but she ignored it.

"I'm sorry," said Thorpe.

"For what?" Gina tore off strips of clear adhesive and taped him tight. "You'll live."

4

Thorpe had barely stepped inside Meachum Fine Arts when he was approached by a well-dressed woman in her thirties, a big-boned Bertha with a prim mouth, plenty of auburn hair, and the beginnings of a double chin. She wore a cream-and-brown suit, the skirt at midcalf, her large feet squeezed into matching two-tone pumps. "Good afternoon." She appraised him with a cool smile, took in the sleek, gunmetal gray suit, black silk T-shirt, black loafers. Vaguely European, hip without trying too hard. She showed her flat white teeth. "I'm Nell Cooper. How can I assist you?"

Thorpe looked around the showroom, raised an eyebrow at the safe contemporary watercolors displayed against the right wall—sailboats and sunsets and dour Navajos. "I'm not at all sure you can."

Reading his distaste, Nell pivoted slightly, inclined her head at the paintings, and raised an eyebrow. "We have to carry a full range of aesthetic options, Mr. . . ."

"Frank Antonelli. I'm moving into a home in Corona del Mar, and I thought you might be able to help me make it livable."

She nodded. "Please call me Nell. I can assure you, Frank, that at Meachum Fine Arts we pride ourselves in finding the perfect fit between our clients and the fine art they choose to surround themselves with."

"A *perfect* fit? That's a terrifying thought."

Nell was knocked a little off stride by that, but she recovered quickly. Meachum Fine Arts was a one-story building in Newport Beach, right on the Pacific Coast Highway, with a black-and-white Op Art mural on the side facing the parking lot, and gold-flaked wood sphinxes flanking the doorway. The ocean was visible from the showroom, a beach volleyball game in progress, but the sound of the waves was muted by the thick tinted windows—you might as well have been watching ESPN. The distressed white pine floor creaked underfoot. The offerings were as eclectic as Nell had said—a red-toned Tenzing carpet, czarist Russian icons, and a museum-quality Italian rococo dresser—but there were too many soapstone sculptures of seals and dolphins. An oil painting got his attention, a realistic image of a traffic cop beckoning in bright sunshine, a bead of sweat rolling down the side of his face, one of his socks halfway down. Thorpe leaned closer.

"Do you like that?"

Thorpe nodded, noncommittal. He strolled around, stopped, then crossed over to a high-gloss ebony desk for a better look. He picked up a small limestone wall panel, held it gently, stared at the image of a man in an elaborate headdress surrounded by Mayan hieroglyphs. The panel was absolutely genuine, a seven-inch-long piece of limestone chipped off a temple wall in Uxmal or Copán or some unknown, overgrown city given up to lizards and dragonflies. Half the man's body was gone, but the face was startling, one of the lords of the Yucatán, a broad, thick-lipped autocrat from seven hundred years ago, more distant from the present than the calendar could count. Thorpe's fingers grazed the regal verdigris countenance, the face staring back at him with blind eyes. A king without a kingdom. In a perfect world, Thorpe would steal the broken panel and return it to the jungle, hide the Mayan lord in some triple-canopy vastness, where the howler monkeys could serenade him for eternity. In *this* world, it was just the kind of thing he was hoping to find in Meachum's gallery.

"Lovely, isn't it?" said Nell. "It just came in yesterday. It was presold, I'm afraid."

"Pity." Thorpe held the limestone king in his hands. Pieces like this hadn't been allowed out of their country of origin for thirty years. "What's the provenance?"

"You'd have to ask Douglas. I really don't know."

"Is the buyer local?"

Nell hesitated. "We have to maintain our clients' privacy. I'm sure you understand."

Thorpe carefully replaced the panel on the desk. He went through the motions of looking at other items in the shop, felt the nap of a classic Anatolian carpet, peered at the signature on a Manolo bullfighter print while Nell hovered behind him.

"Why don't we sit down, have an espresso or a glass of wine, and get to know each other?" Nell gestured to the pale blue leather sofa in a nearby alcove, a cozy nook half-hidden from the main room. "We have a relatively small inventory, but I have access to pieces from all over the globe. I'm certain I can show you some things that would be suitable to your needs."

"How about a martini? That would suit my needs."

Nell started to check her watch, then slipped through a curtain into the back of the shop.

Thorpe sat down on the sofa, draped a leg over one of the arms, and listened to her cracking ice. It was a good sound, and the sound of her jiggling the cocktail shaker was even better. He waited until she came back bearing a couple of martini glasses, a little nervous, probably not sure if she had made the drink to his liking. She had too many clients with misplaced priorities. "Where's the boss?"

Nell's gray eyes heated up. Meachum might be her boss, but she didn't enjoy it. Another reason for Thorpe to like her. "Mr. Meachum is in New York on a buying trip."

"Must be our lucky day, Nell. That way, you get the commission, and I get the pleasure of your company. I hear he's a prick anyway."

Nell had a little-girl laugh, high and nervous, like it didn't get out to play enough. "I really can't address that."

Thorpe winked at her. "You just did."

Nell joined him on the couch, the soft flesh under her chin jiggling slightly. "This new home of yours . . . what kind of square footage are we talking about?"

Two martinis later, they were old friends, chuckling over the latest movies and the best Japanese restaurants, knee-to-knee, Nell confiding that she was tired of covering for Meachum: "Little Nell has her résumé at the Guggenheim and the Whitney, and I'm just waiting for them to give me a buzz."

Thorpe beamed as they went through portfolio notebooks of houses Meachum and Associates had made over. The notebooks were filled with slides and eight-by-ten color glossies, and Nell was eager to let him know the pieces she had chosen, and which ones had been selected by Douglas Meachum. The dates of installation were clearly marked on the slides and glossies, but there was no indication of the clients' identities, and, more importantly, he didn't see any other pre-Columbian pieces.

"The party that purchased the Mayan frieze, have you worked with him before?" asked Thorpe. "Or is it a she?"

"It's a *them,* and they're new to the art world." Nell shook her head. "The Mayan head is the pièce de résistance, but it's only part of the collection we've put together for them. We're doing their whole house." She was slurring her words, her voice a little too loud. "Proof positive that art is wasted on the rich."

"I know just what you mean. Let me guess: They made their money in real estate? Strip malls and parking lots."

"Nope."

"They're doctors," said Thorpe. "Doctors have the worst taste in the world."

"Except for lawyers."

"Okay, *he's* a doctor; *she's* an attorney. Am I getting warm?"

Nell shook her head. "Cold as ice."

"Give me a hint."

"T-shirts." Nell giggled, covered her mouth, as though she had spilled the secret of the plasma warp drive.

"Right."

"I'm *serious,* Frank."

Thorpe turned the page, backing off, giving her a chance to tease him with more information. A circular red-and-white bedroom was filled with paintings, larger-than-life realistic nudes of Bill and Hillary Clinton, Jesse Jackson, Barbra Streisand, and Michael Moore. The sight gave Thorpe a headache.

"I put that whole room together," Nell boasted. She leaned closer and sloshed the last of her drink over her wrist, but she didn't seem to notice. "The artist is a young Chicano painter, totally self-taught. He does Republicans, too. I could talk to him. . . ."

"Anyone working in here?" A woman stood just inside the doorway, tapping her perfectly white sneaker on the bleached pine, a thin, pretty blonde in her early thirties, wearing a white pleated tennis skirt, a scoop-neck blouse showing off the taut musculature of her upper arms. Three gold chains were looped around her neck, a gold stallion dangling from one of them. A red Ferrari convertible was double-parked out front. She scanned the room, her face sharp and hard. "I'm *waiting.*" Her voice was a crow's caw, demanding, and she wasn't so pretty anymore.

Nell quickly got up, smoothed her hair. "Mrs. Riddenhauer, so nice to—"

"What do you look so guilty about?"

Nell reddened.

"Relax," said Mrs. Riddenhauer, her eyes on Thorpe. "No one could blame you." Her body seemed to vibrate at a submolecular level, but she didn't jerk or twitch—it was as though she simply put out more energy than her skin could contain. "Where's Meachum?"

"Mr. Meachum isn't here at the moment, but I'm sure that I—"

"He's never around unless I'm writing a check." Mrs. Riddenhauer caught sight of the Mayan wall plaque on the desk, crossed over and picked it up, her brows wrinkling. "Is *this* it?" She turned it over, handling it roughly. "Not very big for a hundred and twenty-five thousand."

"It's a unique object," Nell said softly. "Size . . . size isn't really important."

"That's where you're wrong." Mrs. Riddenhauer watched Thorpe. "My husband is hung like a Brahma bull, so don't think size—"

"Olé," said Thorpe, snapping his finger overhead, giddy from the martinis and his own good fortune.

Mrs. Riddenhauer squinted at Thorpe, then turned back to Nell. "Still seems like a lot of money for a chunk of rock, and this guy with the headdress is an ugly son of a bitch, too." Her eyes narrowed at

Thorpe. "Olé . . . I get it." She hummed softly as she looked him over. "I like clever men."

"If you don't wish to take possession, I'm sure Douglas would be happy to retain the piece," said Nell.

"Don't be snippy," said Mrs. Riddenhauer, her eyes still on Thorpe. "Meachum said every room was supposed to have a—what did he call it?"

"An aesthetic focal point."

Mrs. Riddenhauer put back the limestone panel. "Well, the dining room needs a fucking focal point, and this is it. Just make sure it's installed before my party. You need to come by and rearrange the main living room, too. It's *still* not right." The sunlight coming through the window behind her made her skirt nearly transparent. A thong on center court . . . Thorpe wondered what Wimbledon would say about that. Mrs. Riddenhauer showed him her small, slightly uneven teeth. "You have a name, clever guy?"

"Frank Antonelli."

"Missy Riddenhauer." She slipped her hand in his. "As in *Camp Riddenhauer.*"

Thorpe nodded, as though he knew what she was talking about.

"What do you do, Frank?"

"I sell insurance."

"Sounds dull." Missy held on to his hand, and her grip was warm and very firm, and if she wanted to hang on, Thorpe was going to have to clock her to make her let go. "You don't *look* dull."

"Ah, but I am. I see that Ferrari of yours out front, and all I can think of is what kind of liability coverage you have, and how you keep that short skirt from blowing in the wind when you accelerate."

"Would you like to go for a ride? You can see how well I manage it."

"I can't today."

Missy gnawed her lower lip, and Thorpe wasn't sure if it was a sign of desire or anger. She gave his hand a final squeeze, then released him. "You want to come to my party? It's next Saturday night, and it's going to be loads of fun. Come on, what's to think about? Meachum did a complete makeover on our home—you'll get a chance to see if you like his work, and I'll get a chance to see if you're as boring as you say you are."

"Sure, sounds like fun."

"I'll put your name on the guest list." Missy slipped him a business card. "Send me an e-mail if you need anything. Nell, give the man the details." She turned on her heel, strode out the door, and slid behind the wheel of the Ferrari.

Thorpe tucked away Missy's business card as she roared off.

5

"Best behavior now, Warren. This is a dangerous man," said Billy, introducing them. "Everybody in the shop thought Frank was a brainiac, but I knew better."

Warren looked up from his beeping GameBoy, pushed aside a nest of light blue hair, the silver chains around his wrists making slinky sounds. He was in his twenties, a sullen punk in torn jeans and a black leather jacket, a barbell stud through his left eyebrow, blue mascara matching his hair and nail polish—the geek as rough trade. He propped one black engineer's boot on the plastic bench of lane number 24, the last lane of the Hollywood Bowlerama, eyeballing Thorpe.

Thorpe held up his right hand. "I come in peace."

Warren went back to his GameBoy, one of those modified units sold only in Japan.

"You'll have to forgive Warren—he's very territorial," said Billy.

"I'll survive." Thorpe felt like he had to shout to be heard over the thundering din, but Billy's silky voice somehow cut through the noise, slipped under the disco blaring on the sound system. No wonder Billy had wanted to meet here: there wasn't a parabolic mike or laser recorder that could pick up conversation through the auditory soup.

"Of course you will," purred Billy, a tall, powerfully built man in his mid-fifties, with large liquid eyes, a broad, flat nose, and skin the color of polished anthracite. His gray hair was cropped and thick, an aristocrat in burnt-orange trousers and a shimmering yellow rayon bowling shirt. He plucked his bowling ball from the return chute, hefted it in his huge hands. "Good to see you, Frank. The shop should have never let you go, but then, Hendricks always had a limited imagination."

"Maybe I was due for a change."

"Nonsense." Cheers erupted from the next lane. Old ladies in green team shirts—Keglar Kuties—were clapping, high-fiving each other. A wizened bottle redhead called to Billy, and he waved back, then moved to the approach line, stood there, the bowling ball clasped to his chest. His matching yellow bowling shoes whispered across the polished hardwood as he glided forward. A smooth release and the ball whipped down the alley. Strike! He sauntered back.

"Two forty-one," said Warren. "Today's three-game average is two twelve. Two seventeen for the week."

Billy tapped the side of his head. "Warren keeps it all up here. You should see him at the supermarket—he knows the final bill before the clerk scans the last item. Comes in handy, Frank. They can't subpoena what's not written down." His face reflected the red neon lane lights as he took inventory of Thorpe's dark gray Versace. "*Très* chic, as always. You're the best-dressed killer I ever met." He grinned. "One dead in the parking lot, another cut down charging out of the underbrush, and another so badly wounded, he died that afternoon." Pins crashed around them, echoing off the concrete-block walls. "My whole career, I never hefted anything more dangerous than a butter knife, and you kill three men in the fifteen seconds it took you to reach your car." Billy's eyes were bright now. "What does that *feel* like?"

"Like it wasn't nearly enough."

Billy nodded. "Yes, Kimberly was a talented girl, intellectually very agile. Weeks . . . well, I always thought he was a little careless."

"Shut up, Billy."

"Eggs and omelettes, Frank, and you *did* draw blood yourself. If you were an ancient Egyptian, those three dead men would be added to your slaves in the afterlife."

"I don't want any slaves."

"Might be nice to have someone to send out for ice water."

"You think I'm going to need a cold drink, Billy?"

Billy reached for his rum and Coke. "We're *both* going to be parched for all of eternity. Of that, I'm certain." He peered at Thorpe over the rim of the glass, a lepidopterist examining a particularly interesting butterfly, imagining how he would look with pins through his wings. "How are you *physically,* Frank? I heard you were lucky not to lose your spleen. I warrant you've been doing push-ups for weeks now, building your strength, working up a good healthy sweat—"

"Did you check out the Engineer like I asked?"

"Congratulations." Billy rattled the ice cubes in his drink. "You were right. He *was* a virus. You have no idea how many markers I had to call in to get confirmation."

"Does the Engineer's shop know where he is?"

"What are you guys talking about?" Warren looked from one to the other, his narrow fox face framed by the upturned collar of his leather jacket. "Speak English, okay?"

"A virus is a player who inserts himself into an existing criminal enterprise, then directs it toward his *own* ends, or the ends of his shop," explained Billy.

"I should have picked up on him," said Thorpe. "Lazurus was into extortion, credit card fraud, money laundering . . . nothing particularly interesting. Then the Engineer joined the crew and they shift into overseas transfers of dual-use hardware. I figured Lazurus had brought him in to oversee the technical part of the operation, but I should—"

"You weren't the only one fooled." Billy chuckled. "Lazurus probably thought it was *his* idea to go into the arms business. The Engineer was going to roll up some very nasty operators when the time was ripe. He was going to take down the whole network. You can understand him being vexed when you stepped on his toes. All that hard work spoiled."

"*Vexed?* You saw what he did at the safe house."

Billy shrugged. "These deep-cover boys are always twitchy, and the Engineer was positively subterranean. The way you and Kimberly duped him must have touched a nerve."

"Why didn't he just say something?" asked Thorpe. "We were on the same side."

"Actually, no." Billy played with the crease in his trousers. "Different shop."

"Same fucking side, Billy."

Billy flicked a speck of lint away. "The Engineer took out Lazurus's crew before he disappeared. Did you know that? Wiped the slate clean, every one of them, except for his own bodyguard. Disappeared with an unknown amount of cash and the cigar box of D-flawless diamonds that Lazurus was so fond of. The Engineer's old shop is as interested in finding him as you are."

"Sure they are."

Billy smiled. "Perhaps I *have* overstated their commitment."

"I want to talk to your contact at his old shop. I want to find out—"

"Who would ever trust me if I did that?" Billy laughed. "Besides, I've already asked about the Engineer. He's as much a mystery to them as he is to you." He stroked his chin. "I have good news, though. Your personnel file got hacked yesterday afternoon."

Thorpe stiffened. "Who was it? Did you run him down?"

"Regrettably, no," said Billy. "Warren put in a trip wire, but the intruder managed to cover his tracks. Temporarily at least. We can't be sure who it was, but the Engineer is the most likely candidate."

"He's got some sweet moves," said Warren, his eyes on the Game-Boy. "I've been slingshot all over the planet, bouncing from one ISP to another, but I'll find him."

"Warren changed the file, just as you asked," said Billy. "I had him tweak your postdischarge assessment. Fine piece of work, too, getting past the shop's fire walls."

"A defcon four–quality crack job," said Warren. "I could bring down the space shuttle if Billy asked me to."

"But you can't trace the Engineer."

"Not *yet*," said Warren.

"According to your file, you're now a very bad boy, Frank, as corrupt as they come. There's even a notation that you may have lifted a few million in cash from an al Qaeda banker who didn't survive his arrest. For your sake, I hope the Engineer doesn't take the bait."

"We're not done with each other," said Thorpe.

"I'm sure it will be a lovely reunion," said Billy. "Give Warren time to locate the Engineer. Warren's an artist. When I met him, he was wasting his time as a card counter in Vegas, and hot-sheeted at most of the casinos. Now he has a calling." His face was radiant. "I hate seeing talent wasted. That's the only sin there is."

"Oh, there's a few more," said Thorpe.

"Indeed." Billy sat on the bench, arms and legs spread wide, staking his turf. "How do you like it on the beach, Frank? Not much fun being just a taxpayer, is it?"

"I'm still getting used to it."

"You don't have to get used to it." Billy crunched the ice cubes from his drink between his strong white teeth. "Retirement is overrated. Even with perfect weather and congenial companions, I couldn't *wait* to get back into action. We've been spoiled, Frank. Playing God, it's the best game in the world." He winked at Thorpe. "You can talk about the nobility of the cause, but if all we cared about was the red, white, and blue we could have just bought a war bond."

Thorpe was going to disagree, but Billy would have known he was lying.

"I've started a . . . consulting firm, Frank. I'm in the process of assembling a team, the best of the best. Strictly corporate accounts. My clients are as eager for information as our former employer, just as ready to secure an advantage over their competitors, but without any presidential findings or pesky oversight boards to finesse. For us, there's just the paycheck and the pleasure of making the chickens tap-dance."

"What do we need him for?" asked Warren. "Just another soldier boy grown up and no place to go."

"Not just a soldier boy," said Billy. "Frank was Delta Force, the warrior elite, and freelancers by nature and training. No snappy salutes in Delta, no parades or public ceremonies; they actually call their officers by their first names."

"That's enough, Billy," said Thorpe.

"You should be proud of yourself," said Billy. "Frank here actually started a war by himself, set a leftist guerrilla army up against a Colombian drug cartel, and they never even knew who lit the match. Sadly, though, our government doesn't take kindly to such initiative. If I hadn't stepped in, Frank here might have ended up in Leavenworth."

"Are you done, Billy?"

"I just wanted to explain to Warren why I value you so highly," said Billy. "You're a rare individual, Frank, creative and highly adaptive, willing to spill blood, but not enamored of violence. Kimberly was the same way." He showed his teeth. "She was tougher, though. You're a little too tenderhearted."

"You want to bet?" said Thorpe.

Billy folded his hands in his lap. "Actually . . . no."

"What about Gavin Ellsworth?" Thorpe said lightly. "Is he on your team?"

"One of my first hires," said Billy. "A *very* cautious fellow, but a brilliant forger." He bent forward, started unlacing his bowling shoes. "We're going to have such a grand time working together again. I've got a new client, a software-development firm under considerable pressure in the marketplace. They have their sights on a rival firm's chief designer. I need one of your signature three-cushion shots, Frank. I need to get the man fired, to make his work product suspect to his former employer, and then have our client pluck him from the depths of despair. Nothing more grateful than a rescued man, right?" He slipped off his shoes, grinned at Thorpe. "When can you start?"

Thorpe didn't answer.

"The shop isn't going to take you back, if that's what you're counting on. The shop isn't even going to exist much longer, not as an off-the-books entity. *None* of them are." Billy wiggled his toes. His burnt-orange socks had a pattern of tiny black clocks. "Control and accountability are the watchwords of the day. Your imbroglio with the Engineer is already being cited as a rationale for the shops' being subsumed into traditional agencies. No fun in that, I can assure you. I can just see you sitting at an FBI meeting when the agent in charge starts droning on about work sheets and . . ." Billy narrowed his eyes, wagged a finger at Thorpe. "You *rascal*. I must be getting rusty."

"Just a little."

"You asked me about Gavin Ellsworth, and I let it slip right by," said Billy, annoyed with himself. "What do you want with him?"

"I can fool you, Billy, but I can't fool you for long."

6

Pinto was on his knees, tightening the chain linkage on Danny Duck, when the staff-only door opened behind him. "I told you, it's going to take me at least another hour," he called, concentrating on the lag bolt. The torque wrench slipped and he scraped his knuckles on the housing. *"Fuck."* He licked his hand, tasting blood and grease, as he turned. "See what you done. . . ." Vlad and Arturo stood in the open doorway, the two of them outlined by the morning sun, and Pinto's Cocoa Puffs did a backflip in his guts. He smiled. "Hey . . . you surprised me."

"Imagine that," said Arturo. "It's not even your birthday, either."

Vlad quietly shut the door, and the interior of the Down the Bunny Hole ride was darker after the flash of sunshine, illuminated only by the overhead lights.

Pinto gripped the torque wrench.

Arturo walked over to Gloria Goose and sat down, propping one foot on her plastic beak as he leaned back against the red upholstery. He folded his hands in his lap, a powerfully built middle-aged man in a black suit. His face was broad and deeply pocked, his hair brushed straight back. "You're late, Pinto."

Pinto stood up, wiped his hands on a rag, his forearms so heavily tattooed that it looked like he was wearing blue lace gauntlets. "Not so late . . . just a few eight balls behind."

"A few?" Arturo admired the shine in his loafers. His oldest son, Preston, shined all the shoes in his father's closet every evening after finishing his homework. As a boy, Arturo had helped support his family by shining shoes in the business district of Los Angeles. His sons would never need to shine another man's shoes, but it was good training. "I think it is more than a few. What do you think, Vlad?"

Vlad didn't answer.

Pinto slouched against Danny Duck, a gristly, hollow-eyed speed freak in jeans and a T-shirt, his face a skull, his hair in clumps. An irregular reddish purple scar ran from his left ear, across his cheek, and down his neck—a souvenir of a meth explosion years earlier. Pinto had been cooking up a batch in his uncle's storage shed, but he was in a hurry, as usual, and added the anhydrous ammonia too quickly. Rookie mistake. He was twenty-seven now, and a pretty good cooker when he wanted to be, but he preferred sales. He had the knack, and he got all the samples he wanted. His foot wouldn't stop tapping. No idea what the tune was, either. He saw Arturo watching him. "You know me, man. I'm good for it."

"Sure . . . we know you, Pinto. You are the man who is late."

Pinto laughed too loudly.

Vlad stared at the brightly colored cartoon characters on the walls: mama rabbits feeding lettuce sandwiches to their bunnies, Mr. and Mrs. Quack-Quack at the swimming hole with their ducklings. He did a slow turn; a tall, pale man wearing thrift-store pants and a striped short-sleeved shirt. His face was sharp and angular, his wispy hair the color of wet straw. His eyes reminded Pinto of the Canadian glaciers in the bottled-water ads on TV, clean and blue and frozen.

The three of them were inside the Down the Bunny Hole ride at the Kids Unlimited Karnival, located for the next two weeks in the north parking lot of the Yorba Linda Mall. The carnival wasn't open for another two hours. Pinto was doing regular maintenance on the rides. He had already finished adjusting Mrs. Piggly Wiggly's Tunnel of Fun, and rewired Dr. Frog's Lily Pond Party, which still gave off sparks, lights flickering. The rides were falling apart, reeking of spilled cola and orange drinks, and dangerously loud, the insulation worn away—to compensate, the management turned up the happy-music sound track to the maximum. Pinto heard "I Am a Friendly Fuzzy Bunny" in his nightmares, woke up wanting to kill the asshole who wrote that song.

"How did you know I was here?" asked Pinto. "I only got this job a couple days ago."

"Your girlfriend told us," said Arturo, his full lips barely moving.

"You talked to Lily?"

Arturo shrugged. "It was unavoidable."

Pinto let that one slide. "She's not supposed to answer the door when I'm not home."

"I think we forgot to knock," said Arturo.

"This is a pretty picture. . . ." It was the first thing Vlad had said since they slipped inside, his voice soft and lightly inflected. He pointed at Harvey Hare spray-painted on the ceiling, a bright blue Harvey with a cowboy hat and chaps, a carrot in his holster. "Pinto, do you know the artist who painted it?"

"Ah . . . no, man."

Arturo patted the pockets of his jacket, found a carob power-protein bar. He sat there listening to Vlad sing along to the piped-in music. Vlad liked to sing with the commercials and kids' songs on Radio Disney. They sometimes sat in their car for hours, Vlad singing while Arturo squeezed the hand-grip exerciser he kept under the front seat, right next to the Red Devil–brand lye. It had to be Red Devil. Not just because it was the best—lye was lye, after all—but because Arturo had started out with Red Devil a long time ago, and it had never let him down.

Vlad finished the last verse of "I Am a Friendly Fuzzy Bunny." He had a good voice, too, high and clear. "How wonderful to work in such a beautiful place," he said to Pinto.

"Yeah? Then you must think having brain cancer is wonderful." Pinto spit on the floor. "Like the bumper sticker says, 'I'd rather be tweaking.' " Think it, do it—he pulled a power hitter out of his jeans, gave it a twist, grinding the flaked methedrine inside, then slipped the plastic torpedo into his right nostril. First the right, then the left. He felt the top of his head lift, the chill running down his brain stem. He glared at Arturo. "You and Vlad didn't have to bother coming around this morning. It's fucking insulting."

"Is it?"

Pinto hated when Arturo used that tone. A Yuppie beaner and the man from Transylvania giving him shit, hassling Lily . . . He pushed back his hair, hit both nostrils again, heart racing. "Look . . . Arturo, I fronted some weight to this guy runs a landscaping business. Guy's got all kinds of clients on his route who like a taste, and don't mind paying top dollar for curb delivery. Mr. Greenthumb is supposed to come by my place tonight and pay me. I was going to call you this afternoon, tell you not to worry about your money."

"We're not worried." Arturo finished the protein bar, then swallowed three B_{12} capsules and a fat blocker, washed them all down with a couple swallows of bottled water. He took his pulse, then pulled a PDA from his jacket, entered in the data.

Arturo took thirty-eight vitamin and mineral supplements daily, monitored his bowel movements, and worked out every morning. Only five-eight, he weighed a brick-solid 201 pounds, about the same weight as Vlad, who was at least six-three and never exercised. Sometimes Vlad accompanied him to the gym, watching as Arturo went through his bench-press routine, not saying a word; then, when Arturo would max out around 410 pounds, Vlad would lie down and, without even a warm-up, crank out fifteen or twenty reps. It was unreal. Vlad wasn't on the juice, either; Arturo had never seen him take drugs of any kind.

Arturo's PDA beeped, alerted him to a new e-mail. He tapped the password, checked his mail, his face getting red. "Quentin's having trouble with the batch," he told Vlad, then glared at Pinto. "We cut too much slack; everyone tries to play us."

"Don't put me in that category, man," said Pinto. "You'll get your ten thousand—"

"You don't owe us any money," said Arturo. "It's been taken care of."

Pinto looked from one to the other. His sinuses dripped the bitter chemical into his mouth. He loved that taste.

"We hauled away your Mustang, so now we're even," explained Arturo. "Left another quarter pound of frost with the little woman just to show your credit's A-one again."

"You can't have my—"

"It's not yours anymore. We just came by to have you sign over the pink slip."

Pinto felt the scar tissue on his neck get warm. "That's a 1967 convertible. The *four*-barrel. Took me over three years to restore it. It's *cherry*." His scars were even warmer now. "Got to be worth at least twenty thousand . . . maybe twenty-five, and I wouldn't sell it for thirty. I love that fucking car."

Arturo unfolded the pink slip.

"I ain't signing that," said Pinto. "Fuck the both of you."

Lounging on Gloria Goose, Arturo sucked the last bits of protein bar from his eyeteeth.

Vlad reached under his shirt, pulled a black pistol out from the waistband of his pants.

"Hey . . . no, no." Pinto backed up, tripped over Danny Duck, and fell onto the floor.

Vlad squirted the right leg of Pinto's jeans, twirled the pistol around his index finger, and slipped it back into his waistband.

Pinto sat up, laughing. "A water pistol? Shit, Vlad, who knew you had a sense of humor?" He looked at Arturo. "So you were just fucking with me about the Mustang?"

Arturo ignited a wooden match with a flick of his thumbnail, tossed it at Pinto. His leg flared with a bright blue flame.

Pinto squealed, beat out the flame with his hands. "That ain't cool."

Vlad quick-drew the squirt gun, pumped a couple of blasts of gasoline into Pinto's chest.

Arturo tossed another match but missed. His next two matches were batted aside by Pinto, but the fourth match set his chest on fire, singed his chin before he put it out.

Pinto backed up, eyes wide. He tried to dodge, but Vlad was good with the squirt gun, hitting him in the leg, the crotch, and even his scalp with the cold gasoline.

Arturo kept up a steady rain of burning matches, he and Vlad working in tandem, herding Pinto from one end of the room to the other. Pinto twisted and ducked around the bright plastic animal cars, but no matter what he did, he kept blazing up. The back of one hand caught fire, and when he tried to wave it out, he just made it worse. The stink of burning hair followed every move he made, and it was like the meth explosion that had scarred him happening all over again—the burn, the smell, the fear.

Arturo held up the pink slip.

Pinto flipped him the finger.

Vlad pretended to fan the water pistol like a six-shooter, splashed gasoline on Pinto's shoes an instant before one of Arturo's matches landed on his foot.

Pinto stomped like that Lord of the Dance faggot trying to put out the fire, screaming, while Arturo laughed and Vlad doused him. He stood there, out of breath, his clothes smoldering, soaked with gasoline, waiting for Arturo to torch him.

Arturo struck a match, held out the pink slip in the other hand.

Vlad blasted away with the squirt gun, splashing gasoline across Pinto's face, drenching him.

Arturo waved the pink slip.

Tears rolling down his gaunt cheeks, Pinto slowly held out his hand.

Arturo blew out the match.

Arturo and Vlad stepped outside a few minutes later, blinking in the sunlight. Some of the carnies were clustered around the snack bar, scraggly men and women gobbling hot dogs before the crowds came. Others leaned against their rides, drinking beer out of paper bags.

Vlad stared at the biggest ride in the parking lot. "I want to ride the Tilt-A-Whirl."

"The carnival isn't open yet, amigo," said Arturo.

Vlad was already on his way.

For the next half hour, Arturo watched Vlad going round and round on the Tilt-A-Whirl all by himself, smiling broadly, whooping it up.

The first time Arturo had invited Vlad over for dinner, his wife had been furious. Fortuna had said that Vlad was too white, that he was in league with *el diablo.* Vlad had been on his best behavior that night, bringing presents for the children—coloring books and remote-control race cars, Barbies and G.I. Joe walkie-talkies—but the toys did not soothe Fortuna. Cradling the crucifix that he had bought for her in

Mexico City, the one blessed by the Holy Father himself, she had collected the gifts after Vlad left, and thrown them all away.

Arturo thought Fortuna spent too much time at Mass, but she was his wife, and the children were her responsibility. If she wanted to throw out perfectly good toys, that was her decision. But when she told him that she didn't want Vlad in the house anymore, Arturo told her that such things were for *him* to decide, and when she insisted, clutching at his arm, Arturo threw her down with a flick of his wrist, told her if she asked him again, he would break her jaw, and then his mother would have to stay with them while she recovered. They never spoke of it again, and Vlad came over for dinner at least once a week.

"Arturo!" Vlad waved from the top of the Tilt-A-Whirl. "Arturo!"

Arturo waved back. If Fortuna could see Vlad now, she would be ashamed of herself. How could someone who took such delight in small things be in league with the devil?

1

"This good deed of yours, Frank, what a colossal waste of talent." Billy hadn't said a word during Thorpe's story, just sat there, impassive, but he couldn't hold back now. "A wake-up . . . just because some businessman smacked a child in the face? You think the boy has never been smacked before?"

"Not in front of me."

"What do you expect the art dealer to do, *apologize?*"

"I already gave him a chance to do that, but he declined."

Billy stared at Thorpe, the tumble of bowling pins crashing around them. "You're serious." The three of them sat on the bench of lane number 24, secure in their privacy. "Look, if you want to sharpen your claws, that's a *good* sign, a healthy sign, but why bother with this art dealer? I have more challenging targets for you."

"Software engineers? No thanks."

"You'll use your talents for Uncle Sam but not for me? Not for *yourself?* What are you, a patriot?" Billy's laugh boomed. "You were bounced out of the military, bounced out of the shop; you don't owe your country anything. It's time to grab what's on the table."

"I'm going to pass."

Billy shook his head, amused. "Have it your way. The offer still stands." He took a deep breath, spread his hands in an attitude of forgiveness. "I'm simply suggesting that this wake-up of yours is a thoughtless indulgence, as narcissistic as your vendetta against the Engineer."

Thorpe leaned closer, right in Billy's face now. "I don't need your approval."

"Temper, temper, but do you honestly think Kimberly would be targeting the Engineer if *you* had been the one murdered in the safe house?"

"You didn't know her, Billy."

"I *hired* her, Frank. Just like I hired you."

"You didn't know her."

Billy eased back. "I'm simply suggesting that getting emotionally involved is risky, risky for you, risky for everyone around you. You're a professional, so is the Engineer. You squeezed him, and he turned it back on you. If you could get some distance—"

Thorpe put a hand on Billy's shoulder, felt the big man tense as he drew him closer. Billy liked touching, but he didn't like being touched. Thorpe kept his hand where it was. "That's the problem, Billy. I *can't* get any distance from it. None at all." He slowly released him.

Billy adjusted his shirt, smoothed out the wrinkles where Thorpe had grabbed him. A tiny vein throbbed on the side of his skull. "If you think this foolishness with the art dealer is going to help you get back into shape for some *real* work, you have my blessing."

"I don't think it's foolish," said Warren.

They both turned and stared at him. Warren hadn't said a word since Thorpe had started talking about the wake-up.

Warren looked up from his GameBoy, surprised. "What? The guy hit a *kid*."

Thorpe nodded. "That's right."

Warren pushed his light blue curls away from his face. "My mother's boyfriend was a hitter. That shit would come out of nowhere, too. One minute, I'd be watching *Power Rangers;* the next, I'd be slammed up against the wall. Never did figure out what I had done wrong." The barbell stud gleamed in his left eyebrow; it looked like a tear falling upward, freed of gravity. "I say *do* it, Frank. Fuck him up good."

"Well . . . that was interesting," said Billy, lips pursed. "Warren has given you his seal of approval, so I guess there's nothing more to be said. How do you intend to use Ellsworth? You plan on selling one of his bogus masterpieces to the art dealer?"

"Something like that."

Billy waited, then gave up. "There's no need to involve Ellsworth. I can simply have Warren crash the dealer's credit history. We could even get him audited, if you like. Take Ware five minutes—"

"*Two* minutes," said Warren, tapping away at his GameBoy.

Thorpe smiled, enjoying seeing Billy try to find out what his plan was. Billy *hated* not knowing things. It wasn't a matter of personal safety, or gaining financial advantage, or even power. Billy just liked being at the absolute apex of the information pyramid. The "Prime Mover," he called it.

"Why not just tell the art dealer's wife that he's cheating?" said Billy. "Or just make the threat. That should do the job." He rested his chin on his cupped hands, his expression serene, and Thorpe was reminded of the Mayan lord in Meachum's gallery, distant and alien and implacable. "No? All right . . . well, considering your style, I imagine you're planning something simple, something with the personal touch."

" 'Something borrowed, something blue,' " said Thorpe.

Billy slowly brightened. "The art dealer's wife . . . is she lovely, Frank?"

"I only met her once."

"Sometimes once is all it takes," said Billy. "Love at first sight, that's the only kind that counts." He cocked his head at Thorpe. "Just one look . . . wasn't that the way it was with you and Kimberly?"

Thorpe raised a forefinger to his lips. "Shhh."

Billy forced a smile.

"I'm just going to give Meachum a wake-up," Thorpe said quietly. "I'm not saving the world or buying my way into heaven. I just want something to keep me busy while I wait for the Engineer to surface. Are you going to help me or not?"

"Of *course* I'll help you," Billy said, preening, and Thorpe remembered all the reasons he had for not liking him. "What kind of a friend would I be if I didn't? I'll have Ellsworth contact you immediately."

Thorpe stood up.

"You should stay off the Net for a while," said Warren.

Thorpe looked at him.

Warren's fingers danced over the GameBoy. "Me jumping around after the Engineer . . . if he's good enough, and I'm not saying he is, but *if* he is, he may be able to backtrack on me. He may be able to smoke out my connections. Billy uses my system when he contacts you, so that's a vulnerability." His fingers stabbed at the keys now. "I've got enough black ice in my program that he's never going to home in on my location, but you, Frank, you got that off-the-rack security. I'd be careful if I were you." He peeked at Thorpe. "If you have to hit the Net, don't hang around, that's all I'm saying."

"Thanks, Warren."

Warren went back to his game. "I just don't like the Engineer playing cute with my trip wire. Pisses me off."

"I'm glad we've got that settled," said Billy. "Go ahead, Frank, give the art dealer a wake-up. Buy the kid a baseball mitt and take him to a ball game, load him up with hot dogs and Cracker Jack. See if it makes him all better. See if it makes *you* all better. When you're finished, we'll get to work, you and I. It will be just like the old days."

Thorpe didn't answer.

8

"I told you, *buddy,* you're not on the guest list."

"Just check with Mrs. Riddenhauer," said Thorpe.

"I don't *need* to check with Missy. The guest list is my responsibility, and I don't see your fucking name on it. No name, no invite, no can do." The man in the doorway jabbed the list, his round face getting redder. He was a beefy redhead in white linen trousers and a short-sleeved sports shirt with a pattern of exploding volcanoes. "You going to take off on your own steam, or am I going to have to help you?"

Thorpe saw Missy walking toward them, dressed in a black leather micromini and a matching halter, her white-blond hair dangling in dozens of braids. An S-M Medusa. Thorpe stood there in a gunmetal gray single-breasted suit and a black silk polo shirt, watching her bear down on him.

"Problem, Cecil?"

Cecil's freckles flared. "Mr. Style Fuck here is trying to crash the party."

"I invited him."

Cecil waved the list at her. "His name ain't on the list."

Missy smacked the paper aside, air-kissed Thorpe, and led him inside. "You'll have to forgive my brother. He's the family idiot."

"DNA plays some nasty jokes," said Thorpe.

"You don't put the names on the list, how can I do my job?" Cecil yelled after them.

Missy's high heels went *clickity-clack* against the hardwood floor. She squeezed Thorpe's hand as they reached the edge of a huge sunken living room filled with people. Waiters in tuxedos gracefully navigated the room, keeping their silver trays with drinks and canapés aloft. "Olé, Frank."

"Olé?" A young guy patted Missy on the hip, sloshed his cocktail on the carpet. "What does that mean?"

"Private joke," said Missy, her eyes on Thorpe. "Frank, this is my husband, Clark. Clark, this is Frank . . . something or other."

"Greetings, dude." Clark was a lanky, barefoot beach bum with stringy shoulder-length hair and sleepy blue eyes. He wore baggy madras shorts and an orange tank top with a CAMP RIDDENHAUER logo. A Superman Band-Aid crossed his chin, and even that added to his look of insouciant cool. "Glad you could make the party. *Mi casa . . .* well, you know the drill." He tossed his empty glass into a potted palm. "Rock on."

"Mingle, baby!" Missy called as Clark staggered off, bumping his way across the room and down a flight of stairs. "He's a genius, you know."

"Yes, I could tell."

"Clark's really hooked into youth culture, but I hope when he gets older, he dresses more like you. European suits, plain but sharp. Above it all. Is that how you feel, Frank? Like you're above it all?"

"Eight miles high."

Missy squeezed his arm. "I love an arrogant man. They're such a challenge."

The house was a sprawling, gated oceanfront estate with natural wood, high ceilings, and full-length windows open to the beach. The sound of the waves rolled in over the hum of conversation. Nell had filled Thorpe in on the Riddenhauers after Missy had stalked out of the art gallery. Clark Riddenhauer designed a line of sportswear geared toward surfers and would-be surfers—he was a talented slacker, a guy who acted like he would have been happy to live in a VW van, eat fish tacos for breakfast, smoke dope, and surf. Missy's job was to crack the whip.

"Clark started the Camp Riddenhauer line just three years ago, and now we've got five shops." Missy smoothed Thorpe's lapels. "I don't fuck around on my husband, just so you know."

"So you're only practicing now, in case you get divorced?"

Missy started to laugh, then spotted someone across the room—a blue-haired matriarch wearing cat's-eye glasses and a paisley muumuu, a cigarette jutting from the corner of her painted mouth. Missy waved, but the woman ignored her. "I hope that old cunt gets cancer," Missy hissed. She waved again, and the woman acknowledged her with a curt nod this time, ashes floating down. "We'll talk later. I have to make nice right now."

Thorpe watched Missy scurry over, take the older woman's arm, chattering away. He took a passing glass of champagne, then made his way through the house, listening to conversations and checking out the security. Thorpe had met with Gavin Ellsworth earlier in the day, and the master forger had delivered the goods, Ellsworth hunched over a bowl of chicken noodle soup at Denny's, goggle-eyed behind his thick glasses as he crumbled crackers into his soup, reminding Thorpe of the federal penalties if he got caught. Thorpe smiled at the memory. Billy was right, as usual: Thorpe *had* decided on the simple approach for his wake-up, one that required the minimum of detail work and the maximum of bravado. He touched the wallet in the breast pocket of his jacket, deftly avoided a drunk in a purple tuxedo, and worked his way deeper into the party.

The talk in the room was mostly about the house, the new art, the encroachment of the wrong sort into the colony, and the lovely ass on the new tennis instructor at the club. The crowd was California chic, the women in leather and silk and skin, most of the men in yacht club finery—every man a commodore! Claire would have loved the scene, everyone's ego on full display, with a full-fantasy kicker.

"I was *wondering* if you were really going to show up," said Nell.

"Nice party."

"I can't wait to leave." Nell pushed back a strand of hair. She was overdressed in a formal blue cocktail dress and jacket, a single strand of pearls around her neck. "What do you think of the art?"

"Who's the woman Missy is talking to?" asked Thorpe.

Nell peered across the room. "That's Betty Berquist, Betty B . . . local doyenne. Lived here forever, drinks her way through every party and charity gala. Writes a weekly column for the *Gold Coast Pilot,* very bitchy, very on point. *Everyone* reads it." She nodded. "Those're the Enersons. He's in commercial real estate; she collects cloisonné pig figurines." Another nod. "Carla Schmidt. Husband owns a Mercedes dealership. Won't come *near* us. Strictly New York galleries." Another nod. "Mark Kelly. Halogen lighting. Did over a hundred million in sales last year. We did his game room. Contemporary erotica, the cruder the better." She grimaced. "I sometimes think I don't have the stomach for this job. Ah, there's Douglas. I have to go over and schmooze with some prospective clients. Would you like to meet him?"

"You go ahead." Thorpe spotted Halley Anderson on the other side of the room, the blonde from the red Porsche, pretending to listen to some Botoxed duffer wearing a new Harley-Davidson jacket with the collar turned up. She kept smiling and looking past him at Meachum. Thorpe eased his way into the dining room, hearing Missy's voice. He found her standing in front of an antique glass case displaying some dull, unglazed Incan pottery and shards of green jade. The Mayan plaque rested at the center.

"I *personally* selected the pieces," said Missy to a group of women clustered around the case. She pointed to the limestone plaque. *"This* is the centerpiece of my collection. The man with the elaborate head-dress is probably a Mayan king."

"He looks like a Vegas showgirl," said an icicle-thin woman with a two-carat diamond in each earlobe. "It's *broken,* too."

"Well, *Jackie,* it's got some jagged edges because it was chipped off a Mayan temple in the middle of the jungle and then brought down-river in a dugout canoe," said Missy. "You ever hear of Indiana Jones?"

"You ever hear of being ripped off?" sniffed Jackie, walking away.

Thorpe edged after Jackie, body-to-body through the crowd, the air heavy with perfume. He watched her summon a drink, then stand around fingering a display of orchids, making sure they were real. He had planned on coming back tomorrow or the next day, but he could finish things now. All he had to do was sidle up to Jackie, whisper a few words in her ear, and she would take care of the rest of it, the rumor spreading through the party like a virus. Thorpe could be on his way. He watched Jackie tapping her foot, saw her tear off an orchid blossom and toss it onto the carpet, and decided to keep walking. Using her against Meachum was overkill, and besides, Missy would be equally hurt by the gossip. Missy was a climber, spikes on at all times, but she hadn't done anything to Paulo, or Thorpe, either. No, he was going to stick to his original plan. But he was going to check out the rest of the house first.

As he eased past an alcove, he stopped, seeing a pale man standing alone in a corner, trembling. His cheekbones were sharp as blades, his blond hair bled of color. Looking at his high-water trousers and badly ironed white shirt, Thorpe thought at first he was a party crasher, but if so, he wasn't enjoying himself. "Excuse me . . . can I help you?" said Thorpe.

The man's blue eyes were wide. He kept trembling.

Thorpe put his hand on the man's arm.

The man stared at Thorpe. "The room is too . . . *full.* I . . . I cannot breathe."

Thorpe squeezed the man's arm. It was like trying to compress a steel beam. "Take it easy. What's your name?"

"Vladimir." The man was gasping now. "Vlad."

"Okay, Vlad, how about if I walk you outside? It's not that far."

Vlad clung to Thorpe, sweaty and sour. "I am scared in here."

"Don't worry, I've got you," Thorpe said gently, leading him out. "Just breathe—"

"Arturo!" Vlad jerked. *"Arturo."*

Thorpe turned, saw a stocky man in a perfectly tailored black suit. He looked like a middleweight boxer turned hedge-fund manager.

"What's going on?" growled Arturo.

"Too many people," said Vlad, panting. "I am choking on them. This man . . . he wanted to help me." His watery eyes turned to Thorpe. "Thank you, *sir.* You're very kind."

"I hope you feel better." Thorpe watched Arturo guide Vlad toward the front door, then headed off in the other direction. At the far wall, he took a short flight of stairs down, following the sound of laughter, louder than and different from the sounds above. He came out into a large room that smelled faintly of epoxy resin. There were half-made surfboards stacked nearby, Styrofoam shavings curling underfoot, black respirators hanging next to an industrial ventilator on the far wall.

Clark and four other men stood around a finished surfboard that was laid out on a rack at waist height, their fingers curled around beer bottles. The board must have been twelve feet long, with blue and silver decorations, ancient Hawaiian motifs. Other finished boards leaned against the walls, old-style longboards, not meant for hotdogging, but for elegantly cruising the waves. The men with Clark were in their forties and fifties, deeply tanned, wearing surf jams and T-shirts washed too many times, potbellied and losing their hair, but utterly at ease with one another. They were having the best time of anyone Thorpe had seen at the party, and he envied them. Clark was right in the middle, talking fast, in a half crouch, pivoting as though he were riding a wave. One of the other men spotted Thorpe, and they all turned.

"It's cool, boys," said Clark. "This here's . . . Fred, or Farley, or . . ."

"Frank." Thorpe reached into a cooler filled with crushed ice, pulled out a bottle of beer.

"You surf, Frank?"

Thorpe twisted the cap off. "No."

"I was telling Kelsey about a board I'm making for him," said Clark. "Plastic core for—"

"If you don't surf, what do you do with your life?" demanded a man with frizzy hair.

"Piss it away, mostly," said Thorpe.

"Good for you." Clark cracked his bottle against Thorpe's. "Me, too."

"You still haven't told us what happened to your chin, Clark," said Frizzy Hair.

Clark took a swallow of beer. "Did a wicked face plant at Trestles yesterday."

Frizzy Hair belched. "My money's on Missy closing her legs without warning."

The other longboarders laughed.

"What money?" Missy stood at the bottom of the stairs. "You said for *your* money, I had closed my legs without warning." She walked toward them. "What I want to know, Mr. Mack Sinclair, Mr. *Second* Place, Waimea Invitational 19 *fucking* 87, is what money could you possibly have to bet on what my legs did or did *not* do?"

Frizzy Hair shrugged, lowered his eyes. "I didn't mean nothing."

"You don't mean shit," said Missy. "None of you freeloaders do." She shook her head. "Clark, honey, you need to get back to the party. Frank . . . I don't know how many wrong turns you took to find your way here, but you better come with us before the boys here start telling you about the good old days and the good old waves, and then Mack asks you to spring for another keg."

Clark hurried after Missy, but Thorpe finished his beer. "Nice meeting you fellows." He walked out, keeping his eye on Missy's ass hitting all cylinders in that tight leather skirt.

Missy didn't turn around, but she must have known he was there. "Hanging around with those fools . . . I'm disappointed in you, Frank."

"*Already?* That's a new record."

Missy looked flustered.

"You shouldn't talk to Mack like that, baby," said Clark. "He's got his pride."

"That's all he's got," said Missy.

Clark grinned at Thorpe. "When she's right, she's right."

The three of them separated in the dining room. Clark and Missy walked toward the living room, while Frank headed for the front door. He took a shortcut through the game room, made his way past the people clustered around the pool table, playing arcade games. Glancing into the living room, he could see Meachum and Nell talking to a husband and wife combo, pitching hard, Meachum with his chest puffed, jaw thrust forward, the hard charger in all his glory. Nell laughed at his jokes, nodding reflexively, and Thorpe wondered how much longer she could keep doing it without her head exploding. Probably longer than she would have believed. You start out with grand ambitions, but you find out you have an almost infinite capacity for betraying them.

"Why so sad, Frank?"

Thorpe turned, saw Gina Meachum beside him, a drink in her hand. "*Hello.* I'm surprised to see you here."

"I could say the same about you." Gina was a little tipsy, a little uncomfortable in casual jeans and a short-sleeved sweater the color of sweet cream. It probably wasn't her kind of a party, which spoke well of her. "How do you know the Riddenhauers?"

"I don't. I just got an invitation and thought it might be fun."

"A terrible miscalculation." They laughed together. "My husband is Douglas Meachum. That's him over there, going to town on the Cushings. He selected the Riddenhauers' artwork."

"So you're playing the part of the loyal wife tonight."

"Actually, Douglas didn't want me to come, but I insisted. He's afraid I'll say something he'll regret." Gina finished her drink. "How's your knee?"

"I had a good nurse."

"You look like you're ready to leave. It's early."

"It's overdue." Thorpe kissed her on the cheek. "Good night."

"Lucky man."

9

"Just give me the name," typed Thorpe. He had logged on after coming home from the party, given it one more shot. "Give me the name. We can both go to sleep."

"Not sure."

"Give me what you've got, then." It took even longer to get a response this time.

"I'm sure of the name. Not sure I should give it to you."

Thorpe stared at the screen, trying to determine the best tactic. The wrong approach would shut down this avenue for good. It had taken him four days to connect with this man, ever since Billy confirmed that the Engineer had been working for another shop. Thorpe had been passed from one contact to another, before finally reaching him tonight. His fingers hovered over the keyboard, then banged out, "I won't insult you by offering money, but I can promise you my help with any problems you might have." He changed the word *problems* to *problem* before sending the instant message.

The courtyard gate squeaked, and Thorpe got up from the computer. He heard Pam giggle as he peeked through the blinds, saw her staggering through the moonlight toward her front door. A guy with a crew cut had his arm around her, a lumbering jock in khakis and a red-and-blue-striped rugby shirt. Thorpe went back to the computer, laid the 9-mm on the table.

"Money is never an insult."

Thorpe waited.

"Still, a favor is a nice thing to be owed."

Thorpe turned at the sudden welter of voices from outside, Pam yelling, the jock barking out obscenities. He forced himself to stay seated, to give the man on the other end of the conversation time to decide. Impatience was a sign of weakness.

"So many problems in the world, Frank. It would be good to have someone to call."

Thorpe glanced toward the curtains, then back at the screen.

"Dale Bingham is the name you're looking for."

Pam started shouting again. He could hear Claire trying to smooth things over, repeating over and over that it was late, that it was after midnight. Thorpe was already out the door by the time the jock called somebody "a fucking bitch."

Lights came on in a couple of other apartments as Thorpe ambled over, deliberately slowing his pace. The three of them were clustered on the steps of apartment number 4, Pam just inside the open door, while Claire blocked the jock from following. Pam was dressed sleek and sexy, hennaed hair piled high, glitter dusted across the tops of her breasts, but Claire must have been in bed already, her hair tousled, barefoot, wearing a Raiders jersey that hung to her knees.

"Have you seen my cat?" asked Thorpe.

The jock whirled. There was a fresh scratch on his cheek, two pink parallel lines. "What's your problem?"

"Looking for my cat," said Thorpe, closer now.

"I *told* you I was celibate," Pam said from behind Claire. "That's the first thing I said when you asked me if I wanted a drink. I'm celibate."

"Fine, you don't have to cum." The jock tried again to get through the door, but Claire held her ground.

"I just wanted to dance—that's what I told you." Pam's mascara was smeared. "You seemed like such a nice guy, Don. That's why I let you drive me home."

"My name is *Ron,* you fucking bitch."

Thorpe stepped onto the porch. The air was heavy with booze. "Here, kitty, kitty."

The jock turned on Thorpe, fists balled. "Get out of here, man, or I'll kick your ass."

"I'm just looking for my cat. She's a beautiful fluffy white Persian."

Thorpe smiled at him. "You probably should go home, Ron; Snowball is scared of strangers."

"I don't give a fuck about your cat, man." The jock went to push Thorpe, but Thorpe dipped his shoulder, and the guy pushed air, lurched off the porch and onto the grass. The jock quickly got to his feet, his eyes hot now. "You *tripped* me."

Thorpe stepped off the porch, leading the jock away. "Here, kitty. Snowball?"

"Be careful, Frank," called Claire.

The jock jabbed a forefinger at her. "You, *shut* up." He advanced on Thorpe.

Thorpe stood there in his baggy shorts and a T-shirt. "I'll walk you to your car, if you want, Ron. Or call you a cab."

The jock swung at Thorpe's head, but Thorpe slipped-dodged the punch and threw him off balance. Another punch, same result. Another and another, the jock slipping on the damp grass, scrambling up, breathing hard, cursing. He kept kicking and punching, but Thorpe stayed just out of reach, moving loose and easy, sometimes gently tugging at the jock's rugby shirt, sending him sprawling. After a few minutes, the jock was on his hands and knees in the grass, dripping with sweat and trying to catch his breath.

Thorpe helped him up. "I'm really tired, and it's way past my bedtime. How about we call a truce. You go back to the club and find someone who hasn't taken a vow of chastity, and I'll go make myself a cup of warm cocoa and look for my kitty cat."

The jock wiped his nose, nodded. "You're lucky I don't want to hurt an old guy."

"I appreciate that." Thorpe watched him leave, waiting until the jock had gone through the iron gate before walking back onto the porch. Miss Edwards upstairs had turned off her light, but he knew she was still watching. "You ladies all right?"

"Snowball?" Claire pinched him, laughed.

Thorpe smiled back at her. "That's a *nice* name for a cat. If I had a cat, I'd probably name her something like that. Or Tabby."

"I bet when Gandhi said he was celibate, nobody argued with him," said Pam.

Claire and Thorpe looked at each other.

Pam yawned. "You coming in?"

"I'm going to stay out here for a little bit," said Claire, sitting on the porch steps.

Thorpe sat beside her.

"I shouldn't have left her alone at the club," said Claire after Pam had closed the door. "It's just that I have a busy day tomorrow and—"

"It wasn't your fault."

"She's got lousy taste in men," said Claire. "Not that I should talk."

"How long has this celibacy thing been going on?"

Claire laughed. "Three days. A new record."

They sat there, not speaking now, enjoying the quiet of the surrounding apartments, aware of the odd intimacy that existed between them, an unacknowledged intimacy. A soap bubble of desire. Miss Edwards had given up and gone to bed. Just the two of them alone in the courtyard, hearing the hum of the freeway traffic in the distance. It felt like being shipwrecked on a desert island, listening to the sound of surf and not caring if they were rescued.

Claire shivered, pulled the football jersey down over her knees. "That was nice what you did. Not hitting that jerk."

"Guys like that, all meat and attitude, you hit them and they resent it. They make excuses. They say they were drunk or you sucker punched them. You're just giving them a reason to come back for more." Thorpe plucked a blade of grass, peeled it down the center. "This way, you let them tire themselves out. If you pretend not to notice, they go away with their dignity intact and they never bother you again."

"I shouldn't have been surprised by the way you handled him." Claire scratched behind her knee, and he knew the skin was baby-soft back there. "Question number sixteen."

"Okay . . ."

Claire nodded again. "Question sixteen of the Minnesota Multiphasic Human Relations test. 'You usually walk, A: fairly fast, with long steps; B: fairly fast, with short, quick steps; C: head up, looking the world in the face; D: slowly, head down.' You answered, 'C: head up, looking the world in the face,' which indicates that you approach situations without any preconceived notions, with creativity and openness."

"What about Ron the jock? How would he have answered the question?"

" 'A: fairly fast, with long steps.' A 'tromp right over you' guy who doesn't take no for an answer."

Thorpe smiled. "That stuff is bullshit, you know."

"I *have* had my doubts lately. I've been asking you questions for months now—Iowa, Stanford-Binet. . . . Your test results are contradictory. Not inconclusive, *contradictory*." She was wide-awake. "Sometimes I think you do that deliberately."

"That's impossible. People with Ph.D.'s put those tests together."

She pinched him again, harder this time. "I've been taking course work in criminal profiling. The certification process is pretty rigorous, but police and federal agencies are hiring, and I could use a full-time job."

"A hundred years ago, cops used phrenology to solve crimes, convinced that the bumps on the heads of suspects could determine guilt or innocence. Profiling is in the same category. All those TV experts . . . the killer is a white man in his early thirties who wears boxers, not briefs . . . except when he isn't, and doesn't."

Claire wiggled her toes. She had long ones, too. "Maybe I should sell insurance, like you."

"You wouldn't like it."

Claire's face was close, her breath warm on his cheek. "Why haven't you ever made a move on me? I know you're attracted."

Thorpe looked back at her. "You're too smart for me. I wouldn't have a chance."

"Liar." Claire put her arm around him. "We'd have some fun."

Thorpe half-closed his eyes, enjoying her touch, almost giving in.

Claire must have sensed his hesitation. "I used to see that one girl come by late at night. Cute brunette . . . acted like she knew just where she was going. She seemed like the kind of girl you'd go for. I was a little jealous." She brushed her lips across his neck, and he raked his hands through her hair, the night humming now. "I kept waiting for her to show up after you got carjacked. Take care of you, maybe bring some chicken soup . . . at least see how you were doing. So, I guess it's over with her."

Thorpe pulled away slightly. "Yeah, it's over."

Claire stiffened. "You're still carrying a torch?"

"No . . . not exactly."

She watched him. "But not exactly free, either?"

He missed her touch already. "No."

"No one is totally free, Frank. You can wait around forever for the perfect moment. Sometimes you just have to take what's in front of you and enjoy it." She waited. "Not tonight, huh? You don't know what you're missing."

"No . . . not tonight."

"Pretty sure of yourself, thinking you're going to get asked again. Must be nice to be God's gift to women." Claire kissed him and he kissed her back, her mouth warm. "Good night, Frank," she breathed into him, getting up. Another kiss and the door closed behind her, gone before he could tell her he had changed his mind. The night was lonely without her.

Thorpe went back to his apartment. He had left the computer on, something that Warren had warned him against.

"You're up late, Frank. Or is it early where you are?"

Thorpe stared at the instant message flashing. He didn't recognize the screen name, but he knew immediately who it was.

"Don't ignore me, Frank. You had better manners that morning in the park."

Thorpe shivered. That's what happens when you get what you wish for. He typed "About time. I had about given up on you."

"Keep the faith."

"We're way past that, you and I."

"You got fired, Frank. I hope it wasn't something I did."

"How did you find me?"

"Trade secret. I took a peek at your personnel file. You've been a naughty boy, Frank. Got your fingers in the honey pot, according to what I read, but then, you should hear what they say about me. We should get together sometime. Exchange notes."

"I'm pretty busy these days."

"You're not just playing hard to get, are you, Frank?"

"I don't see what you have to offer. You had to burn down Lazurus's operation to get away. Makes you seem kind of desperate."

"Why so hostile? I've always treated you with the utmost courtesy. Is that belly wound still giving you problems? I hope you don't blame me for that."

"Of course not."

"Can you still eat everything you like? Fried foods and such? You seem like the kind of person who likes things spicy. I'd hate to think you were on some bland baby food regimen."

"I've got a healthy appetite, thanks."

"Glad to hear it. We have to take our pleasures where we find them."

"Where are you?"

"I'm here, Frank."

"You know what I mean. Can you smell the ocean from where you are?"

"I went beachcombing just this morning. The offshore swells brought in all sorts of interesting things. What about you?"

"I can smell the surf from where I'm sitting."

"We might be neighbors and not even know it. Sad, isn't it? We should get together."

"You think we have anything to talk about?"

"Absolutely."

"I'll think about it."

"Be bold, Frank."

"I have to get my beauty sleep." Thorpe logged off. His hands were shaking. He stared at his fingers until they stopped trembling, waited until they were perfectly still. It took longer than he would have liked.

10

"I still don't know why *I'm* the only one who can fix coffee," grumbled Cecil, bumping the table, the Pyrex pot held high. " 'Cecil get me some coffee.' 'Cecil make me some eggs. . . .' "

Missy looked up from dealing out her tarot cards, annoyed at being interrupted, the precognitive *flow* totally ruined now. She scooped up the cards and then straightened them as her brother refilled her cup. Normally, she would have been furious with him for distracting her while she was doing her morning reading, but after last night's triumph, she was willing to overlook his stupidity.

She watched Cecil's clumsy fingers holding the pot, coarse red hairs in waves across the back of his hands. Hands just like his daddy's. Their mama had hated those ugly hands, those farmer's hands, but she had put up with them, and that was her own damn fault. Cecil reached out and steadied her cup as he poured. He'd be thinking of filling the cup until it overflowed, imagining the scalding coffee slopping onto the table, splashing her tarot cards. Cecil might be thinking that, but he didn't do it, stopping so that the fresh coffee was exactly one inch from the rim, just like she had taught him. Missy could train an orangutan to be a proper English butler if she put her mind to it.

"How come it's always *me* on kitchen duty?" Cecil scratched his belly. "That's a fair question, isn't it?"

Missy picked up the deck of cards, shuffled. She was wearing only a loosely knotted black silk robe, her blond hair unbraided now, a wild corona after the party.

She cut the deck, flipped up the top card. "*That's* why."

Cecil peered at the card.

"Ten of swords." Missy tapped the card with a finger. "That's *you,* Cecil. Ten of swords. Means you exist to serve the queen of swords."

"That's *her,* Cecil." Clark snickered from the other side of the table, sitting there in just a pair of heart-patterned boxers.

"Kitchen duty, yard duty, fucking *doorman* duty, ten of swords or not, it just ain't right." Cecil sat back, rolled one of his syrup-soaked pancakes into a tube, and took a bite, pointing it at her. "You should hire beaners to do all that, not put it off on family."

"I've told you before: I won't have strangers living with us, poking their noses into our affairs." Missy wiped her lip with the tip of her pinkie. "You don't like it, you can get your ass back to sweet home Alabama and I'll send for Cousin Leroy. I expect he'll be happy to take your place."

"Leroy is a retard," said Cecil.

"Then he won't have any trouble filling your shoes." Clark pushed aside his half-eaten sunny-side up eggs, looked over at Missy. "What's wrong?"

"You're beautiful, baby," Missy leaned over and kissed him, her tongue probing his mouth. "I didn't hurt you last night, did I?"

Clark fingered the welt on his neck, shook his head.

"That's good." Neither of them had slept after the party finally tapered off, too excited, too happy. The caterers had packed up and moved out by 4:00 a.m., just in time for the cleanup crew to take over, twelve Mexican women, who had scrubbed, cleaned, and vacuumed the house, all under Cecil's watchful eye.

"The party went all right, didn't it?" asked Clark.

"Sure, long as Cecil is here to fetch and shuffle, help people with their coats and tell them where to take a piss, everything's fine," said Cecil, retreating to the kitchen.

"The party was just *perfect,* baby." Missy beamed at Clark. "Betty B said she was going to give us a big write-up in her column."

"When does it come out?" asked Clark. "Tuesday?"

"Alison Peabody was positively green," Missy bubbled, her black robe rustling with every movement. "You see the way she was looking at the artwork, walking from room to room, trying not to let her jaw drop? Kept asking who helped me with it. Wait until she reads the article, sees the pictures. She's going to need a deep-tissue massage just to unkink her asshole."

"Vlad and Arturo didn't stay long." Clark tossed back his stringy hair. "I tried to make them comfortable, but—"

"No way to make them comfortable," chided Missy. "Arturo's too uptight, and Vlad . . . well, he just doesn't know how to act around normal people."

"I offered him something would have mellowed him right out," said Clark, "but he just shook his head."

"Oh *please.* You know Vlad's not going to do any drugs. That boy had more drugs shot into him than you and I could take in a dozen lifetimes."

"Vlad should count his blessings."

"Don't talk foolish, baby. Those doctors treated him like a lab rat."

"Sure, poor Vlad, let's cry in our beer for poor Vlad," Cecil called from the kitchen. "I ask for a little help with the chores, and it's 'Go fuck yourself, Cecil.' "

"Vlad is special," said Missy.

"I'm special, too," replied Cecil, coming back to the table.

Missy glared at Cecil. "Vlad is like a unicorn. He's one of a kind. You, Cecil? *Shit.*"

Cecil threw his dish towel down and stomped off toward the media room. Probably going to watch porno or *World's Fastest Police Chases II, III,* and *IV,* drinking bourbon and talking to himself. Special? He was about as special as a toilet seat.

Missy smiled, sipped her coffee. She stared out the window, watching the cold green sea. Clark loved the ocean—the sight, the smell, the rush. Called it 'Mother Ocean' and all that other surf nonsense, but when she looked at the waves, all she thought about were sharks and jellyfish and fat octopi waiting to pull somebody under. Octopi, that was the right word for when there was more than one octopus. Not many people knew that.

Clark stood up. "I'm going to take a shower."

Missy watched him stride toward their bedroom, slim and lean and skin so smooth, like he'd never done a day's work in his life. She hummed softly to herself. It had been a *great* party last night. Not bad for a girl who had grown up without ever getting a birthday party, none with a cake anyway. She had shown them. Shown them all. She crossed her legs, reveled in the sound the silk made. Best money could buy. Fuck those symphonies Alison Peabody was always going on about; good silk was all the music she needed. Next thing, the very next thing, she was going to step up the business. The *real* business. Clark was a genius, but he was too easygoing for his own good, willing to waste his time with those damn surf bums. Well, not if she had any say about it. They had already come a lot further than he had ever expected, but *she* wasn't surprised. Wasn't satisfied, either. You let your guard down, you thought you could just kick back and ride the waves, next thing you knew, you were fucked good and fucked permanent.

Her coffee was cold, but she didn't feel like calling to Cecil and telling him to brew up a fresh pot. She replayed the party in her mind. All those guests and neighbors, the fancy ones, the rich ones who had it all handed to them, the sportswear industry contacts and country club honchos, they had all been there. It had taken three years, but she had finally cracked the social scene. She was an equal now; she was one of them.

She was glad that cutiepie from the art gallery had been there to see it. Frank, the sharp-dressed man. She reached for the tarot cards, curious about him, but Cecil had thrown her off. Tonight was soon enough to deal out a reading on Frank. She remembered hearing his voice last night, saw him standing at the front door while Cecil gave him a hard time about being on the guest list, Frank not mad, not throwing his weight around, just beaming, like he had it all under control. She shifted her legs again, the silk warm as a man's breath. That grin of Frank's . . . Clark was lucky she was true-blue.

The front gate buzzed.

"Cecil!" No response from that useless toad. Missy strode to the front door, checked the security monitor.

Thorpe smiled at her from the screen. "Good morning."

Missy smiled back, even though he couldn't see her. She glanced over at the tarot cards. "You believe in fate, Frank?" She pressed the button that opened the electronic gate before he could answer.

II

"Sorry to barge in without calling first," said Thorpe.

Missy inhaled the fragrance of the bouquet he had brought. "A man who brings flowers is always welcome." She took in Thorpe's gray suit, black cashmere sweater, and gray half boots. "Specially when he looks as good as you." She went into the kitchen, came out a few minutes later with the flowers in a crystal vase, set them on the table. She had her robe loosely knotted, and her hair was brushed out, zigzagged like the Sphinx. She hummed softly to herself as she arranged the flowers. She looked tired, little pillows under her eyes, but happy, and Thorpe almost regretted being about to burst her balloon. "How about a cup of coffee, Frank?"

"I can't stay long."

Missy waved toward the tarot deck on the dining room table. "You got time to have your fortune told? I could give you a heads-up on what's coming at you."

"No thanks. If I knew what was coming, I'd never get out of bed."

"Don't be like that," said Missy. "I'm kind of a white witch, if I do say so myself. That's why I invited you to the party without even knowing you. I checked out your energy at the art gallery and knew you were good people."

"That's probably not the only thing she checked out." Clark walked toward them, grinning. "She's right, though, Frank, the cards don't lie." He hitched up his shorts. "I wouldn't be where I am right now if it wasn't for Missy and her gift."

Missy kissed Clark, nipped at his throat like a she-wolf. "The first time I met Clark, I was working in a Hallmark shop in Riverside. He walked in looking for a Mother's Day card, wearing an eye-in-the-pyramid T-shirt—you know, like on the back of the dollar bill? I took one look at him in that shirt and I just *knew* I was going to marry him."

Clark nodded in agreement. "Find yourself the right woman, Frank. I know you got that Mr. GQ thing going, and that's cool, but you find yourself a babe like Missy, that other pussy just won't interest you. Somebody like Missy, she changes your whole life. It's like you never were really awake before."

Missy touched her hair, pleased. "Clark's a romantic."

"I'm serious, babe," said Clark. "No telling where I would be without you. I know one thing, though, I wouldn't be enjoying myself nearly as much." He blushed, suddenly awkward. "Hey, I got an idea. It's a beautiful day, Frank. How about you ditch the fancy pants and let me loan you some trunks. I'll give you a surfing lesson."

"I've got the day planned out."

"Franks sells insurance," said Missy.

"Wow, sorry to hear that," said Clark.

"I don't really sell insurance." Thorpe reached into his jacket, pulled out the federal ID that Gavin Ellsworth had made him, and flipped open the wallet. Showed the six-pointed star, the tips worn as though it had been in use for years. "My name is Frank Antonelli. I'm an investigator with the Import-Export Division of the U.S. State Department."

Clark stared at the badge. "Yikes."

If Missy was surprised, she didn't show it, her eyes so hard that you could have struck sparks off them. "I don't see any warrant."

"I didn't see the need for a warrant. You're not the focus of my inquiry." Thorpe flicked the wallet shut, tucked it back into his jacket. He had practiced that insouciant open and shut flip for fifteen minutes before driving over this morning. A quick show of the tin and the official seal, and that was it. No big deal. The lazy mannerisms of authority were crucial, almost as important as the credentials themselves. Thorpe could have made do with an off-the-shelf badge and ID, but he trusted

Ellsworth's skill. He never knew when a citizen would want to give his wallet more than a cursory glance, and Missy appeared to be someone who wouldn't be cowed by a federal officer. Or anyone else.

Missy knotted her robe tighter. "Just who *is* the focus of your investigation?"

"Should I call our lawyer, Missy?" asked Clark.

"That's up to you," Thorpe said to Missy, "but I think it's unnecessary. I'm looking into possible violations of the 1987 Federal Antiquities Act by Douglas Meachum."

"Antiquities?" said Clark. "Like the History Channel?"

Thorpe smiled. "Some dealers import historically significant artworks into the United States without the proper release forms from the country of origin." He looked at Missy. "Meachum never filed paperwork for the Mayan plaque you bought last week."

"*That's* why you're here?" said Missy.

"I'd like to take a closer look at the plaque," said Thorpe. "I was hoping to get your cooperation without a subpoena."

"See Clark," said Missy, watching Thorpe, "that's the polite way to put your foot on somebody's neck." She stalked off, led him through the house, and finally stopped in front of the cabinet. On her tiptoes now, she retrieved the key hidden on top and unlocked the glass doors, stood there with her arms crossed, daring him to make a move. "I thought we hit it off, Frank, I really did. You must have gotten a good laugh."

Thorpe could see a vein pounding in the hollow of her throat. "I never laughed at you," he said quietly.

"Come on, you can be honest now." Missy patted his jacket pocket. "You're the man with the badge; you don't have anything to worry about."

"I used you to get at Meachum," said Thorpe. "I'm not proud of it, but I'm not ashamed, either. It's my job. I had a good time last night."

"See, that wasn't so hard." Missy roughly pushed her hair back, her eyes warming slightly. "It was a good party, wasn't it?"

"A very good party." Thorpe carefully took the limestone plaque out of the cabinet, the Mayan king in noble profile, his earlobes elongated in the early classical manner. "If it makes any difference, I could have done this last night, but I didn't want to embarrass you in front of your guests. There was that skinny brunette with the diamonds and the fake boobs . . . Jackie. I didn't want to give her the satisfaction."

"That *skank*," said Missy. "Yeah, that would have given her the first orgasm she's had in years."

Thorpe examined the plaque, taking his time. The surface was lightly pitted, every tiny crevice rimmed with moss the color of raw emeralds. It was so beautiful, he didn't want to let it go. "What kind of provenance did Meachum give you?"

"Provenance?" asked Missy.

"A declaration of authenticity," said Thorpe. "A history of the piece. Where it's from, who its previous owners were, all the appropriate documentation."

"It's from . . . Mexico or Guatemala," said Missy. "Someplace in the jungle. It's *old,* that's all I know. We got a receipt."

Thorpe turned the plaque over, noted the chisel marks where it had been hammered off a wall in some dead city where it deserved to stay. It made him angry. He slipped it back into the cabinet. "I'm sorry to have taken up your time. We had a complaint about Meachum, and our office had to investigate, but he's in the clear. At least regarding this piece. Have a good day." Thorpe took a couple steps before Missy stopped him. He could barely hide his smile.

"What's going on?" asked Missy.

"It's not Mayan and it's not old, so it doesn't fall under the Antiquities Act," said Thorpe. "It's a very good fake. I'm sure your guests will never know the difference."

"You're saying that Meachum ripped us off?" asked Missy.

"I deal strictly with federal crimes, so it's not really my business, but . . ." Thorpe leaned closer. "Speaking unofficially, if you paid for a genuine artifact, you got ripped off."

"You're sure?" Missy's mouth was thinner than a fishhook. "You *know* what's real and what's not? You're an expert on this stuff?"

"I'm an expert," said Thorpe. "If it's any comfort, this sort of thing happens all the time, so you needn't feel embarrassed. Meachum may not have done it deliberately—a lot of dealers aren't particularly knowl-edgeable about pre-Columbian art, and, like I said, this is a good copy."

"I didn't pay a hundred and twenty-five thousand dollars for a fuck-ing *copy*," said Missy.

Thorpe pretended to think about it. "Take the piece back to Meachum. I'm sure he'll return your money. He won't want to be taken to court. A sale like this constitutes fraud. You would win easily."

"If I take him to court, it's going to be all over the papers. I'll look like a fool."

"Meachum has his own reputation to consider. He'll want to avoid publicity as much as you do." Thorpe took out his wallet, handed Missy his business card. "Just in case he gives you a hard time, slip this to him when you return the plaque. Tell him I was checking on his paperwork. Let him know I was the one who told you the piece was a fake. He won't argue. The last thing he'll want is to draw attention to himself."

Missy ran a finger over the raised lettering on the business card, cir-cled the gold federal seal next to his name and cell phone number. She looked up at him. "I don't like being taken advantage of. Not by you, and most definitely not by Douglas Meachum."

"I can see that."

Missy nodded. "I appreciate your trying to make things right . . . and not blowing things in front of Jackie Simpson at the party." Her eyes flashed. "I would never have forgiven you for that, Frank."

Clark snickered. "Lucky for you, dude." A glance from Missy and he was conciliatory. "See, babe, in a way, you *were* right about Frank's energy. He's a good guy."

Missy watched Thorpe, and it took everything for him not to blink.

12

Missy didn't waste any time. It was barely five hours since he had told her that the Mayan king was a fake. Thorpe put away his pager, called the number on the State Department business card he had given to her, then keyed in his message code.

"Hey, Frank, this is me. Just wanted to let you know that Douglas Meachum pissed all over himself apologizing for selling me a fake, and wrote a refund check on the spot. I can't tell if he's more afraid of me or of you, but I guess it doesn't matter. Just between us, I don't think he's got any of that . . . provenance that you told me about. Like you thought, he doesn't want anybody to know about the fake art, either, so I guess everything has worked out. I'm still a little pissed at you for telling me you were an insurance salesman, but thanks for wising me up about the art world, and don't be a stranger. Clark says his offer to teach you how to surf still stands. Ciao!"

Thorpe sat in the last pew of Holy Innocents Church, smiling. He wished he could have seen Meachum's face when Missy told him about the federal agent who had been looking into his paperwork.

Holy Innocents was a small Catholic church in East L.A., cool and dark inside, the carpet worn, the cracked wooden pews polished to a dull sheen. A huge stained-glass window of the crucifixion loomed over the altar. Red glass blood dripped from Jesus' side and from his brow, while angels and saints watched from overhead, unwilling or unable to do anything about it. The church was empty at midafternoon except for a few Hispanic women lighting candles in the vestibule, the women keeping up a quiet conversation.

Thorpe selected a small catechism card from the back of the next pew, the image on the front of the card showing a youthful Jesus seated on the grass with two white lambs and three children. Thorpe wrote on the back: "Next time, be kind to strangers and small children, Doug. You never know who's watching." He tucked the card into his jacket. After he mailed it to Meachum, the wake-up would be complete, but Thorpe was going to give him a few more days to sweat. No permanent damage, but maybe Meachum would think twice the next time he was in a hurry. A small thing, but Thorpe found pleasure in it. He checked his watch. In a couple hours, he was going to take another step closer to finding the Engineer, but right now . . .

Father Esteban strode down the aisle, his cassock swirling around his knees.

Thorpe stood up, noted the priest's black high-tops. "Thanks for seeing me."

Father Esteban was wary. "Usually when I get called from my prayers on a matter of urgency, it is to give confession . . . or last rites." His voice was low and raspy, like a boxer who had taken too many hits to the throat.

"Right. . . . Well, I'm good on both counts."

Father Esteban was in his early thirties, a lean, serious Hispanic. Almost as tall as Thorpe, he had smooth caramelized skin and short black hair. A scar curved from his left ear to the side of his mouth, and a drop of sweat had stained his white collar. The cross around his neck was a plain wooden one.

"I've got a bicycle outside," said Thorpe, starting for the double doors. "I'd like you to pass it on to one of your parishioners, Paulo Rodriguez."

Father Esteban walked outside with him, stood beside the bicycle. It was a good bike, not new, no flashy paint job, and a little big for Paulo, but that way he'd get some use out of it. Father Esteban looked the bicycle over. "An interesting choice, Mr. . . ."

"Frank."

"Sometimes people who donate things to the church, people from outside the parish, they like to give the very best. A beautiful twenty-speed mountain bike thick with chrome, a backpack suitable for climbing Mount Everest, titanium running strollers. This is much better. New bicycles are stolen very quickly, or worse, taken by force. This one . . ." He shook Thorpe's hand, his grip strong and calloused. "Paulo will be very happy."

"One more thing . . ."

Father Esteban walked back inside, and Thorpe had no choice but to follow.

Thorpe stopped just inside the doorway. "A week or so ago, a man at LAX was hurrying to his ride and he struck Paulo, knocked him down. Let Paulo know that the bicycle is the man's way to tell him how sorry he is."

Father Esteban stared at Thorpe. "You weren't that man; I can see that."

"No . . . I'm just sort of the messenger."

Father Esteban laughed. "You're no messenger, and this fine bicycle didn't come from the man in a hurry."

Thorpe didn't answer.

"Are you uncomfortable in the house of God?" His voice was a hoarse whisper.

"I feel like I'm trespassing."

"I used to feel the same way myself." Father Esteban folded his hands in front of him. "This man who hit Paulo . . . you saw him do it?"

"I was too far away. The man left before I could reach him."

Father Esteban's eyes were dark and deep. "You found where Paulo prays. Did you also find the man who hit him?"

Thorpe was lost in the stillness of the priest's gaze. "Yes, I did."

"You didn't call the police, though." It was a statement, not a question.

"No."

"Did you hurt this man?"

"Not physically, but yes, I hurt him."

Father Esteban nodded. "Good."

"That's a strange attitude for a priest. I thought you were more into the 'turn the other cheek' thing."

"Turning the other cheek is a useless lesson for those without power." Father Esteban put his hand on Thorpe's shoulder, and the sleeves of his robe slid up a couple inches. Thorpe glimpsed a tiger tattoo snaking up his wrist, crude work, too, jailhouse tats done with a needle, spit and carbon from burned match heads. Father Esteban tugged his sleeve down. "I'll tell Paulo the truth. I'll tell him that you saw what happened to him and decided to do something about it. That way, he'll learn that there are good men as well as bad men."

"You don't want to get his hopes up, Padre."

Father Esteban held on to him as Thorpe started to leave. "A very wise priest brought me into the light about ten years ago. This priest, may God bless him, once told me, 'Esteban, never underestimate the positive power of guilt.'" He winked at Thorpe. "So . . . what in heaven's name did you *do*, Frank?"

13

Dale Bingham crashed into the right wall of the squash court, managed to dink the small black ball against the left corner. It was a kill shot, but the club pro was nimble and incredibly quick, a nationally ranked Pakistani, who tapped it up and over Bingham's head and scored. Bingham drove down his racket in frustration, stopped it an inch from the hardwood floor. He glowered at the pro, sweat dripping down his face. "Nice shot, Hassan."

"That's game, set, match, Mr. Bingham," said Hassan, not even breathing hard. He gave a curt nod, walked off the enclosed court, and closed the clear plastic door behind him.

Bingham toweled off, his movements abrupt, still talking to himself. Hassan was clearly the superior player, but Bingham hadn't given up a point without making the maximum effort, diving the boards and smashing into walls without thought of the consequences. He was thirty-two years old, tall and muscular, one of those upright Dudley Do-Rights that the FBI or Secret Service scooped up right out of Dartmouth or Yale. Bingham had been a poor fit for an off-the-books outfit like the Engineer's old shop. His current job with the state organized crime task force suited him better, requiring fewer moral and legal compromises.

"Good game," said Thorpe as Bingham stepped out of the court.

"Not good enough." Bingham wore a soaked polo shirt, terry wristbands, and baggy shorts, his calves meaty and rounded—he reminded Thorpe of a draft horse, plenty of power and determination, but no speed. He was playing the wrong game, dooming himself to endless frustration. Thorpe wondered how many rackets he had broken.

"Mr. Bingham, we haven't met. My name is—"

"I know who you are." Bingham blotted his forehead with the towel, his face flushed. "Surprised? I know all about you, Frank."

Thorpe was more than surprised. He glanced around, saw only a few other jocks relaxing after their games, watching CNN from benches and chairs. "You've got the better of me here."

"That would be a first, wouldn't it?"

Thorpe had no idea where Bingham's anger came from. "Why don't we go somewhere and talk?"

"Aren't you the calm one?" Bingham laughed. "That must have taken some work . . . a man like you, with your inclinations." He tapped Thorpe lightly on the chest with the squash racket, like an Iroquois counting coup. "I bet you practiced not raising your pulse rate with biofeedback. Or was it meditation?"

"I just think happy thoughts."

Bingham tapped him again with the racket, his eyes like slate. "What are you thinking of now, Frank?"

Thorpe smiled. "I'm thinking you shouldn't do that again, Dale."

Bingham considered it. "How did you find me?"

"That's not important."

"To you, maybe." Bingham blotted his face again, tossed the towel aside. "You want to talk? Step into the court. I've got it reserved for another twenty minutes." He opened the door. "Come on, Frank, it's private in here. We can say anything we want."

Thorpe stepped inside and closed the door behind him. "I'm looking for the Engineer. You're the only one in the outfit who spent any time with him before he linked up with Lazurus."

Bingham kneaded the squash ball. "I don't like thinking about the Engineer."

"I think about him all the time."

Bingham glared at him. "I imagine you do."

"Did . . . did you know Kimberly? Is that what this is about?"

Bingham slammed the ball, sent it rocketing off the front wall. Thorpe jerked his head, the ball grazing his cheek. "One to nothing," said Bingham, picking up the ball as it dribbled toward him.

Thorpe's cheek burned. "Do I get a racket?"

Bingham hit the ball again, even harder this time. Thorpe caught it as it flew by. "Two to nothing." Bingham held his hand out. "Still my serve."

"You blame me for Kimberly's death." Thorpe held on to the ball. "See, we have something in common."

Bingham wiggled his fingers, impatient. "My serve."

Thorpe tossed him the ball.

Bingham bent forward at the service line, not looking at Thorpe. "I only spent a couple of days with the Engineer. That was ample."

"You and he were doing surveillance on Lazurus." Thorpe darted to the side as Bingham served, then scampered forward, the serve a cream puff that hit just above the line. He managed to get it, made the return with the palm of his hand.

Bingham stepped into the return, slammed the ball off the side wall, hitting Thorpe's forehead on the bounce. "Three to zero." He stepped back to the service line. "The Engineer was doing surveillance, I was monitoring the conversation between Lazurus and his crew with a laser microphone." He hammered another serve past Thorpe's head, then went and picked up the ball. "Four to zero." He got back into position. "I was the outfit's bug man. Not quite the glamour of your work, but necessary."

"You spent a couple days sitting in a van with the Engineer."

Bingham rocked forward and back. "You want to know what we talked about? If we exchanged addresses, pet peeves?" He worked the ball over between his fingers, warming it up. "Sorry, Frank. Mostly, we just sat and—" He slam-served.

Thorpe was ready: He turned and smacked the ball as it bounced off the back wall, made a perfect cross-court shot, which was unreturnable. "My serve." He walked to the service line. "The Engineer's a talker. I know that much."

"Yes, but I'm not." Bingham adjusted the grip on his racket. "Aren't you going to ask me how I knew Kimberly?"

"We'll get to that. First, I want—"

"Does it always have to be what *you* want, Frank?"

"It *is* my serve." Thorpe bounced the ball. "What kind of food did he like? Did he ever mention a restaurant, someplace special?"

Bingham shook his head. "Just serve."

Thorpe served, put some side spin on it, so that the ball barely hit the line, and Bingham hit the floor trying to reach it, his racket outstretched. He made it, too, but Thorpe returned the shot before he could get up. "Four to one."

Bingham slowly got back into position, wincing with every step.

"Did the Engineer have any health problems? Did you ever see him use an asthma inhaler or take any prescription medication?"

"I was with her before you were." Bingham was rocking again, eager to get another whack at him. "Then Billy recruited her and things changed. Not at first, but later. There wasn't anything I could do about it, either."

Thorpe's head still throbbed from where the ball had hit him before. "Did the Engineer collect anything? Stamps? Coins? Comic books? Baseball cards? He must have said something—"

"You didn't replace me, Frank." Bingham swished his racket through the air, and Thorpe felt the breeze. "We shared her attentions. Your share was just bigger than mine." The racket flailed the air again, closer this time. "Not much fun finding out you're not special."

Thorpe punched him, knocked him down, the racket flying across the court. When Bingham got up, he knocked him down again.

"You don't play fair," gasped Bingham, wiping his lip with the tail of his shirt.

"I just want to know about the Engineer."

"The first time I met Kimberly, she wanted somebody to sweep her new apartment for devices," said Bingham. "She was always a careful girl, well organized, a very . . . compartmentalized mind. That's important in your line of work, isn't it? That's how you people do the things you do." He glared at Thorpe. "Me, I'm just a glorified technician. No real creativity. Not like Kimberly. Not like *you*."

Thorpe bent down beside him but kept his guard up. "I'm not your enemy."

"I came back a month later to do another sweep, and her apartment was clean, just like before, and she asked me to stick around. The next time, I showed up with a bottle of wine that cost me a week's salary, and she didn't even open it. She was honest—you have to give her that. I would have come by every night, but she had a schedule, and after she joined Billy's shop, her schedule seemed to get busier all the time." Bingham dabbed at his lip again. "I asked her if she was seeing someone else. 'Of course,' she said, with that little laugh of hers. Take it or leave it, right, Frank?"

"That's right."

Bingham stared at Thorpe now. "You *knew* about me?"

Thorpe nodded.

Bingham stepped closer. "You took it, too, didn't you?"

"I told you I wasn't your enemy."

Bingham sat with his back against the wall. "You knew."

Thorpe sat beside him. He ran a hand across the smooth floorboards, thinking of Kimberly's face by moonlight, how she raised herself up on one elbow in bed, deciding whether they had time for another round. Deciding whether he should go home.

"I didn't give her any ultimatums, never told her to make a choice," said Bingham, looking straight ahead. "It wouldn't have made any difference. She would have laughed."

"I remember the first time I saw her," Thorpe said softly. "Billy introduced us, said she was incredibly bright, not a classic beauty, but had 'a real way with the male of the species'—those were his exact words—and I could hear him, but it was like he was a million miles away, because my attention was so focused on her. She just looked back at me, amused, knowing what I was going through, and I played along, pretended I was the smitten suitor while Billy droned on about me, and it was like she and I were in on some private joke. We didn't say a word, but by the time Billy was done with the introductions, I was in love." His voice was even softer now. "I thought she was, too."

"Maybe you were right," said Bingham. "She certainly didn't love me. I didn't care."

"Love wasn't something she was interested in. It would have made her too vulnerable. I probably would have felt the same way if I'd had a choice . . . but I didn't."

"Did you ever wonder about me?" said Bingham.

"Sometimes."

"You never did anything about it, though, did you? You never tried to find out who she was seeing. It wouldn't have taken much effort on your part, but I guess I didn't count. You *knew* I was no threat to—"

"When I was with Kimberly, it was just the two of us. That was as much as I could expect. It was enough. I told myself it was enough, anyway."

"It *wasn't* just the two of you." Bingham jabbed a finger at him. "You see, I *did* something, Frank. Like they say, when you're number two, you try harder." He tried to laugh. "I bugged her bedroom. That's how I found out who you were. So you were never alone. I was there, too."

"You might have had your ear pressed up against the wall, but there was just Kimberly and me in the room." Thorpe had never talked about his feelings for Kimberly with anyone. "That's why I can't let go. I was used to being alone, happy with it, and then I met her, and everything changed. *Everything.* Now she's gone, and I can't stand being by myself, because now I know what I'm missing."

Bingham looked over at him. "I thought about going after the Engineer myself. I know you don't believe me, but I did."

"I believe you."

"Go ahead, Frank, humor me. I might still be able to help you, right?"

"That's right."

Bingham laughed, tears running down his cheeks. "You don't miss a trick. Well, I'm not like you. I wouldn't know what to do with the Engineer if I found him. I wouldn't last five minutes, but you, you're just the man for the job." He cleared his throat. "That's not a compliment, by the way."

"The Engineer was a contract employee," Thorpe said gently. "Did he ever talk about what he was going to do with the money if the operation was successful? Things he wanted to buy, things he wanted to do?"

Bingham rested his head against the wall, exhausted from the burden of his secrets. It was what Thorpe had been waiting for. "Most of the time, I sat in the van, monitoring the recorder while the Engineer listened to Lazurus and his crew. The Engineer could hear that they were crude, so he decided to play the effete Eurotrash intellectual. He had a closet full of personalities to choose from. You should have seen him working out the accent, the mannerisms. He made me laugh." His head seemed too heavy to hold up. "The Engineer was really talented . . . but then, you know that."

"Try to remember what he talked about. *Anything.*"

"Do you really think you're going to find him?"

"One way or another."

"My outfit won't give you any help. You bring him in and they'll deny everything. So will yours. They're all afraid of him. The Engineer knows too many secrets for them to prosecute him."

"That's okay—I don't intend to arrest him."

"Nice not to have to worry about the niceties of the law, to make it up as you go along. Kimberly must have liked that. Well, I'm not built that way. I'm a better man than you, Frank. I'm the better man, but it didn't do me any good."

Thorpe didn't respond, waiting.

Bingham turned away from him, expressionless now. "He liked movies."

"What kind of movies?"

"Weird stuff. Horror, science fiction . . . half of the movies he talked about, I never even heard of."

"Did he catch them on video or at a movie theater? Maybe some midnight art house like the Strand or the Varsity or the Palomino?"

Bingham shrugged. "I don't even remember the titles."

"You remember his voice, though. That's your specialty, right, the barely audible inflections, the intensity. You *know*, Dale; you just have to remember. Replay the scene in the van, replay the sound of his voice. What was the movie that he sounded most excited about? Film buffs love to go on about their discoveries—they can't help themselves. If you don't remember the title, tell me what it was about."

Bingham nodded. "You should have heard him. There was this one he really liked. . . . I don't remember the title, but he said it was a Nazi/zombie classic. He was serious, too." He shook his head. "All I know was it was set on some deserted island and there was a blonde—"

"*Shock Waves,*" said Thorpe.

Bingham stared at him.

"It *is* a classic. These Nazi zombies have been resting on the bottom of a tropical lagoon in the South Pacific for fifty years when ship-wrecked tourists accidentally wake them up. The blonde is Brooke Adams."

"You're as bad as the Engineer. He kept going on about the opening scene, where the Nazi zombies are goose-stepping underwater as the lifeboat drifts overhead."

"Thank you."

"This actually helps?"

"It might."

"You want to tell me how?"

Thorpe stood up.

"I see. You're done with me now. Fine. Well, fuck you, too, Frank." Bingham stayed sitting, back against the wall, his voice flatlined now. "She picked you. I wasn't interesting enough, so she picked you . . . and you let her get butchered."

"If it makes you feel better, maybe when I find the Engineer, he'll kill me first."

"Promise?"

"You know, Dale, some people tell you to let things go, to forgive and forget, but that's all bullshit. You're a poor loser, and so am I." Thorpe looked down at him. "Don't let it bother you. There are lots worse things to be."

14

Quentin wrapped his arms around himself as the jitters hit, holding on while his teeth chattered, jerking like one of those Dodger bobble-heads every Mexican in L.A. had on the dashboard of his Camaro. He sagged when it was over, his mouth sour. He looked over at Ellis, who was hitting on a pint of Southern Comfort while his knees bounced, racked with the jitters, too. "*Told* you the batteries were a bad idea."

"Recipe called for batteries," Ellis said, watching the Westminster dog show on the big screen with the sound off. He sat in the living room of the double-wide trailer, a pasty scarecrow in threadbare cut-offs, scabs crusted across his arms, hair hanging down to the middle of his back. The air conditioner rattled in the side window. It was ninety-eight degrees outside, but the heavy-duty conditioner kept things at a frosty sixty-five degrees inside. He was sweating anyway. Ellis was always hot. So was Quentin. Their nerve endings were too close to the surface—that's what Quentin said. Ellis shifted on the recliner, eyes on the dog show. "Recipe calls for batteries, I add batteries."

"Recipe calls for *lithium* batteries, not rechargeables," said Quentin. "You ruined the batch, admit it. You're the one got to explain it to Vlad and Arturo."

Ellis scratched the scabs on his arms. "Batteries is batteries."

"Rechargeables don't have no lithium in them," sputtered Quentin, his guts cramping up again. He groaned, a bony motorhead in a Green-peace T-shirt and greasy jeans, his dirty bare feet curled up under him on the flower-print sofa. "It's the *lithium* the recipe calls for."

"You . . . you got to admit . . ." Ellis took another drink, trying to hold his hand steady, the neck of the Southern Comfort bottle clicking against his front teeth. "You got to admit, Quentin, it's a *fine* buzz."

By way of response, Quentin bent over the coffee table, hooked a half gram of crank with the long nail of his pinkie, and snorted. It burned like drain cleaner. Damn Ellis had run out of coffee filters and used paper towels to filter the ephedrine brew, left in all kinds of impurities. He shook his head, hit the other nostril, jerked with the brain freeze. He smiled at his reflection in the glass tabletop, his brown hair spiked out. He would have liked to grow his hair long like Ellis, but it kept breaking off. Skin hung loosely from his arms and waist, sagged over his belt, dripped from his jawbone. He looked like he was a melting wax candle. A former all-state tackle at Huntington Beach High, Quentin had lost over one hundred pounds since he discovered the wonders of bathtub speed. He had never felt better in his life, really, but he no longer watched football on TV. He watched everything from Jap cooking contests to soap operas, but never football. Not even the Super Bowl.

Through the back window of the double-wide, Quentin could see the carcasses of half a dozen stripped cars rusting in the desert heat, hoods gaping, engines and tires missing. Ellis collected cars. Said it was the sport of kings. Most of them had bullet holes through the windshields from when they got bored. Plenty to be bored about, too, living out beyond the outskirts of Riverside, eighty miles from H.B. It might as well be 80 million. Fuck it. Riverside was Crank Central. He flicked his lighter, held it overhead, honoring his new alma mater. He looked over at Ellis, thinking he might get a laugh, but that crater-head was glued to the big screen.

Ellis watched a standard-size white poodle flounce across the floor of the pavilion, puffy balls of fur on the dog's head and the tip of its tail bouncing with every step. "I'd like to get me one of them dogs."

Quentin stared at the poodle's handler scampering beside him, an old guy in a black tuxedo, breathing hard. He shook his head. The things some people would do to make a buck. Fucking pathetic.

"Beautiful dog," said Ellis. "Looks like Julia Roberts."

"You said the same thing about the cocker spaniel and the terrier and the Afghan hound. They *all* look like Julia Roberts to you."

Ellis dragged a hand through his greasy hair. "I'm just saying we should get us a dog."

A couple of weeks ago, some lady and her kid had walked down the private driveway to the front door, the kid in a Girl Scout uniform crisscrossed with merit badges, the lady carrying a paper bag loaded with cookies. Ellis had answered the door, listened while the kid went into her sales pitch. The lady had sniffed, wrinkled her nose, catching a whiff of the ethyl ether cooking in the garage. Ellis, for once in his life, had a smart reaction—told the lady they had cats and he was overdue to empty the litter box. "Gosh, mister, how many cats do you have?" asked the kid, gagging. No sale, bitch.

For the next couple of days, Ellis had jabbered on about how they should get a cat in case anyone else came around wondering about the smell. Quentin said no way, he had allergies, so now Ellis had switched to wanting a dog. Quentin tried to tell him that dog piss didn't smell like cat piss, but once Ellis got his mind around an idea, he didn't let go. It was just a matter of time until he came home with some puppy that would get into the acetone, go into convulsions, and then there would be a three-hour argument over who was going to dig the hole for it.

Quentin grabbed the remote and switched channels. Dozens of hot rods streamed around an oval track, kicking up dust. "That reminds me. Any of them cars of yours run? My sister's kid wants one bad. Just turned sixteen and that's all he talks about."

"Nothing out there is worth a damn," said Ellis, "but I can put something together for him. Clean VIN numbers guaranteed. Just give me a week or two."

"How much?" asked Quentin.

"Don't worry about it."

Quentin watched the hot rods go round and round. They looked like windup toys. "My sister's kid, he can tell you everybody won the Daytona Five Hundred. He can go clear back to 1946 or '47, tell you what they were driving and what their time was, too."

Ellis peered at the screen. "I'll put a real nice car together for him. Anybody who can remember all that shit, he deserves it."

"I don't know . . ." Quentin repacked his nose. "I tried to tell him, when you pencil it out, it hardly pays to own a car. You figure in the DUIs, it would be cheaper to take a cab."

"How you gonna pick up supplies if you don't got a car?" asked Ellis. "You going to ask the cabbie to wait while you buy a couple hundred road flares, a crate of Sudafed, and twenty gallons of anhydrous ammonia?"

"I'm not talking about *us*," said Quentin, "I'm talking about *him*. You start figuring in gas, oil, retreads, DUIs . . . and jail time, you can't forget that. Even if you make bail, you're still gonna lose a day, assuming you don't get popped on a weekend, when it's gonna be worse. Like I said, all things considered . . ." He turned around, hearing something. Two men stood just inside the side door. They were wearing Bozo the Clown masks with orange hair and big red noses. If it hadn't been for the shotguns, he would have thought it was Halloween.

"Oh wow, I love this part," whispered Ellis, oblivious to their visitors, as one of the hot rods veered into another, the cars behind them unable to stop, tumbling end over end.

The shotguns had focused Quentin, brought his mind to full attention. He couldn't bring himself to look at those Bozo faces—that was too much to ask—but he was thinking better now, with all the time in the world, because things had slowed down, the way they always did when he was behind a load of crank, and the more he thought about it, the more the fact that they were wearing masks seemed like a *good* thing. If you were going to waste somebody, you didn't need to bother wearing a mask. Yeah, the masks were a hopeful sign, but he still couldn't bring himself to look at anything but the shotguns, a sawed-off double-barrel and a pump Mosburg. The shorter Bozo, the one cradling the Mosburg, had lacy tattoos scrolled over his forearms, spiderwebs with spaceships caught in the strands, and Quentin recognized the design, *knew* who they belonged to, but he didn't say anything. Not a word.

"Give up the goods, motherfuckers," demanded the tall Bozo.

"What?" Ellis tore himself away from the TV. "Hey . . . what's the deal?"

The tall Bozo waved the double-barrel. It had been sawed off unevenly, the metal still shiny, not filed smooth, and that bothered Quentin for reasons he couldn't even fathom. "The deal is, you hand over your stash, and I don't blow your shit away."

Ellis peered at the shorter Bozo's arms. "Pinto? Is that you, man? What up, dude?"

"He recognizes you." The tall Bozo pulled back the hammers on the double-barrel. "Time to make a commitment here, Pinto."

Ellis looked at Quentin. "Did I fuck up?"

Quentin wanted to cry.

Pinto pushed back his Bozo mask. "Damn thing was too hot anyway," he said to his partner. He raised his shotgun.

"Quentin?" wailed Ellis. "I fucked up, didn't I?"

Quentin closed his eyes. He covered his ears, too, covered them tight.

15

"You look chipper this morning," said Billy. "What's the occasion?"

Thorpe slid into the booth beside Billy, the two of them facing the entrance. "Maybe I'm just happy to see you."

"Perhaps that's it." Billy's plate was piled high with a Turbo omelette, the specialty of the Harbor House Café in Sunset Beach—four eggs, three kinds of cheese, bacon, sweet onions, and sliced avocado. They sat in the corner of the patio overlooking Pacific Coast Highway, and though the surrounding tables were filled, the traffic noise masked their conversation. Billy sliced into the omelette with the side of his fork. He was a big man, but he took small bites, his manners impeccable. "Although I suspect your bonhomie has more to do with that wake-up of yours."

"Just coffee, thanks," Thorpe said to the waitress. He had sent the "be kind to strangers and small children" card to Meachum's gallery—he should get it today. Thorpe watched the waitress walk away. A sunny day, Meachum getting his wake-up, and a waitress in running shorts with the legs of a marathoner. He should call Father Esteban and tell him to light a candle in gratitude.

Billy wore dark slacks and a Hawaiian shirt with hula dancers on it, their grass skirts shimmying as he ate. On him, it had a look of casual elegance, a planter from the 1920s with five thousand acres of pineapples to be harvested, and never a doubt in his mind that the offshore hurricane would strike the next plantation, not his. "Have you settled everything with the art dealer?"

"All settled."

"You should thank the poor man." Billy dabbed his lips with a napkin. "I haven't seen you look this good since your encounter with the Engineer."

Thorpe watched the waitress approach with his coffee. The people at the surrounding tables were mostly locals and construction workers from the condos being put up across the street, young people in beach attire, and yacht clubbers from the nearby marina, wearing pearls and Rolexes.

"You sure this is all you want?" the waitress asked him.

Thorpe smiled back at her. "I've got all I can handle."

"You should thank the art dealer," said Billy as the waitress left.

"You already said that."

"The truth bears repeating."

"What did you want to talk to me about, Billy?"

Billy's eyes were innocent. "Do I need a reason?"

"No, but you always seem to have one."

Billy laid his fork down. "How did you find Dale Bingham?"

Thorpe was surprised. "How do *you* know him?"

Billy leaned forward. He seemed to engulf the table, the hula dancers on his shirt in perfect syncopation. "You asked me to find out if the Engineer worked for another shop, so I quietly put out the word. It was Bingham who finally provided confirmation. Now you surprise him, asking questions, so he thinks I gave him up."

"I had no idea, Billy. I got his name from another source."

"I told him that had to be the case, but he doesn't believe me." Billy drummed his fingers on the tabletop, restless. "That's what I get for trying to do a good deed. I'm picking up all your bad habits." He glared at Thorpe. "I had hoped to recruit him."

Thorpe shook his head. "I don't think Bingham's right for the job."

"Bingham has a great set of ears. He could have been very useful." Billy poked at his omelette. "I won't ask you who referred you to him."

Thorpe laughed. "Go ahead, ask."

"I don't want to fight." Billy delicately lifted a thin forkful of eggs and avocado, offered it to Thorpe. "Bite?" He waited, shrugged. "Warren said to tell you that he's traced the Engineer to Southern California. He's definitely still in the area."

"I know."

Billy looked surprised.

"He instant-messaged me a few nights ago. We had a little chat."

"He *told* you where he was?"

Thorpe smiled. "He said he was living on the beach, talked about the offshore swells coming in. I told him I was living on the coast, too."

"Risky behavior on your part, don't you think?"

"Why lie when the truth accomplishes the purpose? We both want to get together." Thorpe watched three trim, well-dressed older women at a nearby table, laughing as they worked on their second round of mimosas. One was showing the others something in the newspaper. "The only difference is that the Engineer wants to talk before he kills me. He thinks I've got a few million stashed, and he wants me to tell him where it is. Me . . . I don't need to talk with him. I just want to kill the motherfucker."

Billy rested his fingers on Thorpe's wrist. "Be careful." His fingers flexed. "I wouldn't want anything to happen to you."

Thorpe glanced at Billy's manicure, noted the perfect half-moon cuticles, the thick, healthy nails.

Billy removed his hand. "Come work for me. I've got a very tricky job. It's just your style."

Thorpe checked his watch. *Shock Waves* was out of print, but he had located a bootleg 35-mm copy from a collector in Seattle and had received it by FedEx yesterday. In four days, it was going to be shown as the midnight feature at the Strand, a small theater in Huntington Beach. The local papers were running small notices about the special presentation in the entertainment sections tomorrow. He had thought to publicize it more widely, but he didn't want to scare off the Engineer. If he really *was* a movie buff, he'd see the notice.

"Frank?" Billy pursed his lips. "Remember the account I told you about at the bowling alley? I'm trying to turn the chief software designer of a local firm. He's relatively young, MIT grad, not married, but he has a girlfriend. Interesting woman—breeds Dobermans and is a chess grandmaster. I was hoping to use a variant of what you did with that coven of white supremacists in Bakersfield. A masterful scenario, but difficult to execute, and I don't have anyone on staff I trust with the job. I was hoping you could step in for a couple weeks. Money is no object. The client has given me a blank check."

"I'm busy."

"Nonsense. You're finished with your wake-up. All you're doing now is waiting around for the Engineer to pop out of a cake or something. I'm giving you a chance to earn some money."

"I still have most of the get-lost cash the shop gave me."

"May I give you some advice, Frank?"

"No."

Billy pushed aside his plate, sent silverware clattering. "You've got too much heart. It gets in your way. It limits you. I want you to reconsider what I've—"

Thorpe turned as the ladies at the nearby table exploded in laughter, and he saw a photograph of Missy in the paper one of them was waving.

"I've always been open to compromise," said Billy. "Perhaps you'd be willing to consult on the case. Just give me the value of your expertise. I'll be honest with you—I think once you get your toes wet, you won't be able to resist. Come on, Frank, quit playing hard to get."

"Excuse me," Thorpe said to the woman holding the newspaper. "Could I see that when you're finished with it?"

"Take it, *please,*" said the woman, a taut matron in white silk workout garb, her mouth a lascivious slash. "The girls and I will pee ourselves laughing if we read it again."

Thorpe took the copy of the *Gold Coast Pilot* back to the table, starting to read it as he walked.

"What is it?" asked Billy as Thorpe sat down.

"Trouble," said Thorpe.

16

"I don't think it's so bad," offered Clark.

Missy tore the newspaper out of his hands and stood up from the breakfast table, hovering over him as she read from the paper. " 'Proving the adage that a fool and his, or her, new money are soon parted, wanna-be socialites Clark and Missy Riddenhauer recently discovered that a piece of pre-Columbian art they overpaid for, in a vain effort to impress the cognoscenti, was a fake. It's called irony, children. Fake art bought trying to achieve fake class. Not in my Orange County.' " Missy glared at Clark. "Not so *bad*?"

Clark rested his elbows on the table, rereading the column. He was just back from surfing, his dirty-blond hair snarled, his swim trunks soaking the upholstery of the chair.

Cecil peeked in from the kitchen but didn't say anything.

Clark looked up at Missy. "I always wondered what *irony* meant. So it means being ripped off?"

"It means everybody we know is laughing at us," said Missy. "It means whatever we do is not enough." She stalked around the dining room in her brand-new blue Givenchy suit and a diamond choker with matching anklet. "It means we've been fucked over."

"Harsh language, babe." Clark sipped his breakfast Pepsi. "Come on down to the lab and I'll fix you up something that will mellow you right out."

"I want you to take care of that bitch," said Missy. "Her, and *him,* too."

"Meachum? Come on, the man already called and apologized. He said *he* wasn't the one spilled the beans to Betty B."

"All he needed to do was tell her that the wall panel was such a per-fect fake that even *he* was fooled. Instead, he tells her that he had doubts but that I was the one who insisted that I knew what I was doing."

"Can't blame a man for covering his ass."

"*I* can."

Clark blew a mournful note across the mouth of the Pepsi bottle, serenading her. He loved her like this, up on her high horse, taking names and keeping score. God, she was totally awesome. He kept the tune going. Their first date, he had played her "Smells Like Teen Spirit" on this big glass bong, and she had laughed, coughing out smoke from four-hundred-dollars-an-ounce Hawaiian bud, and he'd thought if there was a more beautiful woman in the world, some king or movie star probably had first dibs.

"I want Meachum taken care of," Missy said quietly. "Both him and Betty B."

Clark shook his head. "Freedom of the press. That's in the rule book."

"Look at me, Clark." Missy did a slow turn, showed off her outfit.

Clark raised an eyebrow. "You look like a prom queen at Martha Stewart High School. I like you better leathered up, hot and nasty."

Missy smacked the table. "It's a designer original; it's *supposed* to be conservative. I'm wearing it because I knew the article was coming out today, and I wanted to make a grand entrance at the club. Now what do you think people are going to be thinking when I walk into the main—"

The phone rang.

Missy looked toward the kitchen, but Cecil quickly took some eggs out of the refrigerator and started cracking them. She picked up the phone on the seventh ring. She never answered the phone on anything less. "Hello," she said brightly, her mouth set. "Yes . . . yes, Vivian, I did see the paper. Such silliness." Her eyes were slits now. "No, of course I don't take it personally." She stood listening. "No . . . I don't need another copy for a keepsake, but thank you *so* much for asking." She slammed the phone down.

Clark spun the empty Pepsi bottle on the table. "Vicodin?"

Missy sat next to him. He trembled as she lightly stroked his arms with the back of her nails. "I told you when we moved here that it wasn't just about money. I said it was about respect, and recognition, and moving on to the next level. Remember?" She raked her claws across his flesh, left pink scratches in his tan. "We made a promise to each other, a solemn pledge never to settle for less than the best."

Clark chewed his lips as she dug in. "I . . . I got an idea for a new product this morning. Double-buffered crank with just enough ecstasy to smooth out the ride. . . ."

"The party was a step in the right direction. A *big* step. Other people have more money than we do, but the *art* we bought, that showed that we were as good as anybody, that we were okay to be invited into their homes and—"

"Here's the secret sauce—an isomer of ketamine for clarity," said Clark, oblivious. "Whole thing came to me while I was paddling in this morning. I could just see the whole chemical structure—"

"Now everybody is going to read about how we were fucked over." Missy drove her nails in, made him gasp, but he didn't move. "Fucked over like a couple of hicks buying velvet paintings off the side of the road, thinking we were art connoisseurs."

Clark stared at the dots of blood underneath her nails. He was breathing so hard, it felt like his lungs were going to collapse.

"Society bitches like Ann Shaefer and Karrie Jeffords, with their orchid club and their opera guild, they're going to laugh and say, 'What did you expect from that white trash?' " Missy punched her nails into his flesh, then suddenly released him.

"Nothing wrong with white trash," said Cecil, coming out of the kitchen. "Elvis was white trash."

Clark sagged, his head falling forward.

"Betty B's column wasn't just an attack on who we are *now;* it's an attack on who we hope to become," Missy said to Clark. "It's like she's trying to ruin our future."

"Clinton was white trash, too," said Cecil.

Missy stroked Clark's face. He was growing a beard along his jaw-line, a half-inch extension of his sideburns that met at his chin, the look all the boy bands were going for. Clark was almost thirty, but he looked barely out of his teens. He said it was due to his drug cocktails, but Missy thought it was because he let her do all the worrying. Smart as he was, if it wasn't for her, they'd still be living in a cinder-block house in Riverside and percolating crystal on the kitchen range.

"I love you, babe," said Clark, his eyes fluttering.

"I love you, too. So, when are you going to kill Betty B? I want her done first."

Clark pulled away.

"It's a matter of survival," said Missy. "If we don't do *something* about the newspaper article, Guillermo is going to think we can be played. Then *we're* the ones going to get killed."

Clark snickered. "You think Guillermo reads the *Gold Coast Pilot?*"

"Maybe Guillermo doesn't read the *Pilot,* but you can just bet that someone he knows does," said Missy. "Some friend of his wife's, or maybe the man who sold Guillermo his last Porsche and wants to sell him the next one. Someone is going to tell him." She kissed him. "That's why you have to—"

"Arturo and Vlad spend half their day keeping our dealers in line and beating back freelancers. They don't need any more assignments."

"If we don't respond, Guillermo is going to think *anyone* can get away with—"

"Arturo and Vlad taught him a lesson last time. You think he wants a replay of *that?*"

Clark was interrupting her more often lately. Missy wondered if he was on some new brain scrambler, or just puffed up from all those people at the party telling him how talented he was. Not that any of them ever walked into one of their shops and bought some shorts or beachwear. She let it pass. For now. "Clark, honey, I'm just saying this is an opportunity to remind Guillermo what happens to people who fuck with us."

"You're not worried about Guillermo," said Clark. "You're just mad because you got embarrassed in front of a bunch of yacht club snobs who don't like us anyway."

The phone rang.

"Cecil, you pick up that *goddamned* phone, and tell them I'm out shopping." Missy's eyes never left Clark's. "I want them dead. I want Vlad and Arturo to run the route on both of them."

"Dude gave you a full refund, Missy."

Missy snatched the paper. She practically had the column memorized. " 'Douglas Meachum, the urbane owner of Meachum Fine Arts, took pains to assure me that the mistake was an honest one, and that restitution was immediately proffered and accepted. In all fairness, the authenticity of pre-Columbian art is notoriously hard to verify, but what lingers in the ears of this columnist is the raucous bleating of Missy Riddenhauer at her soiree, telling everyone within range of her voice that she had personally selected her precious artifacts, and how knowledgeable she was about their history. Doug Meachum made an honest mistake. What's Missy's excuse?' " She threw the paper down.

"Spilt milk, babe."

"If you won't order Vlad and Arturo to kill them, I will."

Clark tried not to smile. "Come on, you know they won't take orders from you." He stood up, beckoned. "I'm going to hit the shower. You want to join me?"

Missy watched him leave. A few minutes later, she heard him singing in the shower.

"What about me?" asked Cecil.

"What about you?"

Cecil licked his lips. "Let *me* take care of Betty B."

"*You?*"

"What's the matter? You have something against a man bettering himself?"

17

The line in front of the Strand theater snaked down the sidewalk, a mix of stoners and surfers, freaks and fuckups, and movie buffs waiting to see the Tuesday showing of *Curse of the Demon*. A joint was passed slowly down the waiting line as a skateboarder rolled past the ticket booth. The Strand was fifty years old, an atomic age relic with sun-faded paint, cracked tiles, and neon marquee lights with half their tubes burned out. One screen. The theater showed second-run features daily, and classic films at midnight, Tuesday, Friday, and Saturday.

Thorpe drove on—he could hardly wait until Saturday. Four more nights and *Shock Waves* would be the late-night feature, replacing *Twenty Million Miles to Earth* on the playbill, a replacement that had cost Thorpe five hundred dollars. He would have paid the manager five thousand if he had asked for it.

Downtown Huntington Beach was still going strong even at this hour, the bars and clubs rocking, the streets clogged with cruisers, the kids rubbernecking one another. Thorpe made a sharp left turn, heading inland on a two-lane road. He checked his rearview, keeping to the speed limit. There were three cars behind him at varying distances: a VW van, a Lexus with the windows blacked out, and a red Mustang with the top down. As Thorpe approached the green traffic light, he deliberately stalled his car. The Lexus was closest of the other cars, easing up right on his bumper. Thorpe started his car, popped the clutch, and stalled it again. The Lexus beeped. Thorpe started his car again as the light turned red, zipped across the intersection, narrowly avoiding a Chevy Suburban. Thorpe took the next right, quickly backed into a dark driveway, and turned off his headlights. He waited a few minutes, watched as the Lexus, the VW, and the Mustang passed through the intersection and kept going. Thorpe started the car, pleased. Old habits. Where would he be without them?

A gray-white gob of bird shit splattered the windshield, a pelican dump, from the size of it, but Cecil didn't flinch. He was used to it. Lucky for him elephants couldn't fly. He turned on the wipers of the minivan, pressed the window washer. The washer motor spun, but it was out of fluid, the dry wipers smearing bird shit across the glass. Typical. He turned off the wipers, sat back, and waited.

No matter how you looked at it, Cecil was overworked and under-appreciated. He had boosted the minivan in record time—slim-jimmed the door latch, cracked the wheel lock with a breaker bar, and popped the ignition in two shakes of a lamb's tail. You think Missy would be impressed? You'd be out of your fucking mind, you thought that.

Cecil squeezed the steering wheel. The gardener's gloves were a lit-tle lame maybe, but he didn't have any of the cool surgical gloves movie badasses always wore. Cecil knew what he was doing. Gloves were gloves. He knew about cars, too. Missy would have given him a smack for boosting a minivan instead of a Hummer or a Mercedes, but those rides all had security systems and satellite monitoring units. No, if you were contemplating murder, a beat-up minivan was just what the situation called for.

He pulled his baseball cap lower, one of those expansion teams from a city no one ever heard of. Another advantage of watching so much television was that Cecil had learned how to get away with murder. Gloves, that was the first thing. Then a hat, so you couldn't be ID'd from your hair, which in Cecil's case was red and thinning. Clark kept saying he was going to work on some kind of hair-growing formula, but all he seemed to do was come up with better ways to get fucked-up. Not that Cecil was complaining. Clark and his new and improved dope kept the money train rolling. Still, the guy could spend a little time and help out his brother-in-law. Cecil's barber suggested he get a crew cut, said short hair put less stress on the scalp, but that was probably just a way to keep Cecil coming back every two weeks for a trim. Everyone was a rip-off.

Betty B had been inside the Rusty Pelican for almost an hour. Cecil had followed her to three other fancy bars this evening. She probably told everybody it was part of her job, gathering gossip, then wrote off her bar tab on her taxes, another reason the country was going down the shitter. Cecil had joined the National Guard about five years ago, but he washed out of basic training because of his bum ankles. He used to feel embarrassed about it, but now he was glad it had happened. You put in your time defending your country, getting up at the crack of dawn, and some old drunk stiffs Uncle Sam for her fair share.

Try as he might, though, Cecil couldn't bring himself to hate Betty B. Yeah, she had written some pretty rank things about Missy, but, like Clark said, it was just a newspaper. Twice tonight he'd had a chance at her, and both times he had waited too long, making excuses why it wasn't the right moment. He beat the steering wheel. It was just this kind of weakness that kept him fetching coffee for Missy and double-checking the pH balance in the swimming pool.

Fuck it. This time, *Cecil* was going to take care of business. *Cecil,* not Vlad, and not that greaseball Arturo. Clark had told Missy no, said he was happy with the piece of the pie they had. Cecil had to admit it was a pretty fine slice, too—big house on the water, fancy cars, trash bags full of cash, but Missy had said how could you be happy with a slice when you could have the whole damned pie? Cecil didn't think Clark was scared of Guillermo, no matter what Missy said. He thought Clark was just . . . satisfied. Maybe after Cecil killed Betty B, he'd be satisfied, too.

Cecil shifted in his seat, practically sticking to it. He could smell his own sweat. If Vlad or Arturo were sitting here, they'd be cool and calm, Vlad probably talking about some cartoon show he had watched that afternoon, Arturo going on about his stock portfolio.

Cecil sat up as Betty B staggered out of the Rusty Pelican. She had to hold on to the doorman's arm, yapping away, breathing bourbon in his face, from the way he turned away. Cecil's chest was tight. He took short little breaths as he watched Betty B look around, probably trying to remember where she had parked her car. He eased the van out from the curb as Betty B started down the sidewalk. She kept patting her hair, as though trying to hold her head in place.

Cecil tugged at his cap for reassurance, and the action reminded him of what Betty B was doing with her hair. *Loser.* He had stolen more cars than he could count, had rolled drunks, beaten up queers, even done a few B and E's. He had hit Gary Jinks over the head with a tire iron for stealing his girlfriend, and once he threatened a club bouncer with a starter pistol, but here he was, sitting in some minivan, thirty-one years old, losing his hair, and he had never killed anyone.

Betty B started down the sidewalk in the cool night air.

Cecil rolled down the street, lights out, accelerating.

Thorpe drove back through downtown Huntington Beach, feeling so light-headed that he wouldn't have been able to pass a field sobriety test. He hadn't had anything to drink, but there was no way he could walk a straight line. He could barely *drive* a straight line. That's what happiness could do to you. He had spent so much time hating himself these last few months, blaming himself, but now he was doing something about it. Come Saturday, he and the Engineer might meet again, a *Shock Waves* rendezvous. Those saints who said revenge never solved anything had never lost anyone. Killing the Engineer wouldn't bring back Kimberly, but it would make the Engineer just as dead.

For some reason, he thought of Claire, the two of them sitting on the steps under the stars, and her asking him why he had never hit on her. He would have liked to have told her.

Thorpe slammed on his brakes as a man and a woman ran across the street, holding hands. He watched them disappear into a Dunkin' Donuts shop. It was the same couple he had seen walking through the alley behind Meachum's house that first day, two old hippies in tie-dye and macramé, teeth missing, hair everywhere. He wondered how they had gotten from Laguna to Huntington, and he wondered what had happened to the man's floppy hat. Most of all, he wondered how they managed to look so much in love. He drove on, shaking his head.

The wake-up hadn't gone as smoothly as he'd thought. The column by Betty B in the *Gold Coast Pilot* had embarrassed Meachum, but it had been even worse for Missy. He had no idea how Betty B had found out. Billy had read the article and clucked about the law of unintended consequences, as immutable a law as relativity or thermodynamics. Thorpe had walked out of the restaurant, called the gallery a few minutes later. Gina Meachum answered the phone. He almost hung up, then asked to speak to Meachum. He wasn't there. "Frank? Is that you?" Gina said. She told him it was Nell Cooper who had fed Betty B the story. "Douglas was so upset, Frank. He said he had taught her everything she knew, and she betrayed him. She didn't even bother giving notice or leaving a forwarding address."

Thorpe remembered the dismay on Nell's face at the party, watching Meachum working the room, the smile she stuck on her face when she went to join him. Thorpe wasn't sure about the law of unintended consequences, but he believed in the law of common courtesy. It wasn't just Statue of Liberty boilerplate. His most successful operations had been achieved by going through an angry wife, a put-upon chauffeur, a secretary who was never thanked, a gardener whose work was stepped on, a bodyguard made to take out the trash. A powerful man who showed contempt for the people under him was the easiest target in the world. Thorpe was sorry that Missy had gotten caught up in the wake-up, but he was glad Nell had broken free of Meachum.

He took a right onto the Pacific Coast Highway, humming along to the radio as he headed back to his apartment.

18

Thorpe lay on his belly, squinting under the couch and wondering what he was doing here at 2:00 a.m. He had just gotten back from his trial run at the Strand when his phone rang. He jiggled around the golf club, a four iron, stirring up dust balls. "Are you *sure* it went under here?"

"I thought so," said Pam.

Thorpe looked back at her. Pam was perched on one of the end tables, legs drawn up, wearing only an XXL 50-Cent T-shirt and pale blue panties. He could hear Claire cursing nearby. "You did see a rat, though?"

Pam nodded. "Big one. He hadn't brushed his teeth for a long time, either."

"You two shouldn't leave the dog door open. You don't even *have* a dog."

"We shut the dog door, how are we going to get in when we lock ourselves out?" asked Pam.

"Keep the dog door closed. That's your problem."

"The problem is the city's cut back on rat abatement for the last four years," said Claire, peering under the brown leather reading chair, her own golf club ready—a putter. She wore dark blue silk pajama bottoms and a T-shirt with Serena Williams's picture on it. Her butt was in the air.

"He's checking out your ass, Claire."

Claire looked over at Thorpe. They were both low to the floor. "Is that right, Frank?"

"Guilty."

Claire shook her head. "*Men.* You call them up in the middle of the night for help, and instead they scope out the goods."

"Just kill the rat; then you two can flirt," said Pam.

Thorpe got up. "Mr. Rat's not under here."

Claire stood up, too, her short dark hair falling around her face. "Ditto."

"Well . . . he's got to be somewhere," said Pam, still on the end table.

Thorpe had been getting ready for bed when Pam had called, still exhilarated from seeing the crowd outside the movie theater, thinking of what he was going to do if he saw the Engineer in line Saturday night. He was going to let him watch the movie, catch him on the way back to his car, him and his bodyguard, catch them unaware. Thorpe imagined asking the Engineer how he'd liked the movie. Then the phone rang and Pam was yelling, and Claire was telling her to relax.

Thorpe walked into the kitchen, yawning.

"I already checked the kitchen," Claire called.

"I'll check it again," said Thorpe. One of the cabinets was half-open. He bent down, started to open it with the golf club.

Claire touched his side and Thorpe jumped. She laughed, clucked like a chicken.

Still laughing, Thorpe opened the cabinet, gently nudged aside cereal boxes with the head of the golf club. The rat stared back at him, a big one, too, just like Pam had said, dirty brown and beady-eyed, his whiskers brushing the face of the white-haired Quaker on the cardboard oatmeal canister.

"Do you see anything?" asked Claire.

Thorpe shifted his weight. The rat followed his movements, turned its head, and seemed to make eye contact with the Quaker. Thorpe whacked the rat with the golf club, but it was a glancing blow. The rat scurried across Thorpe's hands and onto the kitchen floor.

Bam! Claire swung the putter, missed, and smacked the floor. The rat's legs slipped on the tile as it tried to get away, squealing, desperate now. She swung the golf club again, hit the rat a glancing blow, and sent him sailing. The rat bounced off the stove and lay stunned. Claire advanced on him, the putter raised high. The rat got to its feet, reared back, showed its yellowed incisors, snarled at her, eyes bulging.

"I think he's in love with you," Thorpe said to her.

The rat made a dash toward the living room, then cut back as Claire swung and missed, headed back toward the doggy door.

Claire raised the golf club, but Thorpe grabbed her arm before she could take another try, and the rat raced out through the doggy door, out into the night. Claire shook Thorpe off. "That was *stupid.*"

Thorpe walked to the doggy door, slid down the metal locking plate over the entrance. "Tough guy like that, he earned his freedom." He leaned his four iron against the wall.

Pam peeked in the doorway. "Is it safe?"

Claire reached over, pinched Thorpe's bare nipple.

Thorpe howled, rubbed his nipple. "That *hurt.*"

"It was meant to hurt. I wanted to kill it."

"You're licensed by the state of California to offer psychotherapy?" Thorpe's nipple felt hot. The other one had stiffened in sympathy. "*You* need treatment, lady."

"What a baby," said Claire. "And don't call me 'lady.' "

"Are you guys gonna fuck right here on the kitchen table?" asked Pam. "And if you do, can I watch?"

Claire looked at Thorpe.

"I'm celibate," said Pam. "I have to have *some* fun."

Claire took Thorpe's hand, led him toward her bedroom.

"Rat hunting really turns you on," said Thorpe, exhilarated and nervous and trying not to think too much. "Who knew the killer ape was female?"

"Shut up." Claire closed the door behind them, the room in twilight, sheer curtains on the single window. It smelled like Claire. Thorpe had never been there before. There were photos on the walls that he couldn't make out, and a large desk with a computer and books piled on one side. A bed, too, low to the ground, with lots of pillows.

He looked over at her, and Claire was hesitant, unsure, too, and that convinced him. Thorpe kissed her gently, knowing that this was a bad time to start something, but he kissed her anyway, and she kissed him back, eager now. They undressed each other, not speaking, their little bites and nips silent introductions to their dark places, their flesh warming.

"You still think this is a bad idea?" whispered Claire as they eased onto her bed, the flowery sheets cool against their skin, goose bumps rising, her breasts pebbled, and he warmed her with his tongue. "*Do* you?" she gasped.

"Probably."

She arched against him, her hand sliding up along his thigh. "You want me to stop?" Her touch was feathery. "I can stop, if you want."

Thorpe buried his face in her hair, inhaled her fragrance as she caressed him. He groaned, bit his lips shut, shifted his weight, on top of her now, kissing his way past the hollow of her sternum, trying not to hurry, but sensing her eagerness matched his own.

Claire's legs curled around him. "That's good."

He made his way lower, licked her belly button, tasted her sweet salt sweat. She made tiny crying sounds as he kissed her lower still.

"This is okay, what we're doing, isn't it?" Claire's back arched as he licked her, and she was warm and slick, waxed smooth. She reached down, breathing hard, held the back of his head in place. "I . . . I don't want . . . don't want you to be sorry we're doing this."

Thorpe started laughing.

"That tickles. I'm talking too much, aren't I?"

Thorpe looked up at her, his face glistening.

She averted her eyes. "I'll shut up."

Thorpe entered her, and she was soft and deep; then she gripped him so tightly, the two of them gasped. Neither of them talking now. Just the two of them, alone in the vast twilight, driving into each other, lost and mindless and free. He hardly thought of Kimberly at all.

They lay quietly afterward, arms and legs tangled, tickled by the surface-tension sweat, exhausted and exhilarated. Moonlight softened all the outlines, all the sharp edges. Through the wall came the faint sound of the television in Pam's bedroom. Thorpe stroked Claire, felt her pulse beating through her flesh, and he would have ridden that rhythm all night. He loved the afterward more than the sex. Afterward was more intimate. The barriers broken, no illusions, no lies. For the moment anyway. A moment was good enough. He breathed in the warmth of her, knowing it was too good to last.

Claire rested her head on his chest. "Where did you get so much anger?"

Thorpe shifted.

"Don't be upset. I had a good time. A wonderful time. I was just surprised at the rage inside you, that's all." She blew her hair off her face. "Not anger at women, not a bit of it—I know you better than that. I steer away from those kind of men."

"Gee, thanks."

Claire rolled onto her pillow. "Sometimes an angry fuck can be really great, but your anger . . . it just keeps cycling around in your brain. It must be like having a head full of wasps." She traced his mouth with a forefinger. "I've hurt your feelings."

"I'll get over it."

"Don't be like that. The first time is always weird. At least you didn't keep changing positions like a gyroscope, showing off your fancy moves."

"I usually wait until the second date to break out the trapeze."

She played with the hair on his chest. "I've wanted to make love to you since you first moved in."

"Anticlimactic, wasn't it?"

"Not exactly."

Thorpe brushed his lips across her breast, lingering. "Do I get another chance?"

Claire played with his fingers. "Do you want to know the exact moment I was sure it was going to happen?"

Thorpe ran his nails down her long legs.

"It was the day you moved in, and you came by to borrow a couple of eggs, and even though I invited you in, you stayed in the doorway. Hard to get . . . that's very attractive." Claire kissed his fingers one by one. "I could feel your eyes on me as I crossed to the refrigerator, and I didn't hurry. I took the eggs out of the carton, two in each hand, and I offered them, and you stood there, smiling, waiting me out. *That's* when I knew."

"You're a scary date, Claire." He liked saying her name.

"You're not scared." Her eyes were bright as she rocked against him. "That's one of your games. You downplay yourself, pretend to be in over your head, but you're not."

He watched her, knowing why he had kept his distance. So much for following your instincts. His hand traced along the inside of her, the two of them trembling with the moment, that quiet point when all good and dangerous things were imminent.

"Turn on the TV," said Pam.

Thorpe blinked himself awake, Claire beside him, rubbing her eyes.

Pam stood in the bedroom doorway. "Quick, turn on the TV."

Claire fumbled for the remote, popped the TV on. She kissed Thorpe.

"Haven't you two had enough?" asked Pam. "Oh, here it is."

Thorpe sat up as the image of Betty B came on-screen, a still photo of the columnist in one of her signature hats.

". . . The longtime columnist for the *Gold Coast Pilot* was struck and killed last night by a hit-and-run driver as she left the Rusty Pelican in Newport Beach. Police ask anyone who might have information on the accident to please contact them."

"Betty B put me in her column when I did that suntan oil commercial in Huntington a few months ago," gushed Pam. "She called me an 'up-and-coming spokesmodel with a killer bod.' Isn't that just the wildest coincidence?"

Thorpe stared at the screen. "Yeah . . . it is."

19

"How long is he going to stay mad?" asked Cecil.

Missy watched Clark paddling his board out through the breakers, one of his fourteen-foot torpedoes, black with silver rails. "Until he takes something for it."

"This is so unfair." Cecil sat on the very edge of Missy's blanket. "I did the job, didn't I? I didn't get caught, did I? You keep giving me this kind of responsibility, after a while, you won't *need* Vlad and Arturo."

Missy adjusted her pink bikini top. "Dream on."

Cecil picked up one of the newspapers from the stack he had brought, started reading aloud. " 'Betty B, as she was known to her many friends, was killed by a driver unknown to the police at this time.' " He beamed at her. " 'Driver unknown.' That's me. I'm like a ghost or something. Like fucking Zorro. You should be proud of me."

Missy watched Clark as he stopped paddling, turned, and waited for the next set of waves. "I am proud of you."

"Then how come Clark is so pissed?"

Missy waved to Clark, but he pretended not to see. She thumped her taut abdominal muscles with a flick of her index finger. You could have beaten out a tune on her belly. It might not have been the song you really wanted to hear, though.

The stretch of beach just north of Del Mar was almost deserted this time of the morning. Just Clark, a few younger surfers with their stubby boards, and a couple of retirees trudging over the soft sand with metal detectors.

Clark had been so angry when Cecil told him what he had done that he had grabbed his board with hardly a word. Didn't even want to call any of his longboard buddies. He told Missy he didn't want company, wanted to be alone, but she had ignored him, gotten in the 4x4. Cecil had tried to get in, too, but Clark had peeled out of the driveway. If Cecil hadn't let go of the door handle, he would have lost a hand. Cecil followed them in the other car, while Missy gave him directions on the cell, and Clark kept saying, "Tell that fat fuck to go home." Like Missy was going to listen.

Poor Cecil. It really *wasn't* fair the way Clark treated her brother. Cecil had knocked on their bedroom door early this morning, so excited that he could hardly talk, and turned on the news. Missy had clapped her hands with delight, seeing the footage of the ambulance rushing off, lights flashing, and that old photo of Betty B they showed—she hadn't looked so good in twenty years. Clark wasn't pleased, though. He said Missy and Cecil had overstepped, which was a word she had never heard him use before.

"*You're* glad I did it, aren't you?" asked Cecil.

Gulls screamed overhead. "I just wish I had been there to see that bitch go flying."

Cecil grinned. It was the same goofy expression she remembered from when they were kids, Cecil willing to do anything to please her. All she had to do was tell him that some boy on the bus had teased her, and Cecil's fists would start flying. Sometimes he got suspended the very first week of the new school year. If Missy had told him that the Man in the Moon had peeked in her window, Cecil would have tried to steal a rocket ship.

"I felt a little . . . bad afterward." Cecil dug his fingers into the sand. "Not as bad as I thought, though."

"You'll get the hang of it."

Cecil nodded, fully dressed and ridiculous in a straw cowboy hat because he burned easily, his freckles flaring. He looked like the beefy, ignorant redneck he had always been, but this morning, after what he had done to Betty B . . . well, Missy was happy to have him sitting cross-legged on the corner of her blanket, and she didn't care who saw him with her. Of course, it helped that they were practically alone on the beach.

"I'm thinking of getting me a gun," said Cecil. "Big one. Maybe a shoulder holster, too."

Missy watched Clark catch a wave. He rode it in, cut across the crest, picking up speed as he raced toward shore, crouched over the board, legs wide, hair flying in the breeze.

Cecil sniffed. "If you ask me, I think Clark is just mad because now you've got *me* to take care of things. You don't have to ask him to sic Vlad and Arturo on people."

Missy pulled her legs up, wrapped her arms around her knees as she watched Clark. "Gosh, he's pretty, isn't he?"

"Personally, I see a lot of disrespect from those two, not just directed at me, either."

Missy glanced over at Cecil. "Give me a for instance." She waited. "That's what I thought." She shaded her face with her hand, watching Clark again.

Cecil chewed on his lower lip. "I see things. People don't pay attention to me, but I see the way Arturo looks when you talk. Like he knows more than you do."

Missy was thinking that over, when Clark waved, riding the longboard toward shore.

Missy waved back, smiling as he took the board all the way in. He splashed into the shallows, then slung the board under one arm, carried it closer to the blanket, and drove it in the sand. Every move he made was like a Beach Boys song. He waved again, beckoning, and Missy realized that he wasn't waving at her. She turned, saw Arturo and Vlad standing on the shoulder of the road, beside their parked cars.

Clark approached the blanket, shaking his long hair out. He still wouldn't look at her.

"This ain't good." Cecil kept sneaking peeks at Arturo and Vlad. "This ain't good at all."

"Hush."

Cecil got heavily to his feet, stuck his hands in his pockets. "You tell them I didn't do nothing you didn't want me to do."

Missy reached into the cooler, pulled out a can of beer for Clark.

"You tell them I'm *family*," said Cecil.

Clark walked right past the blanket, met Arturo and Vlad halfway. Missy could see them talking, but she couldn't hear what they were saying.

"Dang it," said Cecil as the three of them headed toward the blanket. "*Dang* it."

Missy tossed Clark a beer, smiled as he caught it one-handed. "I get you boys a brew?"

Vlad shook his head and Arturo didn't even respond.

Clark popped the beer, took a long swallow, and wiped his mouth.

"You sure know how to ride that board," said Cecil. "You could probably turn pro if you wanted to, Clark."

Clark belched.

Arturo laughed and Cecil's face got even redder.

Clark picked up a towel, dried his face. He stood there, gazing off toward the water. "Arturo said one of our Riverside houses got taken down yesterday." He blew salt water out of his nose. "Lost about five pounds of crank."

"I *told* you Guillermo was going to—"

"We don't know it's Guillermo, Missy." Clark took another swallow of beer. "We just know we lost about five pounds of crank, and two cookers got wasted."

"Well, who else *could* it have been? Nobody else would have the balls—"

"Arturo and Vlad are going to find out who did it," said Clark, water droplets glistening on his shoulders.

"I guess maybe now Cecil's going to get some credit for what he did last night," said Cecil. "Maybe I can come along with Arturo and Vlad—"

Clark bounced the beer can off Cecil's head.

Missy had no idea what new dope Clark was on, but it had sure turned him into major alpha dog. It was kind of nice, as long as he didn't get carried away with himself. "Clark, honey," she said, blotting his broad back with the towel, "you got to admit this would be a good time to put down Meachum, maybe his wife, too, make an example of them."

"I'm not admitting anything until Arturo and Vlad tell me who wasted my cookers." Clark looked at Missy, and it was like looking into the eye of a storm. "Motherfucker who did it took one of my new recipes."

20

Thorpe shadowed Ray Bishop around the half-built housing development for a half hour, followed him as he made his rounds up and down the cluttered work site. Bishop limped slightly, stopping to clock in at regular intervals with his ID card. Orange Industrial Security kept their rent-a-cops on a tight leash. Quite a comedown, going from lead detective at the Riverside PD to an unarmed security guard with a badge the size of a dinner plate on his chest.

Thorpe waited until Bishop sat down on a nail keg, pulled out a steel thermos bottle, and poured a cup of coffee, waited until he pulled a pint bottle out of his jacket, sweetened the cup. Bishop didn't even know he was there until Thorpe softly spoke his name. The poor bastard bobbled his drink, splashed his pants. "First time I ever drank on the job," he stammered. "I got this cough that—"

Thorpe held his hands up. "I'm not checking up on you."

Bishop wiped his mouth. He was an ugly man with a broken beak and bad skin, a tough guy aging badly, gone soft and sallow. "You're not management?"

"Don't insult me," said Thorpe. Bishop smiled. It didn't make him look any better, but Thorpe was glad to see he still had it in him. "My name is Frank. I want to talk to you about Clark and Missy Riddenhauer."

Bishop stopped smiling. "That's a mistake," he rasped. "You local or federal?"

"I'm not a cop."

"Yeah, right." Bishop looked out at the half-built homes, the piles of wood debris and curling tar paper. "How did you find me? I thought I covered my tracks."

"You had to get bonded for this job."

"That's right, I had to pass inspection to guard lumber and Sheetrock." Bishop fingered the buttons on his gray uniform. "Old partner of mine from Riverside runs the security firm. Matt said I didn't meet their standards but that he would make an exception. Acted like I should have kissed his fat ass in gratitude." He spit. "If he asked, I *would* have, too."

Thorpe had gone to the computer after seeing Betty B on TV this morning. Getting run down the same day her column came out was probably just a coincidence, but Thorpe had a suspicious mind. He kept following the threads on the insurance-industry database, half-expecting the Engineer to send him a message, but he was all by himself on the Net. An hour later, he hit pay dirt, but it gave him no pleasure, just a sick feeling in his stomach. Three years ago, Clark Riddenhauer had won a $1.2 million judgment against the Riverside Police Department, and Detective Ray Bishop, for malicious arrest and prosecution. The arrest had been for production, sale, and distribution of methamphetamines. The PD's insurance carrier, Liberty State Mutual, had settled out of court. Thorpe had read the judgment, hoping that Bishop was an inept cop who had busted a couple of innocent civilians and stepped on his dick instead. So far, Bishop was living up to his advance billing.

"The Riddenhauer case, that was an impressive example of poor police work, Ray." Thorpe picked up a small chunk of concrete, chucked it across the site, and dinged an empty tar bucket. "No wonder you lost your badge and pension. I think the Academy uses you as an example on how *not* to pump up your arrest stats."

Bishop scowled, and Thorpe got an idea of what he had been like before he had taken the long fall. "What's this about?"

"A one-point-two-million-dollar settlement. The Riddenhauers must have had quite an attorney. Of course, you being a falling-down drunk, that didn't help, either."

"I was never impaired on the job, and that didn't have nothing to do with it anyway." Bishop pulled at his wrinkled jacket. There was dried mud on the cuff of his trousers. "It's a little late for the department to be coming after me now. I ain't got anything you want."

"I told you: I'm not a cop."

"What are you, then?"

Thorpe ignored the question. "If you made a good bust, how did Clark and Missy beat it?"

Bishop sat down on the nail keg, looked past him.

"It's life-and-death, Ray."

"Maybe you ain't noticed, Frank, but I don't do life-and-death anymore." Bishop sat there, and Thorpe gave him all the time he needed to rediscover his courage, or anger, or resentment, whatever it took to start him talking. Bishop took off his cap, wiped his forehead. "I busted Clark for buying crystal meth precursors from a chemical supply house." He shook his head. "Just prior to trial, the main prosecution witness, a clerk at the supply house, recanted. He told the judge that I had threatened him, forced him to finger Clark. That the whole thing was a setup."

"A witness who gets cold feet . . . that's what depositions are for."

"Recanting cost the clerk his plea bargain. It meant three years in Vacaville, but he jumped at it. That gave his story serious credibility." Bishop looked up at Thorpe. "I hope you know what you're doing. Missy and Clark . . . you *really* don't want to mess with them."

"Too late."

Bishop fingered his cap, turning it round and round in his hands. "Sorry to hear that."

"They might have killed someone last night. If they did . . . they may not be done."

"Oh, those two are never done." Bishop looked past him again. "They fooled me in Riverside. You seen them, right? Nice-looking couple. No history of violence. Only reason I busted Clark was so I could turn him. He turned me inside out instead." He cleared his throat. "The clerk at the chemical supply store . . . day before he was supposed to testify, the pastor of his church disappeared, him and his whole family. Neighbors didn't see anything, didn't hear anything.

The pastor, his wife, and their two little girls, just up and gone." His face sagged. "Funny thing, they left their clothes behind. Left their toothbrushes and their bank account, too. Church had a prayer circle for them, asked God to do something. That's how the clerk found out. He got this phone call, and suddenly he changed his story. Never did find that family, so I guess God had a previous commitment." He stared at Thorpe. "You don't look so good."

"You said the Riddenhauers had no history of violence."

"They got a crew chief named Arturo who handles the rough stuff. A total hardball, but he looks like the president of the Jaycees. I didn't connect him with Clark until it was too late. These days, Arturo has a helper. Creepy type. Wouldn't think Arturo would need help, but there you go."

"The creepy one . . . tall and skinny, ultrawhite?"

"That's him. I seen guys in the morgue had more color."

"His name is Vlad. I met him at a party. He didn't seem so dangerous."

"I hope you're usually a better judge of character." Bishop buffed his black shoes with his hand. "Are you the one Clark and Missy are after?"

Thorpe shook his head. "A couple of innocent bystanders. I put them in the soup."

"Now you think you're gonna pull them out."

"That's right."

"Well, tell your innocent bystanders to relocate and not look back. That's my professional advice." Bishop checked his watch, stood up. "Duty calls."

Thorpe easily kept pace with Bishop, the man's limp more pronounced now. Bags of broken cement leaked grit into the bare ground. Cardboard coffee cups lay crushed underfoot. "You said Arturo had a helper now. *Now.* You're still keeping tabs on them."

"You're a good listener." Bishop kept walking. "I used to be the same way once. You may not be a cop . . . but you're something." He slipped his ID card into a time clock mounted on a railing. "Couple months after I lost my job, my wife walked out and took the kids with her. This may be hard for you to believe, but I wasn't the best husband in the world. She walked out, and I loved her so much, I didn't beg her to come back. I drifted for a couple of years; then my old partner heard about me, said if I cleaned up, he'd give me a job." His hands trembled slightly. "After I got myself under control, I figured I'd see what Clark and Missy were up to." He shook his head. "Maybe I just wanted to play policeman again. It's hard . . . hard to leave something you're good at."

The wind kicked up sand. Thorpe checked the area without making a big deal out of it.

Bishop stepped on an empty pack of Marlboros, crushed it flat. "Missy and Clark live in a fancy house in Newport with her brother, Cecil, who don't seem like much, from what I could see. Arturo and the new guy come and go as they please. I set up outside one of Clark's surf shops for a few days. Kept track of what went out the front door, what went out the back. That store isn't selling enough shirts and trunks even to pay for the air conditioning. I figured maybe he was dealing dope out of the stores, but I watched the clerks—they're not moving anything except their lips. I think Clark is using the stores to launder drug money."

"You take what you had to the locals?"

"Didn't have anything in the way of proof, and I'm not what any DA would consider a reliable source."

Thorpe shook his hand. "Thanks, Ray."

Bishop hung on. He had a good grip. "You're really going to try to stop them?"

"I made the mess; now I have to clean it up."

"Haven't you heard? Nobody picks up after themselves anymore." Bishop lowered his eyes. "When I first met Clark, he was a joke. Idiot lived eighty miles inland and all he talked about was big waves, surfing." He shook his head. "Now he lives in a mansion, and I clock in every fifteen minutes and shit in a Porta Potti. You tell me how that happened, Frank, because I'd really like to know."

Thorpe didn't answer.

"Yeah . . . well, you don't make promises, I like that." Bishop idly touched the pint bottle in his jacket. "I'd be willing to help you, though. Just as long as I keep out of sight."

"You've helped me plenty. It's on me now."

"Sure, I've been a *big* help." Bishop twisted the buttons on his uniform. "I got to make my rounds. Serve and protect."

21

"Oh, hello . . . Frank." Gina Meachum stood in her doorway, a hammer in her hand. A painting leaned against the sofa behind her. Her long dark hair was loosely bound with a strip of white lace, as though she had reached for whatever was handy to hold back her hair. She wore jeans and a cowboy shirt.

"I hate to interrupt," said Thorpe, "but—"

"Who *is* it?" Douglas Meachum called from inside the house.

"A friend," Gina answered, then waved Thorpe inside. "This isn't a very good time. I'm finishing up some loose ends." She pushed back her hair. "Have you found a house yet?"

"No . . . not yet." It was hard to lie to her. Even harder to tell her the truth. Did he start with the suggestion that they get out of town for a few weeks, or end with it? Should he smile when he assured them that he would take care of everything? Have no fear, Frank Thorpe is here. He followed her inside, watched as she hung the painting, trying to decide where to begin. The painting was a realistic bright oil of a playground scene, a little girl pushing a red toy truck through the sandbox while a boy watched her from halfway down a slide. You knew within moments they were going to be fighting over the truck.

Gina stepped back, set down the hammer on a chest. "What do you think?"

"I like it." Thorpe moved closer to her. "I need to talk to you and—"

"Who's your friend?" Meachum said from the hallway, wheeling a large suitcase into the living room. He was wearing the same peacock blue Emilio Zegna suit that he had sported at LAX.

"Frank is house shopping," said Gina. "We may be neighbors soon."

"We're a little busy right now, Frank," said Meachum, setting down the suitcases. He was handsome but stiff and angular, as though there was a clothes hanger across his shoulders. "We're leaving for Hawaii in the morning."

"Two weeks in Maui." Gina looked at Thorpe, made eye contact. "It's kind of a second honeymoon for us."

"No need to be melodramatic," said Meachum.

"Frank was at Missy's party," said Gina, still watching him. "He may be interested in some art for his new house."

Meachum smiled at Thorpe. "Is that correct?"

Thorpe had only two kinds of luck. Very, very bad or very, very good. "Yes . . . I was at the gallery a week or so ago, looking at some pieces. I talked to Nell—"

"You won't be talking to her anymore." Meachum grimaced. "That woman stabbed me in the back. Didn't even have the integrity to tell me what she had done. No gratitude in this world anymore." He took a deep breath, adjusted his necktie. "I'm sure you've read all about our difficulties in the paper. I can only hope that Betty B's column doesn't dissuade you from allowing me to fulfill your aesthetic needs. I can assure you that I maintain the highest standard—"

"The article said you gave Missy a full refund."

"Douglas has never been anything less than ethical with his clients," said Gina.

Meachum glanced at his wife. "Yes, I gave Missy a full and immediate refund."

"Then what's the problem?" asked Thorpe.

Meachum beamed. "Finally, someone who understands the business world. You're a breath of fresh air, Frank. Mistakes happen. What counts is how we deal with our mistakes."

"I think people have an almost infinite capacity for forgiveness, as long as the apology is sincere," said Gina. There was just the faintest edge to her voice.

"If Nell hadn't gone running to Betty B, no one would have had any complaints," said Meachum, avoiding her gaze.

"I thought you came out pretty well in the column," said Thorpe. "Missy was the one who got snakebit."

"Yes . . . well, I did my best. In my defense, I have to say that I attempted to convince Betty B that the story was of little interest to anyone, but she despises Missy—"

"Despised," said Gina, correcting him. She glanced at Thorpe. "The poor woman was killed by a hit-and-run driver a couple of nights ago. It was just so sad."

"Almost makes me believe in God," muttered Meachum. He looked at Thorpe, sniffed. "That was in poor taste. I apologize, but the column was very bad for business. I've been doing damage control for the last two days. It just seemed like a good idea to give things time to settle down."

"A very good idea," said Gina.

"Can we make an appointment to discuss some art when I get back, Frank?" said Meachum. "I'll be back in the gallery on the fifteenth."

"I'll see you then."

Meachum forced a handshake on him. He probably thought that sealed the deal. "Is that what you came here for? Forgive my manners— I didn't even ask."

Thorpe turned to Gina. "Have a good trip." He walked quickly toward the front door.

"I hate this song," said Mellon.

"We're not here for a concert," said Pinto as *Hellfire Sonata* boomed out from the other side of the door, the lead guitar from Iron Church howling. He racked the pump Mosburg.

As if on cue, the door to the master bathroom slid open and Weezer stepped out in a reek of chemicals, a fat cracker wearing bib overalls and rubber gloves, swim goggles pushed back onto his forehead, a black war-surplus rubber respirator dangling around his neck. He jerked back when he saw them, then came at them. "What the *fuck* are you doing in my house?" he demanded, shouting to be heard over the music.

Mellon started laughing. "You look like a deep-sea diver."

"Hey, Captain Nemo, we came to pick up the load," said Pinto.

Weezer slid the door shut behind him. It was quieter now. "Do you morons *know* who I work for?"

"You're one of Clark's cookers." Pinto sniffed. "Smells like fresh crank, too."

Weezer didn't back down. "When Vlad and Arturo get done with you, there won't be hardly anything left." The respirator bounced under his chin as he spoke. "Two flushes and you'll be sent down the sewer with the rest of the turds."

Mellon cocked both barrels of his sawed-off gun.

"I had guns pulled on me before." Weezer spit on the floor, looked at Pinto. "You and your sidekick should take off now, while you still have a chance."

"My *sidekick*," said Pinto. "I like that."

"Knock that off, Pinto," said Mellon. "I ain't nobody's sidekick."

"No harm done." Weezer slowly turned his back on them, slid the door open. The music pounded around them. "I'm going to go back to work, and let you two be on your way. We'll just call this whole thing a misunder—"

Mellon unloaded both barrels into Weezer's back, hurled him into the bathroom. He looked at Pinto, waved at the smoke and spray. "I truly do hate that song."

22

Thorpe heard Hathaway coming a block away, the full-size Ford 4×4 pulling into the parking lot, bouncing over the speed bumps, glass packs trumpeting as Hathaway pumped the accelerator. The metallic blue truck was tricked out with oversize blackwalls, gold-flecked chrome wheels, and matching chrome bed rails, bumpers, and mirrors. A decal beside the gas tank showed a cartoon bad boy pissing onto a Chevy insignia. He revved the engine again as Thorpe opened the door.

"Subtle ride, Danny," said Thorpe, stepping up into the cab. It smelled of weed.

Hathaway peeled out of the parking lot before Thorpe was completely inside. Thorpe banged his head, hanging on with one hand as Hathaway cackled, gave it more gas.

"I missed you, too, asshole," said Thorpe, buckling himself in. At the small of his back, he felt the 9-mm semiauto clipped to his belt. He had been carrying since he talked to Ray Bishop and found out who Clark and Missy really were.

"You really missed me, you would have got in touch sooner." Hathaway downshifted, the fingers of his right hand caging the devil's-head floor shift knob. Lean and hard as a roofing nail, he wore a WHAT WOULD JESUS DO? tank top, shorts, and huaraches. Hathaway had been in Thorpe's four-man Delta Force squad. He was much younger than Thorpe, moody and high-strung, the only member other than Thorpe to survive. After their courts-martial, Thorpe had gotten Billy to take him into the shop, but the pace of operations was too slow for Hathaway, and his drug habit had flared up. When Billy cut him loose, Hathaway had hired on with the DEA, which always needed deep-cover field agents, and a minor drug problem was part of the job description. Hathaway had flourished at DEA; he could have moved inside to a desk, could have run his own string of informants, but he preferred the street, and the excuse it gave him to play the part.

They cruised the outskirts of Little Saigon, a community of recent Southeast Asian immigrants who had transformed the former white-bread inland slum into a bustling high-density community of minimalls and backyard vegetable gardens. The street signs were all bilingual now, and most of the high school valedictorians had last names that were unpronounceable to the older residents.

"You talked to Billy lately?" asked Hathaway, watching a couple of pretty Vietnamese girls in shorts and crop tops. "Fucker won't even return my calls."

"What's the matter, you tired of your job?"

"Too much paperwork." Hathaway sniffed. "I hear Billy's gone into business for himself. Maybe you could put in a good word for me."

"It would be a waste of a word."

Hathaway smiled, his teeth white and shiny as fresh dice. Hathaway might let everything else go, but he was fastidious about his oral hygiene. Thorpe remembered the two of them dug into the tree line of a Colombian mountainside, hunkered down for almost a week, waiting to spring an ambush, wet and cold the whole time. Thorpe had shivered and kept quiet, while Hathaway had chewed sugarless Dentyne and jabbered about dental caries and gingivitis and the need to floss after every meal, until Thorpe had threatened to knock his incisors out.

Thorpe checked the side-view mirror. "You said you could fill me in about the local meth scene."

"You have to admire Vietnamese people." Hathaway nodded at an old man sweeping the sidewalk in front of a noodle shop. "They have discipline, a sense of order. You drive down the street in Santa Ana, there's trash all over the sidewalk. Huntington Beach is even worse. Surfers, Frank, they want the ocean pristine, but you walk into one of their cribs, you better wear your hip waders. The Vietnamese, they're not afraid of soap and water."

Thorpe checked the side-view mirror again. It was the day after Gina and Douglas Meachum had left for Hawaii. Thorpe wondered how the second honeymoon was going, wondered if Meachum had called the blonde yet, waiting until Gina was in the shower. Maybe he had learned his lesson. Learned it without Thorpe's help. Thorpe had twelve days to make sure that they were safe when they came back home. Time enough. If Thorpe got lucky again, the Engineer would be at the screening of *Shock Waves* tonight. He was out there in cyber-space, circling in the darkness; the smell of blood and money kept him close, but it might be the Engineer's love of oddball movies that forced him into a mistake. A man's passions were always his weakness.

"Asian women, they are the absolute best." Hathaway slowed, checked out a slim, well-dressed woman stepping out of a black Lexus. "No tits, though. If the Vietnamese had tits, I'd marry the whole country."

"Let's talk meth, Danny."

"What's your interest in the wonderful world of speed?"

"There's a married couple distributing chemicals out of Newport—"

"Clark the shark? He and Missy are the only ones who fit that description." Hathaway waited for confirmation, shrugged. "Clark moves high-quality meth, and designer pharmaceuticals he comes up with himself. *Himself.* Only does about fifteen, twenty million dollars a year, but the man's a regular Thomas Alva Edison . . . if Edison'd been a dope fiend." He looked at Thorpe. "You don't want to mess with him."

"That's what everybody tells me." Thorpe checked the mirror again. "There's a white Pathfinder that's been trailing us for the last mile and not doing a good job of it. Young white guy with a goatee behind the wheel. Couple of others with him."

Hathaway glanced at the rearview, then popped open the dash, revealed a .357 Magnum lying among the fast-food wrappers and cat-sup packs. "Why don't you snap off a few rounds, see how committed they are?"

Thorpe closed the dash. "You burned these yokels?"

"Sold them a thousand hits of Midol last week." Hathaway ran a red light. "They seemed to be under the impression it was ecstasy."

The Pathfinder pulled into oncoming traffic, raced through the intersection after them, almost hit a Cadillac.

Thorpe tightened his seat belt as Hathaway made a hard right onto a side street, then veered through an alley, tires screeching. He cut through a car wash on the next block, took a one-way street the wrong way, raced through another alley, and headed in the opposite direction. Thorpe's fingers hurt from hanging on.

"We're clear," said Hathaway. "You could have backed them off with a couple shots from the Magnum, saved my tires, but hey, no hard feelings."

"What do you mess around with this petty shit for?"

"It's not the money, Frank; it's the principle of the thing."

Hathaway thought he was being clever, but Thorpe knew it was the truth. Danny saw the world as two circles. One very tiny circle contained his friends, with barely room inside for Thorpe and one or two others. The other circle contained everyone else on the planet. His friends could count on Hathaway to keep his word, and to keep his silence. The rest of the world had reason to worry. Casual rip-offs, short-weighting his busts for the DEA, strong-arming crack dealers for their bankroll and their stash, it was all the same agenda to him: whatever, whenever, whoever.

"One of these days, some kid you burned for a few hundred dollars is going to kill you."

"Like you're Mr. Safe and Sane. You're the guy asking about Clark and Missy, so tell me about your PTA meetings and your 401(k) and your high-fiber diet. Edge City, Frank. You're as fucked-up as me. You just hide it better."

They touched fists.

"Clark's muscle . . . they as bad as I've heard?" asked Thorpe.

"Worse. A couple of very sick dudes." A wizened old woman in a velour jogging suit and a Dodgers cap leaned against a walker. Hathaway threw her a kiss as they drove by, but she ignored him.

"She looks like the old lady with the Hustler cap," said Thorpe.

Hathaway half-turned in his seat, getting another look at the woman. "You're *right*."

The village had been high on the Colombian plateau, guerrilla country, with stifling days and sharp, cold nights, the stars so close, he'd almost ducked. "That woman must have been a thousand years old," said Thorpe. "Probably spit in the face of Pizarro. Sat there the whole time we dug out that well, a wad of coca leaves filling one cheek, the Hustler cap perched on her head. Never *would* say where she got it."

Hathaway looked straight ahead. "I think about going back there sometimes. See how those people are making out. Then I figure, Let well enough alone."

Thorpe nodded. Never go back. Better to think they had made a difference.

"I'm sorry about Kimberly," blurted Hathaway. "I should have said so sooner. She tried to cover for me when Billy found my stash at work. He bounced me anyway, but I appreciated the attempt. Small kindnesses, Frank, they stick in the memory. That old woman with the Hustler cap . . . she gave me corn cakes one morning. Never said a word, just gave them to me like I was one of her grandkids."

Thorpe remembered the first time he and Kimberly had made love. She had gone into the kitchen afterward, come back a few minutes later with a glass of fresh-squeezed orange juice, stood there, slim and naked, saying, "Don't count on this kind of treatment every time, Thorpe." But he had, and he was never disappointed. Maybe that's why he forgave her for her other lovers.

"Frank? You ever find Lazurus?"

"He's dead. It was the Engineer who killed her. He was running an op on Lazurus the whole time."

"No shit?" Hathaway chewed his thumbnail. "I can believe it. I heard most of the equipment Lazurus's crew shipped turned out to be defective. Games within games. I can't keep it all straight."

"The Engineer and I have been keeping in touch. We might be going to the movies together tonight. I hope so anyway."

Hathaway stared at him. "You need help, just tell me."

"I know."

"Why fool around with Clark and Missy? Haven't you got enough on your plate?"

"I've still got a little room."

Hathaway chuckled. "There's a dude named Guillermo—he's the closest thing to competition that Clark's got. Guillermo moves five or six times the weight, but they've got an arrangement."

"Peace treaty?"

"More like a free-trade agreement," said Hathaway. "Clark's always coming up with new drug combos, and simpler ways to cook meth, so when he moved in a few years ago, his dealers started taking business away from Guillermo right off. They went back and forth for a long time, tit for tat, but Guillermo was preoccupied with keeping out the Mexican Mafia, and then the Aryan Brotherhood started undercutting him with that rotgut crank of theirs. So while Guillermo was scrambling, Clark made his move." He sniffed. "Nuclear fucking winter. Clark had just two men handling the rough work."

"Vlad and Arturo."

"That's right." Hathaway eyed him. "Vlad and Arturo took down five of Guillermo's dealers in one weekend, and that was that."

"Five dealers by *themselves?*"

"By themselves. It wasn't just the dealers who got dead, either." Hathaway looked like he had bitten into some rotten meat. "Vlad and Arturo cleaned house: men, women, babies crying in their cribs, *everybody.*" He set his jaw. "After that, Guillermo decided it was better to give Clark a slice of territory, and buy his overflow, than fight him. Things have been quiet between them ever since."

"Guillermo let just two guys make him back off? I don't believe it."

"If you know these two, you know they ain't normal guys, Frank. They went through those dealers' security like shit through a goose. That's why Clark and Missy can drive around town in a convertible, and Guillermo uses a bulletproof Lincoln Town Car. Nobody blamed Guillermo for calling things off."

"Still . . . letting two guys make him back down . . . If I were Clark,

I'd worry that Guillermo might hold a grudge. I might be able to drive around town with the top down, but I'd still be paying attention."

Hathaway shook his head. "I know what you're thinking. Last time I saw that look on your face, we almost ended up in federal prison, pounding rocks for twenty years."

"Shining Path was murdering our villagers. We did the right thing."

"You started a fucking war, Frank."

"War between monsters. Shining Path guerrillas and the coca lords—it was like *Godzilla versus Ghidra:* You don't care who wins, you just want them to just keep tearing at each other so they don't wipe out Tokyo."

"That wasn't our mission," said Hathaway. "It was fun, though." He scratched at the inside of his arm, the flesh scabbed. "You get involved with Clark and Missy . . . it might not be so much fun. I just hope you know what you're doing now." He sniffed. "Must be quite a payday."

"There is no payday."

"Payday or payback, got to be one or the other."

"You get a regular retainer from Guillermo, or does he just pay you for advance notice of a bust?"

Hathaway hesitated. "Is it that obvious?"

"I know you, Danny. It's the move you'd make."

Hathaway shrugged. "Man has to take care of his needs."

"There're all kinds of needs. I need you to tell me about Guillermo. I need you to tell me about Missy and Clark, and Arturo and Vlad. I need to know all the players."

Hathaway drove for a few more blocks. "I got something you might be interested in," he said finally. "One of Clark's cookers in Riverside was taken down a couple of days ago. Made a real mess of the tweaker's trailer, too. Clark must have lost another cooker, too, because some truly righteous crank hit the market yesterday. Shit had a real sweet, smooth burn . . . might as well have Clark's autograph on it."

"Guillermo?"

"Not a chance. Guillermo's trying to find out who's moving this shit, probably worried that Clark will think *he's* behind it. Nobody knows who the guilty party is, not yet, but it's bound to come out. Somebody always wants to tell the tale." Hathaway grinned at Thorpe. "Stand-up guys are in short supply, Frank—I think you and me are the last two specimens."

23

"That shit will kill you," said Arturo.

Vlad stared at the half-eaten cheeseburger in his hand, watched a droplet of grease slide off the patty and spatter the wax paper on the tabletop. He took another bite, chewing with his mouth open, then reached for an onion ring.

"Onion rings are even worse," said Arturo. "The oil they use . . . Clinton was president last time they changed the deep-fat fryer. You're just *asking* for a coronary."

The onion ring drooped in Vlad's hand, soggy with batter. He stuffed it into his mouth. "I do not think it's food that will kill me, Arturo." He picked up a couple of french fries, catsup running down his fingers. "Or you, either, my friend."

Arturo blotted his forehead with a paper napkin, threw it onto the ground. A uniformed truck driver looked over as the wind sent the napkin billowing against his leg, then went back to his triple cheeseburger. Arturo watched Vlad dredge more french fries through the puddle of catsup on his paper plate. In spite of all his warnings, the man just didn't care about nutrition. Then again, Arturo was the one who had clocked in with a cholesterol reading of over three hundred at his yearly physical. Gringo doctor had looked at him like he was measuring Arturo for a coffin.

A horn blared at the nearby traffic signal, some *puto* in a blue Miata. Arturo took a deep breath, let it slowly out. Stress could kill you as fast as a sledgehammer to the back of the head.

The two of them sat at one of the outside tables at Gutbuster Burgers in Santa Ana. The umbrella over the table shaded them from direct sun, but not from the heat or the gritty auto exhaust from the intersection. Arturo had grown up less than a mile from this spot, breathing this filthy inland air day in and day out—no wonder he had asthma as a kid, his mother coating his chest with Vicks VapoRub every night, which worked about as well as lighting a candle to the Virgin of Guadalupe. His own kids breathed only ocean breezes, salty and clean and healthy. They lived in a house in Laguna del Cielo, an exclusive community in the hills above the Pacific. His mother had wept when she first saw the house, said God must be very happy with Arturo. Or very angry.

Vlad pushed over the basket mounded with onion rings. "You want one?"

Arturo's stomach grumbled, but he held up a can of vanilla Slim Fast. "*This* is what you should be eating for lunch. Vitamins, minerals, fiber, protein, everything you need." He popped the top. "This is what movie stars live on. That's why they look so good."

"I thought you said Atkins was the reason they look so good."

"Well, this is what I say now."

"Okay." Vlad started on another cheeseburger, gawky in pants that were too big, and an orange polo shirt buttoned up to the throat. His eyes were blue and blank as buttons.

They made quite a pair, sitting outside Gutbuster: Arturo barrel-chested, thick wrists poking from the sleeves of his suit jacket, while Vlad was flattened out, knotted with muscle. Even though Vlad was much younger, his face was networked with tiny wrinkles, and there was blood in the whites of his eyes. Arturo had suggested Vlad go to his doctor, get checked out, but Vlad just shook his head. Last week, Arturo had found tufts of blond hair in the car, but he didn't bring it up.

"What are you thinking, Arturo?"

Arturo took a sip from the can of Slim Fast, smacked his lips. "Thinking that I've probably already lost five pounds drinking this stuff, and it's only been a week."

"You look good."

Arturo smacked his belly. "I'm off fast food forever." He stared at the onion rings. "No saturated fat. No refined sugar. No caffeine. No milk shakes, either." He chugged his low-fat drink as Vlad polished off the second cheeseburger. "Not everyone has your metabolism, Vlad. You can eat as much as you want and never gain an ounce, but not me. I got Indian blood. Yaqui, from the deserts of northern Mexico. I read all about it. It's genetics. My ancestors were always on the verge of starvation, so my people store fat easily. Save it for a rainy day. Except it never rains anymore."

Vlad folded another onion ring into his mouth.

Arturo grabbed an onion ring. "This has probably got twenty-five grams of carbohydrates in it. That's about a quarter of my daily allotment." He bit into the onion ring, chewed slowly, as though performing a scientific experiment. He finished that one, reached for another. "If these were fried in canola oil, things would be different, but this thing's full of old grease, just like I told you." He chewed faster now.

"Did you call Weezer and let him know we're on our way?"

"He's not answering his phone, which means he's probably ruined the batch and he's afraid to tell us. I'm so sick of dealing with crankheads."

"We should go before the traffic gets bad."

"I want to let my meal settle. Just that one onion ring probably upset my digestion."

"You ate two onion rings."

"Then my goddamned digestion is *twice* as upset." Arturo watched a slim blond college girl walk to the window and order a double cheeseburger, double fries, double rings.

Arturo's face was hot with anger now. "Clark needs to pay attention to *business* instead of throwing parties for people who don't like him anyway. That's why we got all this trouble with dealers extending credit, and suppliers jacking their prices . . . and cookers getting *killed*. That's an insult, Vlad, and instead, all Clark and Missy want to talk about is some stupid article about their stupid party."

"I feel bad about that party. I embarrassed myself."

"You still thinking about that?"

Vlad shook his head. "So many pretty people in one place, laughing, talking fast . . . I felt like I was drowning on words. If that man hadn't stopped to help me—"

"I didn't like him."

"Everybody else ignored me, pretended they didn't see me, but he was nice."

"He had eyes like a wolf."

Vlad shrugged. Once Arturo had decided on something, there was no changing his mind.

"Forget about *him*. We got other problems." Arturo covered a belch. "I'm getting sick of us driving freeways day and night, making pick-ups, smacking down brainless, crusty-eyed dealers, counting money that's all wrinkled and covered with disease—"

"That's our job, Arturo."

"Clark needs to apply his brain so we don't waste our time with these losers. He should make a drug that burns the fat away. Or makes people smarter." Arturo snagged another onion ring. "If he made a grease with vitamins and minerals and antioxidants, a *good* grease, then we would not have to do the things we do."

Vlad watched him chew through the onion ring. "You should tell Clark about the good grease."

"I *did* tell him." Arturo stood up. "Let's go see Weezer and listen to his sad excuses."

Vlad dabbed at the inside of his nose with a napkin, saw a spot of bright red blood. He bussed the table, depositing their cups and paper in a trash can before following Arturo to their car.

24

Wakened from their long slumber, Nazi zombies trooped slowly across the bottom of the tropical lagoon, their jackboots kicking up little puffs of sand with every step. Thorpe had seen the movie five or six times before, but he had never understood why the zombies were all wearing sunglasses. Except that it made them look really cool. The sound track was a mere whisper from where he stood. He leaned forward, peered down through the second opening in the projection room, checking out the crowd below. Still no sign of the Engineer.

"Who are you looking for?" asked D.K., the projectionist, watching the movie through his own portal. He was a frail old gent in a threadbare brown suit, a proud, liver-spotted lothario with a bad comb-over.

"Nobody."

"Nobody, my ass. If you're checking out the girls, forget it. You're too old and too square for this crowd. You want to turn some heads, you'll need to get some tattoos, and pierce your pecker."

"I'll take that under consideration."

"I remember when all it took to get laid was a Brylcreem pompadour and new Levi's. I wouldn't be young again if you paid me."

Thorpe watched the exits, so disappointed, he wanted to break something. He had no right to be—it had always been a long shot—but he was. It would have been an elegant trap, tripping up the Engineer with a classic bad movie. The fact that *Shock Waves* was also one of Thorpe's favorites would only have made it sweeter. Would have.

"Let me turn the sound up in here," said D.K. "I can't hear a thing."

"I like it quiet," said Thorpe, still watching.

The audience was bathed in light from the tropical island on-screen.

The theater was packed. Thorpe could see rows and rows of surfers with their bare feet up, and street kids slouched like ragged hippies lost in a time warp. Plenty of couples Thorpe's age, too, buffs drawn from all over to the screening of this out-of-print rarity. The *Los Angeles Times* had even included a boxed notice in its upcoming-events calendar yesterday. The Engineer *had* to have seen it. He wasn't here, though. Thorpe had roped off the balcony, found a spot where he could see people walking in past the ticket booth without being seen himself. He had gone to high alert at one point when a group had approached wearing zombie masks, but they weren't the right size for either the Engineer or his bodyguard. He tracked them anyway, waited until they had raised their masks to stuff popcorn into their mouths before returning to his post. He scanned the crowd again. The Engineer wasn't there.

"You got to plan ahead if you want to meet the ladies." D.K. crossed his legs. "See, you're at the wrong movie. Midnight features, that's for the screwballs and freaks and girls wear ripped fishnet stockings. Those kind of girls aren't interested in a man with a job, a man who uses deodorant. You should be going to the matinees we run on weekdays. *Ghost, Dirty Dancing, A Man and a Woman,* early Harrison Ford and Richard Gere, too. The joint is just packed with horny housewives. Fish in a barrel for a good-looking fella like you."

Thorpe smiled. "What about you?"

"Wednesday mornings. Fred Astaire and Ginger Rogers, Doris Day and Rock Hudson." D.K. rearranged the strands of hair on his scalp. "Good thing we only run those movies once a week, or I'd have a heart attack."

On-screen, the shipwrecked survivors straggled ashore, Brooke Adams's blouse clinging to her. One of the paradigms of any great zombie movie was a fetching ingenue with great cleavage. In a few minutes, the survivors would traipse through the jungle to the abandoned laboratory of a renegade Nazi scientist and the fun would really start.

"People been saying for years that Rock Hudson was queer, but I'll never believe it," said D.K., watching the movie.

Thorpe watched Brooke Adams.

———

"If this movie is so good, why don't we go inside and *watch* it?" asked Gregor.

"Because I am a cautious man," said the Engineer. "Frank may be in there."

"Let *me* go in and find out."

"Do you honestly think you could spot him before he saw you?" sneered the Engineer. "Sit back and read your magazines."

Gregor started to say something, then thought better of it. Instead, he tilted back his seat, the motor groaning with the weight of him, opened a copy of *Assbusters*. There was just enough moonlight coming through the window to illuminate the pornographic images, the flesh gray and dead as the lunar landscape.

The Engineer sat perfectly still in the driver's seat of the Buick sedan, watching the Strand theater. They had been there for over an hour, watching the crowd slowly filing through the doors, but had seen no sign of Thorpe. There was undoubtedly a back entrance, but the Engineer couldn't be in two places at once, and he didn't trust Gregor to keep lookout. It was hard to be unobtrusive when you were over three hundred pounds. The man had other abilities. No, the Engineer stayed put. He could sit for hours without needing to shift his weight, completely comfortable. He could have been an astronaut, able to live in cramped quarters for months without complaint. He *would* have been an astronaut if there had been money in it, money or ego gratification. What was the point of going to the stars unless you were getting away with something?

Gregor was breathing heavily now, his face bent over the pages.

The Engineer cracked his window. He hated missing the show. He had seen *Shock Waves* only on video, never a 35-mm print. He had no idea how Thorpe could have found out about his predilection for cheesy horror movies . . . but he didn't put anything past the man. He had been tempted to buy a ticket, but the idea of being fooled by Frank was unbearable. Fooled *again*. He remembered the girl, Kimberly. That had rankled. She and Thorpe had gotten him good. Well, the Engineer had laughed last. With Kimberly at least. He smiled to himself. Kimberly was merely a preview of coming attractions. Thorpe was the main feature. He turned to Gregor, annoyed. "Kindly stop smacking your lips."

"Sorry."

The Engineer stared at the marquee announcing *Shock Waves*. If Thorpe was setting him up, they would wait for the theater to empty, then catch him leaving, when his guard was down. If the showing of his favorite movie *was* just a lovely coincidence, then he and Gregor would simply stroll in afterward and confiscate the print. He hummed softly, thinking of the good times ahead.

"That was a pretty decent movie," said D.K., packing up the first reel.

Thorpe watched the remnants of the crowd filing out. The Engineer would have to wait. In twelve days, the Meachums would be back from Hawaii, but Thorpe had come up with a plan to keep them safe. It might even work.

"Don't worry, kid. There's a woman for you out there. You just got to pick your shots."

Thorpe helped D.K. with the other reel.

"That's him," said the Engineer.

"Where?"

The Engineer eased the Buick forward, lights out, barely giving it any gas. He wouldn't have recognized Thorpe from this distance, but the film cans he was lugging down the alley marked him. The Engineer had waited until the crowd had left, then drove past the stragglers smoking under the marquee and found another parking spot. A few minutes later, someone stepped out of a theater exit he didn't even know existed, and he knew it had to be Thorpe.

"Is that him?" Gregor tossed aside his magazine. "I'll grab him."

"Even if you could *grab* him, that's not what I want. I prefer to see where he's going."

"Because of the money?"

"Very good." The Engineer watched the corner. "If we snatch him, it will degenerate into a contest of wills, and he might just choose to die before giving me what I want. The man is sitting on at least two or three million dollars; I'd like to see where he lives . . . . perhaps who he's living with. Frank is stubborn, but he has a soft spot for the weaker sex." Smile. "And he *does* have some idea what I'm capable of."

"I get it."

"Down," hissed the Engineer, sliding lower. Gregor barely got his knees out of view before headlights illuminated their car and then were gone. Gregor was quicker than he looked, a world-class wrestler in his youth, now gone to fat and indolence, but still useful. Loyal, too. That was why the Engineer had spared his life.

The Engineer had drugged Lazurus's whole crew at the party they gave in his honor for escaping, drugged them and shot them in the head, shot them one by one as they snored away. Except for Gregor. He had watched his bodyguard snoring, and the Engineer had actually placed the barrel of his pistol in Gregor's mouth, started to squeeze the trigger . . . and stopped. Sometimes he surprised himself. He had been so angry that night, angry at Frank for not staying at the safe house, angry at having to rush with Kimberly, not being able to take his time. Killing the crew had been necessary for security reasons, but it didn't really diminish his anger.

"Up." The Engineer turned on the ignition, pulled away from the curb. He could see the red taillights of Thorpe's car far ahead. He didn't turn on his headlights until Thorpe turned the corner. He sped up now, afraid they were going to lose Thorpe.

25

Thorpe drove slowly down the alley, lights off, not knowing what he was doing here. He should be home. He should be knocking on Claire's door, apologizing for ignoring her these last few days, but he didn't want to lie to her about his reasons. Instead, he was dodging potholes and overflowing garbage cans at 4:00 a.m., still pissed off that the Engineer hadn't taken the bait. He wouldn't be able to sleep now anyway, might as well check up on the Meachums' house. They might have returned early from their second honeymoon. If they'd had a fight, Meachum would have run off to his girlfriend, but Gina would have come home to her paintings. The front of their house gave no indication of recent activity, but he drove down the alley anyway. He slowed as he passed their back door, continued on, and parked beside their neighbor's garage. He had seen something in the space between the window shade and the frame: the flicker of a television. He walked slowly toward the house, staying to the edges of the alley, where there were no pebbles to make noise.

He edged closer to the window. The TV was on in the back bedroom, tuned to CNN, the sound low. Leaving the TV on when you went out of town wasn't a bad idea. That was one possibility. If Gina had come home by herself, she might not have wanted to sleep in her marriage bed anymore. That was another possibility. Someone changed the channel with a remote, the room momentarily brighter, and Thorpe glimpsed a man in the dimness of the bedroom. He put away the 9-mm, shaking his head. This was a possibility he hadn't considered.

Thorpe knocked on the back door, and the door rattled, unlocked. He knocked again, opened the door. "Ray! It's me, Frank. Ray?"

The kitchen light came on, and Ray Bishop stood there, barefoot, scratching his ass with a .38. "Come on in."

Thorpe closed the door behind him, locked it. "Ray, what are you doing here?"

"Same thing you're doing. Looking out for these people . . ." Bishop was wearing new Bermuda shorts and a sport shirt with a button-down collar. Clean-shaven. He padded over to the refrigerator, barely limping. "You want a soft drink? I got Coke, 7Up—"

"How did you find this place?"

"You think you're the only one who can run an investigation?" Bishop slipped the .38 into his front pocket, took out a can of Coke. "The morning after you came calling, I went to the library, did a search on Clark and Missy. The most recent entry was that nasty column that society broad wrote. I ran her next, and found out she got run down the same day the column came out. Didn't take much to figure out that you were worried that the Meachums were next. The gallery was closed, but it wasn't hard to find out where they lived." He cracked the can, Coke foaming across his knuckles, but he ignored it. "You told me at the construction site that you had put them in the soup, but for the life of me, I can't figure out what you might have done."

"You can't stay here."

"Why not?" Bishop sipped from the can. "The Meachums aren't going to be back for a while. They left their itinerary on a notepad, the hotel they are staying at, everything. They were either in a big hurry or just naïve, I can't make up my mind. The lock on that back door . . . I opened it with a bankcard and a paper clip."

The Meachums *had* been in a hurry. On the counter, Thorpe could see the hammer and the picture hooks Gina had been using when he interrupted her. "Ray . . . you being here, it's breaking and entering."

"You going to turn me in?"

"That's not the point. Vlad and Arturo might show—"

"I hope they do." Bishop flipped off the light. "Come on, you want to watch some TV?"

Thorpe followed him into the back bedroom. In the dim light from the TV, he could see Bishop's security uniform draped over a hanger, an overnight bag on the floor. He stayed standing while Bishop sat in an armchair. "You're planning on being a hero, Ray?"

"After you left, I got to thinking." The images from the TV were reflected in Bishop's face, but he wasn't watching the set. "Vlad and Arturo are expecting to find a couple of Yuppies here, trusting folks who think calling 911 is the answer to all their problems." He finished his Coke, set the can down on a coaster. "Well, I *know* who Vlad and Arturo are, and I'm not about to give them a fair chance—they show up, I'm going to blow their brains out. Self-defense. I may not even stick around to call it in." He belched, proud of himself.

Thorpe sat down. "What about your job? You had a good thing going there."

Bishop gave him the finger, and they both laughed.

"Okay, it was a shit job," said Thorpe, "but you can't stay here."

"You don't think I can handle myself?"

"No . . . it's not that."

"I used to be a good cop."

"I know—"

"I haven't had a drink since I saw you last . . . and, yeah, it's not the first time I've been sober for a few days, but this time feels different." Bishop leaned forward in his chair. "I'm grateful to you, Frank. That night at the site, seeing you all rough-and-ready—that used to be me. *I* was the guy asking questions; *I* was the guy standing up for what was right. I was no saint, but I did my job." His hands gripped the arms of the chair. "Clark and Missy beat me back in Riverside, they took away everything I cared about, and I let them. I rolled over and *let* them. Well, not anymore. I'm not going back to punching a clock, protecting lumber and drywall, and pretending it's all fine." He pointed at his uniform. "I keep that there to remind me. I actually had to buy that thing, you believe it?" He shook his head. "No thanks. I know who I am now."

Thorpe nodded. "You look good."

"I *feel* good." Bishop breathed easily, relaxed now, settling in to his flesh and his newfound certainty. "It's like I lost my way these last few years, but coming here, on my own, making that decision myself . . .

it's like I got a direction again." He blushed, his face pink as a canned ham. "I guess someone like you can't understand what that's like."

"Ray . . . I understand *exactly* what that's like."

Bishop stared at him. "Yes, I believe you do. Otherwise, I wouldn't have felt so envious of you when you walked off the site, on your way to do what I should be doing." He leaned closer, his features grotesque in the flickering light of the TV. "I bet you made some outrageous fuckups in your time. I bet you made some real doozies."

Thorpe just smiled.

"You don't give anything away, do you? I like that. There's too many talkers, you ask me. I'd still like to know how you got mixed up with Clark and Missy, though. I can see how that newspaper column would set her off, but how was that your fault? Did you talk to this Betty B?"

"No, but I might as well have."

Bishop watched him, waiting for more, then gave up. He patted his belly. "You hungry? I'll scramble us up some eggs."

Thorpe stood. "I've got some business to take care of."

"At *this* hour?"

"They'll be awake. If not, I'll convince them that it's time."

"Anybody I know?"

"I don't think so." It was a lie, but Thorpe was comfortable with it. Bishop needed to be here—he understood that—but there was no way Thorpe was going to let the man put himself in jeopardy. He had planned on waiting a day or so to talk with Clark and Missy, but he was going to do it now. Right now. He couldn't take the chance of Arturo and Vlad dropping by. Bishop might have convinced himself he was ready to take them on, but Thorpe knew better. Thorpe had to defuse the situation with Clark and Missy. Bishop could stay here as long as he wanted, on guard for an attack that would never come. Whatever brought him closer to the man he wanted to be.

Bishop got out of the chair, hitched up his shorts. "My wife and kids are in Pennsylvania, living with her sister outside Pittsburgh. Her sister has a big house. . . . They're not suffering. I . . . I've been thinking about paying them a visit. I got some money saved. What do *you* think?"

"I think that's a fine idea."

Bishop nodded, looked away. "I'm not quite ready yet, but I think about it. I was a lousy husband. I was a good father, but I was a lousy husband."

"People can change, Ray."

"That's what I tell myself . . . but I'm not so sure." Bishop looked up at Thorpe, fidgeting now. "How do you think I should go about it?"

"You don't need advice from me."

"The hell I don't," said Bishop. "Should I call first, or surprise them?" he said, whispering, as though someone else might hear. "Do I take flowers or gifts for the kids? I sent cards for every birthday and Christmas, but—"

Thorpe put a hand on Bishop's shoulder. "You don't have to call first, but don't go by the house. You don't want to put any pressure on her, and you don't want to upset the kids. Go to where she's working. Go there just before she gets off for the day and ask her to go have a cup of coffee or just walk and talk. You'll be nervous, but that's okay, because she'll be nervous, too."

"Not her," said Bishop. "That woman's a rock. I got no idea why she put up with me as long as she did."

"*She* knows why. All you have to do is allow her to remember." Thorpe lowered his voice. "Don't promise her the moon; she'll have heard that from you often enough. Tell her the truth, Ray. Tell her that you're making your way back and you know you've got a way to go, but that you love her. Tell her you love her. You can't say that too often. Tell her you love her and you thought about her and the kids the whole time you were apart, and ask her for another chance. Make sure she knows it's her choice and that you will understand if she's had enough. Tell her you love her. Tell her you've been wrong about everything in life but her. Then hope she says yes."

"You sound like a man who's had to beg a woman to take him back a few times."

"No, but I'm ready."

26

The Engineer pulled Gregor back into the shadows as Thorpe emerged from the back door of a house down the alley, the kitchen light illuminating him as he stood there saying his good-byes to some ugly bastard in Bermuda shorts.

"We can stop him," hissed Gregor.

The Engineer yanked on Gregor's earlobe, silencing him. They might be able to shoot Thorpe before he reached his car, but they couldn't surprise him, and the Engineer needed Thorpe alive and talking.

They had barely kept Thorpe's taillights in sight after leaving the Strand theater, staying well back, but had lost him as he entered Laguna Beach. For the last half hour, he and Gregor had been doing a grid search of the residential areas, cruising back and forth, searching for his car. Thorpe didn't live in Laguna—the Engineer knew that much. His wireless Internet connection was someplace in the Long Beach area, so Thorpe must have business in Laguna, the kind of a business that permitted a drop-in visit at 3:00 a.m. Love business maybe. The Engineer felt himself grow erect at the possibilities. A few minutes ago, they had spotted Thorpe's car in the alley and quickly parked on a side street, unsure where he was. They were in the alley when the door to the house opened. The Engineer was frustrated to see the ugly bastard with Thorpe. Not love business, but still . . . there were other possibilities.

"He is *leaving*," muttered Gregor.

"Stay." The Engineer didn't move until Thorpe drove away. He noted how the man on the porch waited until Thorpe left before returning to the house. He also noted Thorpe's license plate number.

Bishop was whisking his eggs with a fork when there was rapping on the back door. "It's open." He smiled, beating the eggs to a froth. "I knew you'd change your mind." He heard the door open behind him, the floorboards creak. Too much weight. He dropped the bowl, reached for the gun in his pocket. . . . The punch caught him across the temple, knocked him down, the .38 sliding across the tiles.

"You're a messy cook, champ."

Bishop slowly raised his head off the floor, trying to focus. There was egg yolk in his hair. A big man, a really big meatball, hovered over him. Bishop could see the hairs in the man's nostrils.

"Back off, Gregor. Give him room."

Bishop pushed himself up with one hand. There were two of them, but it wasn't Vlad and Arturo. . . . It was two other ones. The meatball who had hit him, and another one, a soft intellectual type. He rubbed his head with his fingertips, winced. No blood, though.

"Help him up, Gregor."

Bishop felt himself being lifted effortlessly to his feet. His knees buckled.

"I was hoping to get off to a better start," said the soft man. "Violence should always be the last resort, don't you think?" He stood next to the stove, flipped on the gas, dreamy-eyed at the pop of the pilot light.

"You guys . . . take whatever you want," said Bishop. He knew they weren't here to take anything, not anything that could be carried, but he decided to make the effort. "There's a stereo in the living room and a couple of good TVs."

"Is that right?" said the soft man. "This is our big score, Gregor."

Bishop bent forward, his hands on his knees. He used to be able to take a punch better.

"Where did Frank go?" asked the soft man.

Bishop straightened. "Frank who?"

The soft man smiled. "There's no reason we can't all be friends. Gregor and I, we're the best friends you're ever going to have. I know we're off to a rocky start, but, hey, you were the one who pulled the gun."

"I thought you were someone else."

"A man with enemies. I knew I liked you, Mr. . . ."

"Bishop. Ray Bishop. I'd like to help you boys. . . ."

"Excellent, Mr. Bishop," said the soft man, clapping his smooth hands.

"I just . . . I just don't know any Frank."

The soft man looked genuinely pained. "Gee, Mr. Bishop, I wish you hadn't said that." He turned up the gas, the jets hissing louder, the blue flame four inches high.

The meatball grinned. He was a huge locomotive, well over six feet, thick-gutted, with enormous hands and tiny, hateful eyes.

"Are you talking about the man who just left?" asked Bishop. "I didn't even know his name. He saw my light on and asked directions. Said he was lost."

"Lost was he?" said the soft man. "Where did he want to go?"

"He was a little drunk, if you really want to know," said Bishop. "He said he had been driving around looking for the fire station. Said he wanted to fill out a complaint about a neighbor who wasn't keeping his yard mowed. He didn't make a lot of sense, if you really want to know. I offered to make him a cup of coffee, sober him up a little, but he didn't want any part of it."

"That sounds like Frank," said the soft man. "You offer him your hand in friendship, and he rejects it."

"Sorry I couldn't be of more help to you." Bishop looked from the soft man to the meatball. "Sorry I pulled the gun on you, too."

"I say let bygones be bygones," said the soft man. "What do you say, Gregor?"

"It's late," said Gregor. "It's late and I'm tired."

The soft man sighed. "Gregor *does* have a point, Mr. Bishop. I have enjoyed your little charade, but the reality is that you are going to tell me what I want to know. The only matter in dispute is how much pain you're going to endure before you do."

Bishop licked his lips. He didn't turn his head, but he knew the hammer was on the counter behind him. "I don't like being hurt. I got no pain threshold at all."

"Now we're making progress," said the soft man. "So, where was Frank going?"

"There's a Denny's in South Laguna that's open all night. He wanted me to meet him there for breakfast, but I prefer my own cooking."

"Does Denny's still have that Grand Slam Breakfast special?" asked the soft man.

Bishop smiled. He was fucked no matter what he did.

"It's a very good deal," said the soft man. "Pancakes, eggs, sausage . . . How do you know Frank? You must be pretty special for him to drop in like this."

"We worked a stakeout one time," said Bishop. "He was anticrime detail and I was Riverside PD. I transferred to Laguna a year ago, but we kept in touch."

"You're a police officer?" asked the soft man. "I should have known. You have the look."

Bishop felt warm. "Thanks. Frank stopped by tonight and told me he had stepped in some dog shit, couldn't get it off his shoe no matter what he did. Said it was just the worst stink imaginable. . . . I look at you two, and I understand what he meant."

"Can I get started?" snarled Gregor.

"Not yet." The soft man watched Bishop. "Frank must have given you his phone number, the two of you being old buddies. Why don't you give him a call now, tell him you're in very big trouble."

Bishop wasn't trembling anymore. "*Am* I in trouble?"

"Yes, I'm afraid you are, Mr. Bishop," said the soft man.

As Gregor stepped toward him, Bishop grabbed the hammer and slammed it against the meatball's head. Gregor groaned, staggered, and Bishop hit him again. "You're under arrest," he said, swinging wildly now, gasping with the effort, hitting him so hard that his fingers went numb. Gregor fell to one knee. Bishop reared back with the hammer . . . slipped on the omelette spill, the two of them falling into a heap.

Bishop threw punches, struggling, but Gregor easily held him down with one hand, reached for the hammer with the other.

One of Bishop's eyes was stuck shut, but he could see Gregor straddling him, blood pouring down his face. One ear was half-torn off where Bishop had hit him with the claw end of the hammer. Beautiful sight. There was an explosion of bright light, and *pain.* So much pain.

"How do *you* like it?" asked Gregor.

"Put the hammer down," said the soft man, his voice coming from far away. "I want him alive. I want to talk to him first."

"You're . . . busted," Bishop whispered to Gregor. He couldn't seem to move, but he could still talk. A good cop didn't need a gun to command respect; he got it with a tone of voice, an attitude, a willingness to step into a situation. Otherwise, any yahoo with a cannon could be sheriff of Dodge City. "Assume the position, shitbag."

Gregor swung the hammer again.

Bishop heard his teeth skitter across the tile floor. Such a strange sound.

"Stop it." The soft man tried to pull Gregor off him.

Bishop spit blood into Gregor's face.

Gregor shrugged off the soft man, drove the hammer down again.

Bishop smiled. I can still piss the bad guys off, he thought. That's something. He heard things crack as Gregor hit him again and again, but he didn't feel the blows.

Bishop's lack of response seemed to make Gregor madder, the big man cursing as the hammer rose and fell, spraying the kitchen with brightness. Bishop had the thought . . . had to fight to keep the thought—it was like those dandelions that flew away if you breathed on them. He had the thought that even though Gregor was breaking him, Bishop wasn't broken. This man called Bishop was not broken. Not at all. He would have liked to tell Frank about this wondrous insight, but then, Frank probably already knew it.

Bishop could barely see Gregor anymore, the poor fellow shrinking to a smudge of darkness, his cursing fading now, too. Bishop thought of his wife and kids. In a perfect world, Frank would tell them how Bishop had changed in these last few days, how he had stood up, how he had died as a cop. He closed the eye that was still open. It made it easier to hang on to that bright and shining thought.

27

"You know what the fuck *time* it is?" said Cecil.

Thorpe held his State Department badge and ID to the security camera. "Let me in, asshole. You want a warrant, I'll come back with a SWAT team."

"I got to ask Missy."

"Make a decision, Cecil. Use your nutsack for something other than a hand rest."

Silence from the intercom.

"Time's up. Good-bye, Cecil. You explain it to her when I come back with—" The security gate swung open and Thorpe drove in.

Cecil met him at the front door. "Wait here. I'll go wake up her and Clark."

"What's that on the wall?" asked Thorpe, pointing. As Cecil turned to look, Thorpe shoved his head into the wall, drove him so hard, the plaster cracked. Thorpe stepped over him, walked down the hall. It was a cheap shot, and a dangerous move, but Thorpe needed to get into character. He needed to sell a story.

The master bedroom was dimly lit, redolent of good pot and Missy's perfume. Missy and Clark were sleeping in each other's arms, adrift on red silk sheets, the bed a massive heart. It was probably supposed to be romantic, but to Thorpe, it looked like they were swimming in blood. He lay at the foot of the bed, resting on one elbow now, watching the door. While he waited, he slipped a hand under the sheets and played with Missy's foot. She cooed, nestled deeper into the pillow, one slim breast falling free of the top sheet, her nipple hardening. Thorpe looked over, saw Clark's eyes open wide. "Hey, Clark, surf's up."

Cecil staggered into the bedroom waving a .44 Magnum. He saw Thorpe.

Thorpe yawned. "Don't do anything stupid."

Cecil moved closer. There was a lump rising already in the middle of his forehead, bits of plaster sticking to the reddening skin.

"What happened to your head, Cecil?" asked Missy, awake now, rubbing her eyes. "You look like a unicorn."

"I'm going to kill this son of a bitch," said Cecil, freckles flaring as he drew down on Thorpe.

Thorpe winked at Missy, his hand still under the covers.

"Damn it, Cecil, put the gun away before you hurt somebody," said Clark. He looked at Thorpe. "It's the middle of the night, Frank. What's going on?"

Cecil was trying to hold that big .44 steady, but his hand was shaking.

Thorpe smiled at him. Most people had no idea how hard it was to shoot someone who was looking you in the eyes.

"Stop it, Cecil!" snapped Missy. "You get your ass out of here *now*. I mean it."

Cecil's hand was twitching so badly that even if he got off a shot, Thorpe was probably safe. He wiped his eyes, slowly lowered the gun, breathing so hard, it was as if he had been running a race.

"Go on," said Missy, her voice gentle now. "Leave the gun."

"No fucking way," said Cecil, still watching Thorpe.

"Leave it," said Missy. "We're fine. Please? Do it for me."

Thorpe waited until Cecil had laid the .44 down on the nightstand, waited until he had started for the door. "Why don't you go make us some coffee? Black, two sugars for me. You probably already know how Clark and Missy take it." He listened to Cecil cursing all the way down the hall, then pulled his hand out from under the sheets. He backed off the hammer of the 9-mm he had been holding. "I'm glad you spoke up, Missy, I would have hated to ruin your linens."

"What's going on, Frank?" asked Clark. "Are we under arrest?"

Thorpe glanced around. "You see a cop?" He reached into his jacket, tossed Missy his badge and ID. "Here's a souvenir. I don't need it anymore."

"I don't understand," said Clark.

"I think I do." Missy watched him. "Are you here to kill us, Frank?"

She caught on fast. It made Thorpe's job so much easier. "I decided against it."

"What changed your mind?" asked Missy.

Clark turned to Missy. "I'm confused."

About ten minutes later, Thorpe had told them his story. The three of them were still on the bed—Thorpe stretched out, languid as a cat, Clark sitting cross-legged, half-dressed now in a pair of Matrix pajama bottoms, smoking a joint. Missy remained nude, completely at ease, one bare leg sticking out from the sheets. She was so taut and lean, Thorpe could count the striations in her inner thigh. No tan line, either.

"You have more twists than fifty miles of back road, Frank," said Missy, not taking her eyes off him. "I mean that as a compliment."

"You don't have to believe me," said Thorpe. "I just wanted to give you the option."

Clark offered Thorpe the joint. "Where are my manners?"

Thorpe ignored the joint. "Same place I left my sense of fair play."

"So this whole thing with the fake ID and the art was your way of gaining our trust?" She tossed her hair, blond and brassy. "You didn't have to work so hard."

"It wasn't hard. A badge gets a lot of respect, even from people who should know better." Thorpe shifted position, took up even more room on the bed. "You have to admit you were grateful when I told you the art was fake. I wouldn't know a fake from a firing squad, but it worked. I could have killed you any time I wanted after that."

Clark blew a smoke ring. "Killing us isn't really the hard part. It's avoiding Vlad and Arturo afterward—*that's* the puzzlement. Guillermo knows that better than anyone."

"Oh, I wouldn't have killed you until *after* I'd killed them," said Thorpe.

"You think you're Superman?" Clark giggled. "Where's your cape, dude?"

"I don't need to be Superman; I just need to get close." Thorpe patted the sheets. "Look at us here, snug as bugs." He smiled at Missy. "Five minutes after I gave you the benefit of my art expertise, you asked me to stay for breakfast. Remember? Sooner or later, you would have introduced me to Vlad and Arturo, and maybe we would have gone out sailing, or up to Big Bear to ski, and then . . ." He cocked a finger at Clark. "Bang." Turned the finger on Missy. "Bang." He shrugged. "Getting close means the other person has let his guard down. After that, it's just a matter of waiting for the right opportunity, and I'm very patient."

Missy let the sheet slip from her breasts. "Vlad and Arturo might have surprised you."

"Maybe."

"Definitely."

"I got to award this one to Missy," said Clark, "which is why I find it hard to believe that Guillermo sent you." He pulled the sheet back over Missy's breasts. "Me and Guillermo got what's called a 'balance of terror' thing working between us. Vlad and Arturo scare the holy shit out of him, and I'm not a greedy man. Now, Guillermo can throw more troops into the fight, but if things get too messy, too public, the police and DEA move in, and we all lose."

"That's why Guillermo hired me. I clean up after myself."

"*You're* not greedy, Clark, but Guillermo is," said Missy.

"Don't start with that again," said Clark. "Did the Aryan Brotherhood send you to stir up trouble, Frank? Or was it the Yellow Magic boys? I know they're looking to expand operations. Come on, who hired you? I'll pay plenty for the truth."

Thorpe shrugged. "I just wanted to give you a heads-up. You do what you want."

"What I *want* is a hallucinogen that sharpens my reflexes, makes my dick hard, and improves my memory." Clark grinned. "I'm working on it, too."

Missy hadn't taken her eyes off Thorpe. "*Listen* to him, Clark."

"You want a war, Missy and I don't," said Clark. "Vlad and Arturo are good, the best, but they're only two men."

"Frank makes three," said Missy.

Thorpe didn't respond.

"Is that what you're here for?" asked Clark. "You offering your services? Was that stare-down with Cecil supposed to impress us?"

"Putting Cecil out of his misery wouldn't have impressed my grandmother, and I don't want a job."

"Then why the heads-up?" Clark leaned forward on the bed. "Why are you being so nice to us, Frank?" His eyes were all pupil now. "Missy tells me everything. That's the basis of a good marriage."

"I always wondered what the basis was," said Thorpe.

"Now you know." A sharp edge in Clark's voice now. "So why the freebie?"

"No such thing as a freebie," said Thorpe. "I had a deal with Guillermo, but he's backing off, and I'm not about to wait around for the official cancellation. Consider this payback." He eyed Missy. "Besides, maybe we'll meet up again sometime and you'll remember when we were all in bed together. A man has to think long range in my business."

Missy shook her head. "If you're serious enough to take out Vlad and Arturo, no way would Guillermo stiff you." She nudged him with her foot, let it rest against him. "I'm a little disappointed, you coming up with this tall tale, Frank."

"I'm a little disappointed, you killing Betty B," snapped Thorpe. "Guillermo read her column and knew you'd take it hard. He started having doubts that I could pull things off, afraid you'd be mad at me for telling you the art was fake. He thought you might pull in the welcome mat."

"You *did* get pissed off at Frank after the article came out, babe," said Clark. "You got mad at him and Betty B and Meachum, and the Man in the Moon, too. You said you wished you had kept that damn stone plaque. Said it all looked plenty old anyway."

"I couldn't believe it when you flattened Betty B," said Thorpe. "Guillermo saw that on the news and told me to hold off on my end of the deal. He said he wanted to wait and see if you went after Meachum, too. Then all he would have to do was dime you out to the cops. The DA *hates* coincidences. I told him no way you would be that stupid, but Guillermo seems to think you are."

"Guillermo is going to have plenty to think about soon enough," said Missy.

Clark played with Missy's hair. "Actually, when you think about it . . . if Frank is telling the truth, killing Betty B saved our lives." He kissed her on the cheek. "Kudos, babe."

Thorpe slid off the bed, yawned. "You and Guillermo can work it out. I'm done."

"You go home, man, go home and tell whoever you're working for that we didn't buy the bullshit." Clark threw his pillow at Thorpe. "Dude wants to cause trouble. Split the alliance. Go on, get out of here before I make a phone call. You never even *met* Guillermo. He's the Invisible Man. Missy doesn't like him, but me and Guillermo, we got no beef. We got an arrangement."

Thorpe shrugged. "You might want to rethink that arrangement. Who do you think took down those two cookers of yours? Good night, Missy."

"Wait!" said Clark. "How do you know about the cookers?"

"*You* killed them?" said Missy.

"I don't do grunt work. I have too much respect for myself," said Thorpe. "Guillermo sent some *vatos* out to Riverside to do the job. Do it up good and sloppy. He wanted to see how you would respond. Little weakness on your part, Clark. That's blood in the water to someone like Guillermo."

Missy glared at Clark. "Exactly."

"You might want to make that phone call," said Thorpe. "I hope Vlad and Arturo are as ferocious as you think they are, because Guillermo has the taste now."

They called out to him, but Thorpe kept walking.

28

It was barely dawn as Thorpe closed the front gate behind him, the familiar squeak comforting, more from the implication of safety than for the suggestion that he was home. There was no home. He could see lights on in Claire's apartment. It had to be her; Claire was a runner, while Pam slept in. He hesitated, wanting to knock on her door, but didn't move. He was tired, but that wasn't what was stopping him, and it wasn't Kimberly, either. He had used her memory as an excuse long enough. She was dead. No, Thorpe's life was filled with secrets; there was no room for Claire inside. No room for anyone else.

He closed his door behind him, slid down to the floor, and held his head in his hands. He should have been happy. The Engineer hadn't shown up for *Shock Waves,* but Clark and Missy had bought his story. He had saved Douglas Meachum's life tonight, and probably saved Gina Meachum's, too. They would never know it, and that was fine. Let them go back to their house in a couple of weeks, flower leis draped around their necks, their vows renewed. Let them never know how close they had come to a visit from Vlad and Arturo.

In a few weeks, Gina might question where Thorpe was, ask around to see if he had bought a house. Meachum would curse Thorpe for missing their appointment, tell her that he'd never expected the man to buy anything, say Thorpe could at least have given him the courtesy of a phone call, though. Let them go on with their lives, uninterrupted. He smiled, thinking of Bishop. The bright spot in the whole fuckup. He had been so happy tonight, talking about his new life, his new plans. So rare to see change that happened for the best, not some vast unraveling or a series of missed opportunities. Bishop was going to make it. That was something.

Thorpe got up, went and started the shower. Warm, then cold, then warm again. When he was done, he changed into clean clothes, checked himself in the mirror, but not too closely. He moved quickly now, hurried out and across the courtyard, not making a sound. He knocked on Claire's door. He heard footsteps, saw the peephole darken, and then the door opened.

Claire looked him over, hands on her hips. She was wearing nylon shorts and an L.A. Marathon T-shirt. "You always manage to surprise me. That's one of your best qualities."

"I didn't know I had any others."

An hour later, Claire gazed at him from her side of the bed. She pushed back the covers, the two of them hot and steamy. "You're just one surprise after another."

"I said I was sorry about not getting back to you."

"Don't flatter yourself, Frank. I can handle a one-night stand. I just didn't think that was your style." Claire put her hand on his heart. "No, what I was surprised at is . . . *this*."

" 'This'?"

"You were so angry before that I couldn't keep up with you, didn't want to keep up . . . but now . . . you're so tender. We were together the whole time, every minute. What *happened* to you since the last time?"

Thorpe lightly stroked her belly, watched her eyes.

"No answer?" Claire sensed the lies; she just didn't know what the truth was, and sooner or later, that would ruin everything.

"I'm just glad I'm here," said Thorpe. He kissed her neck, slid his hand across her hips, dipping lower, his touch feathery.

She groaned, pushed him away slightly. "Don't get me started. I have to give Pam a ride to the airport in about a half hour. She's going to New Orleans with this guy she met."

"I thought she was celibate."

"He's an attorney. I think they're having fun finding loopholes."

Thorpe pulled her closer. "Tell Pam I'll pay for a cab."

"Big spender. Don't let her find out; she'll want you for herself."

Thorpe shook his head. "I'm already taken." If it was a lie, it was a lie to himself as well as to her.

Claire kissed him.

"Tell Guillermo you got word that Clark is making a move on him. He'll probably give you a bonus. Try answering your phone once in a while, Danny. Love and kisses."

Thorpe hit SEND, watched his e-mail to Hathaway disappear. He glanced out the window, the courtyard empty in the soft light of evening. He had slept all day after Claire left to take Pam to the airport. Claire was working this afternoon and tonight on stuff for her Psych 101 class. They would get together tomorrow, maybe go out for breakfast, see if he could persuade her to ditch class. He could still smell her on his hands, on his face. He didn't want to wash until he saw her again.

He called the Meachums' house, waited until the machine picked up, then began talking. "Ray? It's me, Frank. Call me at 555-0609. I've got good news." He had tried the same thing earlier, without response, but he wasn't sure where the machine was located in the house, wasn't sure Bishop could hear his voice. No sense for Bishop to stick around there until the Meachums got back. Bishop had put himself on the line; he could go home now.

"Enjoying the evening, Frank?"

Thorpe stared at the instant message flashing on-screen.

"It's me, Frank."

"I know who you are."

"I missed you. Did you miss me?"

Thorpe fought back his anger, thinking of himself standing in the projection room, hoping to get a glimpse of the Engineer. Thorpe had missed him all right, but not in the way the Engineer meant it.

"Not in a talkative mood today? PMS?"

"Could be. We should get together and discuss it."

"I would like that."

"How about . . ." Thorpe thought of his plans to spend time with Claire, but he put them aside. "How about tomorrow?"

"Tomorrow's not good for me. Sorry."

"Pick a date."

"You're so abrupt. I don't remember you being so curt. We only met that one time, but you seemed like a man who loved the sound of his own voice."

Thorpe checked his watch. "I'm a busy man."

"Good for you, Frank. Idle hands are the devil's workshop . . . or something like that."

Thorpe looked up as the gate creaked. Claire had come back, was walking toward his front door. "Let me know when you want to get together," he typed.

"Don't go. You're always in such a hurry."

Claire knocked.

"Time is money." Thorpe looked toward the door, glad he had locked it.

"Don't I know it, and never enough of either, is there?"

Claire knocked again. "Frank?"

"You're not still mad about Kimberly, are you? Because if you want to talk about it, I've been told I'm a good listener."

Thorpe watched Claire leave. Halfway across the courtyard, she turned around and stared at his window, then walked quickly to her place. She knew he was there.

"Frank? You still there? Maybe we can work out our troubles together."

Thorpe watched Claire's door close. "I don't have any troubles."

"Then I envy you, Frank. I truly do."

"Got to go."

"Let's make a date. I'm going to be out of town for the next week, but why don't we get together on the eleventh?"

Thorpe was disappointed. A week was too long. A minute was too long. "Sure."

"Wonderful. How about 1:00 p.m. at Black's Beach?"

"The nude beach?"

"You're not shy, are you, Frank? Not ashamed of the body God gave you, I hope. This way, we can be certain we're equally unarmed. Ha-ha. So, one o'clock, Black's Beach. I'll be lying on a towel, facing the large set of rocks offshore. Pelican Rock, they call it."

"I know what they call it."

"We're going to have a swell time. I think we have a lot in common."

"I don't."

"See, that's something else we can talk about. I hope—"

Thorpe shut down the computer. It was only then that he realized how fast his heart was beating. Claire's lights were on, but he stayed where he was.

29

Thorpe knocked on the Meachums' front door this time. The curtains were drawn. He knocked again. "Ray?"

There had been too many unanswered knocks in the last twenty-four hours. First, Claire rapping on his door while he was busy with the Engineer last evening, Thorpe unwilling to let her in, as though the Engineer could see through the computer screen. Then afterward, he had gone over to her place, knocked, called out her name, but she didn't answer, either. He didn't blame her. Now it was Ray Bishop who wasn't responding.

Thorpe looked around. A man across the street was mowing his lawn with headphones on, grass spraying his shanks, oblivious to Thorpe and everything else. Thorpe went around back, uneasy now.

"Ray?" Thorpe knocked on the back door again. "It's Frank." Thorpe used a credit card to spring the lock. It was easy. He'd barely opened the door when he caught the smell and knew Bishop was dead.

Ray Bishop was sprawled beside the refrigerator, faceup, his head beaten in. Blood was everywhere—splashed on the floor, sprayed across the walls, dark fingers dripping down the stove and refrigerator like the hand of God. Not a forgiving God, though, but a raging, petulant God who smote believers and nonbelievers alike, women and children and tired old men who had turned their lives around.

Thorpe knelt beside him. Bishop's face was barely recognizable: swollen and bruised, crusted with black blood, his jaw shattered, the orbit of one eye caved in. A line of tiny red ants streamed from one of the baseboards, up Bishop's arm, and to the corner of his mouth. Thorpe flicked them away, but they kept coming, and he grew angrier, squashing them with his fingers, flattening them with his shoes, smearing them to paste. They would return—there were always more ants—but not for a while.

He kicked aside the blood-caked hammer on the floor, sent loose teeth caroming across the tile. Thorpe felt sick. He sat beside Bishop again, wondering what his last moments had been like. The knuckles on his right hand were raw—he had gotten a few punches in. It wasn't much consolation, but Bishop might have taken some small pleasure in that. He didn't go gently, and that was all Thorpe was hoping to ask for himself.

Vlad and Arturo must have come by a couple nights ago, right after Thorpe left . . . or maybe they had surprised Bishop the next morning, before Clark and Missy had had a chance to call them off. Thorpe was certain he had convinced those two, but Vlad and Arturo had already been told to kill Meachum, kill anyone else they had found there, and they had found Ray Bishop and pounded his skull apart. Bad timing.

Thorpe looked at Bishop's ruined face, forced himself not to turn away. "I'm sorry, Ray. I'm not sorry you were here . . . because you made that choice yourself, and it changed you, it changed you back, and I'm *glad* you got the chance, *glad* you took the chance, because there's not one in a hundred who would have done what you did." Thorpe's vision was blurry, hot tears running down his face, his voice a hoarse whisper. "I'm just sorry I wasn't here with you when they came."

Thorpe wiped his eyes on his sleeve. He cleared his throat, his voice a low rumble now, a prayer for the dead, and a promise. "I'm going to kill the men who did this to you, Ray. I give you my solemn word."

A lone red ant squeezed out from under the floorboard, started toward Bishop's body. He got halfway there before another ant emerged, antennae twitching. Then another. And another.

Thorpe couldn't even give Bishop a decent funeral, couldn't notify his family. If he called 911 to report the murder, the cops would be all over the house, and they would ask around until they found where Gina and Douglas Meachum were. The Meachums would have to fly home, right back into trouble. No, he was going to have to leave Bishop right where he was.

Thorpe watched the ants' slow progress while he considered what to do. By the time he crushed the first ant with a forefinger, he knew. He punched in the number on his cell phone, wiped his eyes again while it rang. "Hey, girl, it's Frank." He listened. "Yeah, well, I knew we'd be talking again, too. It's hard to say good-bye, isn't it?" He nodded. "Tell Clark there's been a change of plans. . . . That's right. That's right. Tell him you won the bet, but don't tell me what it was. I don't think I could handle it." He laughed, his finger hovering over the second ant. "Look, I don't know if Clark wants to go after Guillermo. . . . okay. Well, I'm glad you convinced him. I wanted to let you know that I'm available. I'll work with Vlad and Arturo; that's no problem." He pinched the red ant between his thumb and forefinger. "We can work out the finances later, but I want Guillermo taken care of. He thinks we're still working out our business arrangement, but I spotted one of his homeboys cruising my neighborhood a few minutes ago, and I don't think he's planning to deliver a Candygram."

30

"You're *sure* Guillermo is going to be there this afternoon?"

"I'm not sure of anything, Frank. Shit happens." Hathaway lay on the tanning bed, eyes protected by yellow plastic sun goggles, arms at his side. He had a Ranger insignia tattooed on his left shoulder, just like Thorpe.

"Guillermo has to be there." In the ozone blue light, Thorpe could see faint track marks along Hathaway's forearms. Old injection sites, barely perceptible. He wasn't sure if Hathaway had moved on to more discrete veins, or if he had backed off his habit. "If Vlad and Arturo don't see the Invisible Man, this isn't going to work. I might even get myself killed."

"So, call it off. We'll postpone things."

"I can't do that." Thorpe remembered Ray Bishop lying on the kitchen floor, surrounded by a corona of dried blood. "I want those fuckers dead ASAP."

"There's a difference between being stand-up and being suicidal, Frank."

Thorpe watched Hathaway stretched out under the buzzing incandescent tubes of the tanning bed at Perfect Bronze. The room shimmered with harsh light, Thorpe's baggy white trousers and shirt turned to cobalt in the ultraviolet B. He had called Hathaway after he talked to Missy, told him to contact Guillermo. The offer to Guillermo was the same one Thorpe had made to Missy: a meeting, a face-to-face between Clark and Guillermo to reaffirm the cease-fire and settle the question of who was taking down Clark's cookers. Thorpe had assured Missy this was their best chance to kill Guillermo before he killed them. Hathaway had told the same thing to Guillermo.

Hathaway blindly stuck a hand out.

Thorpe slipped the cold can of Red Bull to Hathaway. "You said you had already run it past Guillermo. You said he agreed to the meet."

"Guillermo hears he has a chance to get Arturo and Vlad served up to him, of *course* he's going to say he's interested, but that was yesterday. He's had a whole night to think about it, consider all the things that can go wrong."

"What's your best guess, Danny? Is he going to show or not?"

Hathaway took a sip from the can, his long bleached-blond hair lank and green in the ultraviolet. He lifted one of his goggles, peeked at Thorpe. "I think he'd like to see Vlad and Arturo dead as much as you do."

Thorpe nodded. "I can hardly wait to meet the man."

Hathaway slipped the goggles back in place. "I hope you can say that afterward."

"Don't worry."

"*I'm* not worried. Guillermo needs me. . . . You're the one who's disposable. I told him you were my inside man, a disgruntled employee of Clark's looking to better himself. If Vlad and Arturo go down, Guillermo will be generous, full weight, too, but if something goes bad, if he thinks you're playing him loose"—Hathaway shook his head—"he'll fuck you up fast and move on."

"I'm ready."

"Sure you are." Hathaway stretched, kept his face pointed directly at the overhead tubes. "I thought you were chasing after the Engineer. Doesn't this business with Clark and his crew get in the way?"

"The Engineer is out of town for the next week. We're getting together when he comes back."

"You and the Engineer keep in touch, do you? The two of you coordinate your social calendars?"

Thorpe smiled. "That's right. My dance card was empty, so I decided to take out Vlad and Arturo." He stared at the posters on the wall, the beaches of Jamaica and Hawaii an alien landscape in the glare. "I doubt Clark will really be at the powwow. Does Guillermo understand that?"

"He figured as much. It doesn't matter to him. I told you that the only reason Clark and Missy are still alive is because of Vlad and Arturo. You deliver those two boys, your problems are over. It could be your own private holiday."

Thorpe had watched Claire walk past his window on her way to work this morning. She hadn't even looked toward his apartment, but he had imagined running after her. Imagined her coming back with him. Sitting around drinking coffee and making love. That would be a real holiday.

"Nothing like sunshine, Frank." Hathaway shifted slightly on the tanning bed. "When I'm done, you should hit the rack yourself, put that melanin to work for you. Fifteen minutes here is like two hours on the beach. Ladies love that extra-crispy look, trust me." He adjusted his white Speedo. "I still think you should just let me turn Clark and Missy over to the DEA. It will take a while to build a case against them, but—"

"Not interested."

"Yeah, you like the personal touch." Hathaway lifted his goggles again. "You really could get yourself killed, you know."

"Thanks, Mom. I'll eat my lima beans and say my prayers every night."

"Keep it simple with Guillermo," said Hathaway, serious now. "He's serene, but don't think he's not paying attention. He won't even raise his voice and you'll already be dead. I've seen it happen, Frank. Seen it with my own eyes."

Thorpe nodded.

"I told Guillermo that Clark will send you in first, to make sure things are up to code, and—"

"I *got* it, Danny."

The timer beeped and the tanning bed switched off, the room suddenly cool and dark by comparison. Hathaway lifted the top half of the bed, swung himself upright, and pushed away his goggles. His skin glowed silver in the after burn, his protected eye sockets bone white. He blinked at Thorpe. "What?"

"You look like a movie star."

31

"He *does* look a little familiar," said the doughy checker at Ralphs supermarket, her tongue stuck in the corner of her mouth, as though that would help the cow think.

"Take your time," said the Engineer. "It's an old photograph."

The checker—her name tag said CARMEN—scanned cans of infant formula, bricks of cheese, and boxes of prepackaged noodle slop while taking another look at the photo of Frank he had laid on the counter. "Thirty-nine fifty-five," she said to the mother with the screaming brat in line, then turned to the Engineer. "What do you want with him?"

The Engineer didn't react, but he felt a wave of pleasure surge through him. She *recognized* Thorpe. He had already taken in her cheap jewelry, her fatigue, and the tiny photos of ugly children that dangled from her key ring in the register. "He's my brother-in-law," the Engineer said, head down, as though he were embarrassed. "Ran out on my sister and left her with a couple kids to raise. I hired a private detective, who tracked him to Long Beach, but I'm tapped out. Figured I'd try to find him myself."

"He didn't seem like that kind of a guy." Carmen took the check from the mother, wished her a good day.

"No one seems like that kind of a guy, Carmen," said the Engineer.

Carmen wiped her upper lip, thinking it over.

"I'm in a hurry, lady," said the next man in line, loading six-packs of generic orange soda onto the counter.

"I got a smoke break in twenty minutes," Carmen said to the Engineer, scanning with both hands.

The Engineer waited for her outside, watching the shoppers come and go. The shit that people shoved into their mouths never ceased to amaze him, but he was in too good a mood to dwell on that now. He had spent the last couple days stopping at every supermarket, mini-mart, gas station, and drugstore in Long Beach, showing Thorpe's photo without result—other than a poor fool who had tried to hold him up while leaving an all-night market last night. The Engineer knew that Thorpe lived *somewhere* nearby; the man's Internet signal emanated from this general area, but that was as specific a location as his equipment could determine.

A white kid in a FUBU sweatshirt pushed a cart toward the parking lot, one wheel wobbling. He gave the cart a push, rode it for a few yards. You would have thought the moron had won the lottery.

Thorpe's license plate number had proved to be another dead end. Not that the Engineer ever had high hopes for it. The plate was valid, registered to Frank Antonelli, but the address listed was a mail drop in Cerritos, and the clerk there said the box hadn't been used in months.

The Engineer watched a couple of seagulls fighting over the remnants of a fast-food cheeseburger, screaming at each other as they tore at the bits of meat and cheese.

Gregor was still in the apartment, nursing his wounds from his encounter with Ray Bishop, the policeman or security guard—whatever he was, he had beaten Gregor's face as if he'd been trying to tenderize it. Almost tore one ear off, too. The Engineer could understand Gregor being angry, but there was no excuse for killing the man before he could be of service. No excuse whatsoever.

The Engineer had insisted that Gregor stake out the house in Laguna, see if Thorpe returned, but Gregor had quickly grown bored, said that too many people were walking past his car, staring at him. When the Engineer finally disposed of Frank, he was going to rid himself of Gregor, too. He should have killed the man when he murdered the rest of Lazurus's crew. Kindness was almost always a cause for regret.

The Engineer waved at Carmen as she walked through the automatic doors. He followed her around to a bench on the side of the building, the asphalt strewn with cigarette butts.

Carmen lit a cigarette, dragged deeply, and exhaled slowly through her nostrils.

The Engineer smiled at her.

"He just seemed like such a nice person," said Carmen. "Always called me by my name, not 'Hey, lady' or 'Hey, you.' Same as you did." She looked at the Engineer, gnawed at her lower lip. "I don't want to get anybody in trouble."

"My sister just wants the child support he owes her. The kids at school are teasing them about their clothes."

Carmen nodded. "Don't I know what that's like."

"Does Frank come in on any particular day of the week? Any particular time?"

Carmen shook her head.

"Did he ever give you any idea where he lived? Maybe he talked about a fire that had happened nearby, or he complained about traffic from the college? Anything that would give you a sense, a *feeling* of what neighborhood he was living in."

Carmen puffed away. "Not really."

The Engineer smiled, wanting to drive his fingers through her eyes. "Did he ever come in wearing workout clothes? Maybe he talked about a fitness center, or someplace where he liked to go running. I know he's a runner. That's where he used to meet women to cheat on my little sister."

Carmen looked pained. "I wish I could help."

The Engineer patted her on the hand, felt her recoil. "Don't you worry. I know something useful will come to you. A sharp-eyed woman like you. I'm sure you'll remember something."

"Uh-huh." Carmen shaped the ash on her cigarette by rolling it along the sole of her shoe. "I got to get back soon."

"Did Frank ever—"

"There *was* this one time. . . ." Carmen scrunched up her face with the effort of thinking. "I remember I asked him if he had gone to the Christmas tree lighting at the pier. It's a really big deal, with fireworks shot off the *Queen Mary*, and balloons and free candy. Anyway, I was complaining because it was so crowded that I had to park like a mile

away, and push my kids in the stroller, and they had to double up, the
two of them howling the whole way—"

"And Frank said?"

"He said he had just walked over to the ceremony from his place. I
told him he was lucky, and he told me he got that all the time, but he
thought *I* was really the lucky one, because Christmas was no fun
without kids." Carmen looked at the Engineer, flicked away her cigarette. "So, I guess he must have missed his kids."

If the Engineer could have resisted the impulse to vomit afterward,
he would have kissed her.

32

"Where's Clark and Arturo?"

"They're on their way," said Vlad.

Thorpe and Vlad sat in Thorpe's rented Land Rover. They were parked on a ridge overlooking the gate to Ungerman Groves, the last independent stretch of orange trees in Orange County, seventy-six acres of stunted Valencia seedless. It was late afternoon, the groves deserted, traffic on the back road sparse. A developer had made old man Ungerman an offer too good to refuse. The trees hadn't been watered in months, completely unattended, bereft of leaves, their fruit rotting on the ground. Thorpe had used a fake ID and credit card for the Land Rover, picked up Vlad at one of Clark's stores in Huntington Beach. Not much conversation on the twenty-minute drive to the grove, just Vlad fiddling with the radio, singing along to various pop songs. He knew all the words.

Vlad turned off the radio, shifted in his seat. He wore checked polyester bell-bottoms, a polo shirt buttoned to the throat, and a cheap nylon raincoat. When he got into the car, the wind rippled the raincoat and Thorpe glimpsed a cut-down H-K assault rifle hanging from a shoulder strap, a forty-round banana clip in place, another one taped alongside it. A real full-auto fire hose. "This is a fine day."

Thorpe looked over at him.

"Once we get finished with Guillermo, Clark says you can come on board." Vlad's skin was white as chalk, his blond hair dull and thinning. Only his eyes were alive, a large broken blood vessel in one eye like a red flag. "You're going to like working with me and Arturo. We have a lot of fun."

"That's what I hear." Thorpe scanned the road, but there was no sign of Arturo, or Guillermo, either. He touched the 9-mm tucked into his waistband, his untucked black dress shirt covering the gun butt. He wondered which one of them had beaten Bishop's skull in with the hammer, Vlad or Arturo. Vlad's face was unbruised, but that didn't mean much. "How long have you and Arturo been working together?"

"I don't know."

"Taught you the business, did he?"

"The business?" Vlad's eyes were such a light blue, they looked diluted. "He taught me to drive, and to use good manners, and how to housebreak a puppy."

"You have a dog?"

"No, but I know how to paper-train one."

Thorpe laughed, but Vlad wasn't joking. He tensed, spotting a black Lincoln Town Car approach from the east.

Vlad saw it, too. "Is Guillermo's car really bulletproof?"

"That's what they say."

The Town Car didn't even slow as it passed on the road below the Land Rover, a big beast with smoked windows, riding heavy and low. The driver took a hard right onto the gravel access road to Ungerman Groves, tires squealing as he accelerated, dust flying. The Town Car smashed through the chain-link fence without any loss of momentum, the gate sailing end over end through the air.

"Wow," said Vlad.

The Town Car careered through the grove, flattened a couple of small trees, and stopped in a little clearing, facing away from them. Dust slowly settled around the Town Car. The windows stayed rolled up, gray exhaust curling out the tailpipe. Hathaway had called Thorpe just before he picked up Vlad, given him the location of the grove. Guillermo had picked a good site for a private meeting—no surprises, not from the outside anyway.

"I hope you and Arturo can be friends," said Vlad. "He didn't want Missy to cut you in. He says we don't need the help, and that you're not worth the money."

"What do you think?"

"I don't care about money, but Arturo has a family to think about. He worries about money all the time. Don't *ever* ask him about the stock market." Vlad adjusted his assault rifle, made himself more comfortable. "We disappeared Arturo's broker last year. All those Internet stocks . . . I never understood that."

Thorpe watched him, not sure whether to believe him.

Vlad ran a finger over the leather trim of the Land Rover. "Soft. The broker had shoes that were soft like this. They fit me good, but Arturo wouldn't let me keep them. He bought me a pair of really expensive loafers afterward. Arturo says nice clothes are an investment, but I like swap meets." He looked at Thorpe. "You have really nice clothes. I think Arturo is a little jealous of you."

"Where's the accent from, Vlad? The Balkans, that would be my guess."

"You're a good guesser." Vlad hesitated. "I was born in Romania." He shifted in his seat again. "I have a photograph of me as a baby; Ceauşescu is holding me up for the camera. He's not smiling, but you can tell he's proud. I'll show it to you sometime."

"You must have been young when he was overthrown."

"I was nine. They had already finished the primary operations on me." Vlad's cheeks colored slightly when he saw Thorpe's surprise, the effect more stark because of the whiteness of his skin. "Romania was a very poor country under Ceauşescu, but the leader had a great vision. His scientists did some of the first experiments with recombinant DNA. Glandular extracts, too, and a full range of drugs and hormone injections. Special drugs for special children. There were a lot of tests you had to pass. It was a very great honor."

"So it was like what the East Germans did? To make superathletes for the Olympics?"

"Not exactly. More like . . . Ceauşescu, he wanted to play God."

"Yes, there's a lot of that going on."

"We were called the 'New Ones.' It was a great honor, Frank." Vlad looked away, his voice trailing off. "Our scientists had high hopes, and they were very successful, all things considered, but it would have

taken decades to achieve their goal. They didn't have enough time."
He smelled like dry leaves. "When the regime was overthrown, the
scientists had really only taken the first few steps into the project. First
steps . . . they are always wobbly." A tiny bubble of blood formed at
the base of one nostril. "The New Ones who reached adulthood, the
few who did . . . we were wobbly, too." He looked at Thorpe. A drop of
blood rolled from his nose, and he absently wiped it away. "You don't
mind . . . you don't mind knowing about me, do you?"

"No, of course not," said Thorpe, stunned.

Vlad smiled at him. "I told Arturo you had good eyes." He nodded
toward a car driving from the west. "Here comes Arturo now." You
would have thought it was Santa Claus, from the sound of his voice.

Arturo parked his Lexus next to them, got out and looked around.
He had a large Band-Aid across the side of his chin. As he walked over,
Thorpe saw a machine pistol in a spring-loaded shoulder rig under his
open suit jacket. He must have thought a claw hammer wouldn't be
much use against Guillermo.

Thorpe and Vlad stepped outside, joined Arturo in watching the
Town Car. Thorpe noticed a distinctive sheen to Arturo's dark green
suit. Woven Kevlar. The cautious man survives—that was one of Billy's
mottoes, and it must have been Arturo's, too. There were only two facto-
ries in the country that made such high-quality protective garments—
their suits cost nine thousand dollars, but Thorpe imagined Arturo
had a closetful. Arturo might worry about money, but some clothes
really were an investment. "You cut yourself shaving?" Thorpe asked
gently.

Arturo touched his chin. "What business is it of yours?"

"You should be careful, that's all," said Thorpe.

"Guillermo just got here," said Vlad.

Thorpe glanced over at Arturo's car. "Where's Clark?"

"He decided to sit this one out. Are you surprised?" Arturo looked
through a pair of small binoculars, methodically scanning the grove,
taking his time. "There's nobody hiding in the trees." His pocket
buzzed, and he pulled out a PDA, checked the message, and shook his

head in disgust. "Missy," he said to Vlad. "She wants to know if we're done yet."

"Missy doesn't like doing business on cell phones," Vlad said to Thorpe. "She says all kinds of people are listening in."

"She just likes telling us what to do," said Arturo. "She thinks she's smarter than anyone else."

"Something's happening," said Thorpe as the driver of the Town Car got out, walked around to the other side, and opened the passenger door. No one there.

"What's he doing?" asked Arturo.

The driver opened the trunk. It was empty, except for the spare tire. The two rear doors remained shut. "He's showing us that there's only him and Guillermo," said Thorpe.

"I can't see from this angle," said Vlad. "The windows are blacked out."

"Guillermo isn't going to show himself until we get down there for our parley," said Thorpe. "He's probably got a couple of *pistoleros* stuffed alongside him on the backseat for insurance."

Arturo checked his machine pistol. "That won't be a problem." He looked at Thorpe. "Time for you to earn your pay, gringo."

Thorpe nodded. "I'll go down, check things out. When I give you the sign, you start down to the clearing. Take it slow. I don't want Guillermo getting jumpy."

"I know what to do; you just hold up your end," said Arturo.

"As soon as Guillermo realizes that Clark's not with you, it's *over*, so as you drive down, keep turning around as if you're talking to somebody in the backseat. Then, when you make your final approach, drive past the Town Car so you can jump out and rake the inside through the open doors."

"I told you we don't need any advice," growled Arturo. "Your job is to convince Guillermo that we're here to settle our problems about the cookers. You think you can handle that?"

"We're going over the plan whether you want to or not," said Thorpe. "If you get killed down there, I get killed, too. Guillermo's only going to hold off on me until you arrive, so the timing is crucial. Don't come on too fast, not too slow, and make sure you kill them all. You think *you* can handle that?"

Arturo slightly tilted the machine pistol. He didn't aim it at Thorpe, not exactly, but his intentions were clear. He smiled. "Maybe I keep you waiting, huh? Maybe I go bird-watching or decide to stop and shoot some rabbits?"

"That's a good plan, Frank," said Vlad. His nose was dripping blood again. "We're all . . . you know, *excited.*"

Thorpe locked eyes with Arturo. "You should watch out for head shots down there. Although, looking on the bright side, there wouldn't be a mark on that suit—they could bury you in it."

"That's not so funny, Frank," said Vlad.

"Sure it is." Arturo's eyes were black and shiny as beetle wings. "Frank is a joker. That's why Missy likes him so much. She likes a good laugh, and there's Frank, ready, willing, and able to tickle her funny bone."

"Don't fight, you guys," said Vlad. *"Please?"*

Thorpe got into the Land Rover. "Wait a minute or two after I wave; then come on down. Don't wait too long; otherwise, Guillermo's going to think something's gone wrong."

Arturo picked his teeth with a fingernail. "What could go wrong?"

33

Thorpe drove over the broken gate and onto the gravel road, keeping it in first gear, taking his time. He had rolled his window down, and the breeze brought in the stink of rotting oranges. He tilted his rearview mirror, tried to get a glimpse of Vlad and Arturo, but the angle was wrong. The Land Rover hit a pothole, bouncing him forward. Looking through the trees, he could see the Town Car, the trunk open wide, ready to take a big bite.

He was sweating, but he kept the air conditioner off. Better to be soaked than to get the shakes. He needed all his steadiness now. One of Guillermo's *pistoleros* lay inside the trunk of the Town Car, crammed into a cubbyhole under the spare tire with a full-auto M249 machine gun, a SAW. Thorpe couldn't see the gun, but he could feel the man sighting in on him. Hathaway had told him the SAW was equipped with a couple of belts of military ordnance, rounds that would go through an engine block like vanilla yogurt, rounds that would tear Thorpe apart as he sat behind the wheel, rounds that would chew up Vlad and Arturo as they approached, before they even stopped their car. All the Kevlar in the world wouldn't save Arturo. Or Vlad, either. A strange, sad duck. Not an evil bone in his body, but he had probably lost count of all the people he had killed. What had Hathaway said? Vlad and Arturo had taken out five of Guillermo's dealers in one weekend, killed everyone they found, men, women, and children . . . babies in their cribs. Not even counting Ray Bishop, and Bishop *did* count. No, he and Arturo both had to go.

The driver of the Town Car pulled an orange off the nearest tree, wound up, and fired it at a nearby sprinkler head, splattering pulp. One of the boys of summer in baggy jeans and a hooded sweatshirt, probably an Uzi inside a rosin bag under his shirt. The driver picked another orange.

Thorpe carefully steered around another pothole, rolled over one of the trees that the Town Car had flattened. He had to blink to keep the sweat out of his eyes, but a tiny rivulet squirmed from his hairline and rolled behind his ear as he stared at the trunk of the Town Car. Hathaway had assured Thorpe that he would be in the backseat, sitting right next to Guillermo to make sure that Thorpe survived the execution of Vlad and Arturo, when the instinct was not to leave any witnesses. "You ain't a witness, Frank. You're a co-conspirator," Hathaway had said, laughing.

Thorpe eased the Land Rover toward the edge of the road, out of the direct line of fire, and slowly rolled to a stop. He turned off the ignition, his hands steady, his mind clear. He touched the 9-mm tucked into his waistband. He wasn't ready for anything, but he was ready enough. That was Thorpe's motto.

"Frank stopped the car," said Vlad. "We should get going."

"Not yet," said Arturo, watching the dust billow across the Town Car through the binoculars.

"Frank said—"

Arturo patted Vlad on the back. "I know you like him, but that's not enough."

"Clark said we were supposed to work with him."

"Clark lets Missy tell him what to do. A real man does not do that. We're going to have to have a long talk with him. Set him straight."

"Frank is getting out." Vlad rechecked the assault rifle slung under his arm, worked the action. "We should *go.*"

"Howdy, Frank, fine afternoon, isn't it?" The driver of the Town Car was Danny Hathaway. The inside of the car was empty.

Thorpe glanced back to where Vlad and Arturo were parked on the ridge above the grove, then back at Hathaway. "What happened?"

"At the last minute, Guillermo decided that he didn't want to get involved."

"He didn't want to get involved, but he loaned you his armored car?"

Hathaway plucked a desiccated orange off the nearest tree, hefted it before letting fly. A miss. "Actually, it wasn't a loan." He grinned. "I kicked him and his two bodyguards out at a miniature golf course in Santa Ana, told them to play a round on me. Guillermo didn't think it was funny, but he never did have a sense of humor."

Thorpe turned his head so that he could keep track of Vlad and Arturo. The Lexus was still parked in the same spot. "What do you want to do now?"

Hathaway opened the rear door of the Town Car, pretended to talk to someone inside, then slipped into the backseat, crawled forward on his belly. "Same as you want to do. I can handle the SAW better than Guillermo's shooter anyway."

Thorpe strolled around to the side of the car, positioned himself so that his face was partially blocked by one of the trees. Even with his binoculars, Arturo wouldn't be able to tell that Thorpe was talking. "Can you see the road from in there?"

"No problem." Hathaway's voice was muffled. "It's hot in here, though . . . and Guillermo's shooter was a lot smaller than me."

"We won't have to wait long."

"We can drive away if you want, Frank. This thing is built like a bank vault. You can flip them the bird as we drive past."

It was tempting. What they were planning was murder, legally anyway, not morally, and the distinction between the two had caused Thorpe grief his whole life. He beckoned to the Lexus. "No, I'm good for it."

"You know the rules of engagement," said Hathaway.

Thorpe touched the 9-mm under his shirt. "Yeah, there are no rules."

Hathaway's laugh sounded hollow from under the spare tire.

"Let's get down there," said Vlad.

Arturo put down his binoculars, started the car. "Forget Frank's little pep talk. Here's the way it will happen. Just past the gate, there's a big pothole. I'll take it fast, so the car will really dip, and when I do, you roll out your door and into the gully by the right side of the road. Guillermo and his *pistoleros* won't be able to see clearly through the smoked glass of the Town Car. Then you scurry up the gully, keeping ahead of me. When I get there, we hit them at the same time."

Vlad shook his head. "Better I move behind your car after I roll out, then cut left through the trees. I'll keep low, move fast; there's enough brush to screen me. They'll be watching you approach in the car, and I'll catch them from behind. They'll all be dead before you hit the brakes."

Arturo considered it, nodded. "You're right."

"Arturo . . . you should be careful when you start firing. You don't want to hit Frank."

"No, we wouldn't want that." As Arturo put the Lexus into gear, his phone beeped.

"At least it's not Missy, asking if it's over yet," said Vlad.

"I've been waiting on this call," said Arturo. He listened as he watched the Town Car. "You're *sure*?" He smiled and then snapped the phone shut.

"Good news?"

Arturo stared through the windshield at the orange grove, his face darkening now. "I just wish the call had come through ten minutes ago."

"What is it, Arturo?"

"Clark and Missy's new best friend is a liar. Guillermo didn't have our cookers killed."

"Maybe Guillermo lied to him."

"Why do you always take his side?" asked Arturo.

"I'm not." Vlad nodded toward the Town Car. "Let's go down and take care of business. . . . We can ask Frank to explain things when we're done."

Arturo shook his head. "If Guillermo didn't kill our cookers, maybe *he's* not our problem." He chewed on his thumbnail.

"You should call Clark. Ask him what he wants us to do."

"I don't need to call anyone," said Arturo. "No, we'll let Frank explain to Guillermo why we backed out. It should be a most interesting conversation. I just wish I could piss on the *pendejo*'s body after Guillermo gets done with him." He slipped the Lexus into gear, pulled out onto the main road. "Let's go to Santa Ana and pay a visit to someone who will be *very* unhappy to see us. Would you like that?"

Vlad stared out the window.

Thorpe watched the Lexus drive away. "You can come out now."

"What happened?" asked Hathaway, emerging from the inside of the Town Car, trying to work the kinks out.

"I don't know." Thorpe kept watch on the road, just in case.

"Too bad. I was looking forward to seeing if this Vlad character could be killed."

"What does *that* mean?"

"Vlad is the reason that Guillermo backed off." Hathaway stretched, popped his neck. "Guillermo thinks Vlad is some kind of *brujo* . . . wizard. I don't believe a word of it, but Guillermo does."

"Maybe Guillermo just wanted an excuse to back down."

"Guillermo doesn't make excuses," said Hathaway. "He told me that when they had their dustup a couple years ago, one of his cousins shot Vlad five times. They found blood everywhere, so they knew he wasn't wearing a vest, but the next thing Guillermo knows, Vlad's back in action." Hathaway snagged a bottle of mescal from inside the car, took a swig, and offered it to Thorpe, who declined. "Guillermo tracked down the ER doc who worked on Vlad, and the guy goes on about patient confidentiality until Guillermo clarifies things for him." He took another swallow of mescal, showed his perfect white teeth. "Doc said he had never seen insides like Vlad's. He showed Guillermo the X rays, and Vlad's organs are all overdeveloped, with scar tissue and . . . *growths* everywhere. Doc told Guillermo that Vlad should have died from the gunshot wounds, but a day later, he walked out of Intensive Care and disappeared. Doc was really pissed. I guess he was working on some article for a medical journal, but his proof walked out on him." He squinted at Thorpe. "I dearly would have liked to have seen how those weird organs of his would hold up to the SAW. Nine hundred rounds a minute, that's some serious firepower."

"Sorry I got you into this, Danny. You ruined your deal with Guillermo for nothing."

"I'm the one owes you," said Hathaway. "I was overdue for a change. I'm done with Guillermo and the DEA both."

"I thought you liked the work."

"Every job gets old, Frank, even the pussy tester for the king of Siam hates Mondays." Hathaway scratched the inside of his arm. "Besides, there's too many temptations at DEA, and I never been good at telling Satan to get his ass behind me. No, you done me good. You woke me up."

"Yeah, you're welcome."

Hathaway put the top back on the bottle of mescal, tossed it onto the driver's seat. "What are you going to do now?"

"I'll think of something."

"You could let it go. That's something."

"Danny, if I was the kind of person who could let it go, I wouldn't have achieved the lofty station in life that you see before you."

"Sergeant Hardass." Hathaway threw a sloppy salute, a Delta Force salute, mocking the regular army feebs. He turned serious. "I guess if you were any different, the Engineer would be sleeping better at night."

"No, the Engineer has no trouble sleeping. He sleeps a sweet and dreamless sleep; I'm counting on that." Thorpe looked at Hathaway. "What are *you* going to do?"

"I don't know. . . . It's a beautiful evening." Hathaway pounded the Town Car with his fist. "I think I'll clean out my crib and then take this baby on a road trip. It's not too late for you to come, Frank."

"Yes, it is."

34

Vlad could see Pinto's knobby anteater-skin cowboy boots protruding from under the white Mustang, heavy-metal music from the boom box drowning out the sounds of work. Fancy boots for the job at hand. He eased into the double garage from the back door, not making a sound. Arturo beckoned Vlad closer, jaw clenched, probably still angry about Thorpe.

For the last few hours, all Arturo had talked about was how he wished he had gotten the phone call sooner. Then he could have taken care of Thorpe himself, instead of leaving it to Guillermo. Vlad felt bad that Thorpe had fooled him, but the feeling didn't really linger. None of his feelings lingered. Arturo was always in a boiling rage, taking everything personally. A dealer was late with a payment, a cooker spoiled a batch, and Arturo acted like they'd had him in mind when they did it.

Vlad picked up a grease rag, wiped at the blood and brain matter on his shoes. *He* didn't act out of anger or resentment; he didn't blame anybody or call names. He just did what he was supposed to do. He tossed aside the rag and was reaching for the handle of the hydraulic jack, when Pinto sensed that he wasn't alone.

"Mellon? That you?"

"It's me," said Vlad.

A socket wrench clattered to the concrete floor. Pinto crabbed the creeper out from under the car, but Vlad turned the handle of the jack, lowered it, pinning Pinto's torso with the frame of the Mustang.

"Fuck!" Pinto clawed at the floor, his knotty forearms scrolled with spiderweb tattoos, a spaceship snagged in the web, hanging upside down as a two-headed spider watched from Pinto's elbow joint. *"Fuck!"*

Vlad lowered the jack a little more, Pinto begging now, his boots flapping on the ground. That was the good thing about a hydraulic jack: You had such fine control over the level of lift, raising and lowering it by quarter inches. Precision work, he liked that. He once told Arturo that he was thinking of taking a correspondence course in watch making, and Arturo said he might just as well study brain surgery. It took a few minutes for Vlad to realize that Arturo wasn't serious. Arturo had apologized, even gave him a shoe box full of watches a few days later, new watches, too, said Vlad could practice on them. The watches were still in the shoe box, untouched. Someday, when Vlad wasn't so busy, he was going to see what made them tick.

"What's going *on,* man?" Pinto said from under the car.

Arturo strolled into the garage, avoided the spots of pink transmission fluid on the concrete floor. It was bright inside the garage, tools neatly laid out. A calendar on the wall showed a nude blonde holding a shock absorber between her legs. Arturo turned off the boom box. They didn't have to worry about Pinto's cries. The garage was in a warehouse district of Santa Ana, and everyone in the vicinity had gone home for the night long ago.

"What's this about?" called Pinto.

Arturo pulled up a stool and sat down. A cigarette smoldered in a tuna-can ashtray by the rear tire. "Did you think we wouldn't find out?"

Pinto's fingers twitched, the nails scalloped with grease. "Find out what?"

Vlad lowered the jack, heard Pinto groan, backed it up again. Not quite as high, though.

"Did you think we wouldn't find out?" repeated Arturo.

"Can't . . . can't breathe," gasped Pinto.

Vlad lowered the jack. He watched Pinto thrash around, then raised it again.

Arturo waited until Pinto had caught his breath, the man making wet sounds as he sucked in air. "Do you have anything to say for yourself?"

Silence from under the car.

"Vlad?" said Arturo.

"It wasn't my fault," blurted Pinto.

"That's better," said Arturo. "Now we're getting somewhere."

"Let me out," said Pinto. "We'll talk."

"You can talk from there," said Arturo.

"Hey, Pinto," said Vlad. "If I wanted to buy a roller coaster like the one at the Kids Unlimited Karnival, how much would it cost?"

"*What?*"

"Vlad asked you a question," said Arturo.

"I don't know, man. Two or three hundred thousand. I never priced them," said Pinto. "Come on, let me out of here."

"Three hundred thousand, that's not so much," said Vlad. "I could ride anytime I wanted then, day and night."

"This Mellon . . . is he the one who put you up to it?" asked Arturo.

"You're cutting off my circulation," said Pinto.

Vlad lowered the jack.

"It was *Mellon*," said Pinto. "It was his idea. I didn't want to."

"I'm glad to hear that," said Arturo. "That makes a big difference."

"Mellon . . . he *made* me do it," said Pinto. "Said he'd kill me if I didn't help him."

"So, you ripping off our cookers was just self-defense," said Arturo.

"That's right," said Pinto. "Absolutely, self-defense."

"Where we going to find this Mellon?" asked Arturo.

"Mellon . . . he's got a place just off Seventeenth Avenue," said Pinto. "I don't know the address, but I'll take you there."

"This is a nice car," said Vlad. "Lot nicer than the other one."

"I guess that's what you did with the crank you stole from us," said Arturo.

"You shouldn't have taken my Mustang," said Pinto, defiant now. "I loved that fucking car."

Vlad tapped the side panel. "What's with the snake emblem?"

"It's a '68 Shelby GT Five Hundred Cobra. Almost cherry," said Pinto. "Zero to sixty in four point eight seconds. Less than fifty of them left in this condition." Even in his position, he couldn't keep the pride out of his voice. "Just let me out of here, okay? I'll show you the interior. All leather. Matched hides and everything."

Arturo's PDA beeped and he pulled it out of his jacket, checked it. "Missy wants to know how things are going," he said to Vlad. He keyed a reply.

Vlad watched Pinto try to squeeze out from under, the creeper's metal wheels squeaking on the concrete. Vlad let him make an inch of progress, then adjusted the jack, dropping the car down slightly so that Pinto retreated, thinking it was some permutation of the Cobra's undercarriage, trying again from a different direction. They went back and forth, Vlad humming as Arturo tapped away on the PDA.

"Come on, man, this is so unnecessary," said Pinto, gasping, farther under the car than he had been before, only his knees free now. "Mellon is the one you want to deal with. He's a total crank maniac. . . . I'd go in guns blazing if I was you. Let me out and I'll take you right over. We'll settle this, then go back to business as usual."

Arturo put away the PDA. "You don't know his address?"

"I wish I did, man. Just let me out, and I'll take you there."

"His address is 1209 Plesa, right off Twenty-fifth, not Seventeenth." Arturo smiled, but Pinto couldn't see it. "I was having a little fun with you. Don't worry about taking us over. We've already been there."

"Place was a real mess," said Vlad. "Smelled bad, too. I don't think Mellon had taken out the garbage in weeks. Drugs . . . they ruin a person's perspective."

"Fuck *you,* man. Fuck the both of you."

Vlad lowered the jack and Pinto screamed, the sound uncoiling from his chest, echoing in the garage.

"Mellon only had about a half ounce of that gold meth you took off Weezer," said Arturo. "He said you kept the rest, promised to move it out later this week. Where is it?"

Pinto made gurgling sounds, boots kicking feebly.

Arturo beckoned to Vlad, waited until the jack was raised. "Where's the rest of the meth?"

"Fuck . . . *you.*"

"You need to work on your vocabulary," said Arturo.

Pinto gagged, legs twitching.

Vlad raised the car slightly.

"Better?" said Arturo.

"My ribs . . ." Pinto tried to scuttle out, but his legs weren't working. "You *fuckers . . .*" His voice was high-pitched now, like a little girl's. A brave little girl's. "I think . . . I think you broke something important."

"I'm sure it's nothing that an Ace bandage and a little bedrest won't cure," said Arturo. "Come on, Pinto, just tell us what we want to know, and then we'll let you finish working on your beautiful car."

"Sure . . . *sure* you will."

"You can trust us," said Arturo. "Have we ever lied to you?"

Pinto's breathing was ragged.

Arturo looked over, and Vlad raised the jack, kept going, lifted the car three feet off the floor. Arturo squatted down, keeping his knees clean, and looked in at Pinto. Vlad looked, too. Pinto's head lay against the floor, his eyes half-closed. Blood dribbled from his mouth and nose. "Pinto? Pinto! Where did you stash our goods?"

Pinto opened his eyes, stared back at them. "Fuck . . . *you.*"

"*Bueno.*" Arturo nodded, then took the smoldering cigarette from the bent-can ashtray, puffed it back into life. He reached under the car, offered it to Pinto, but the man's hands just twitched. Arturo stuck the cigarette into the side of Pinto's mouth, then backed away, squatting on his haunches, watching. "Good for you, hombre. I wouldn't talk to me, either."

Pinto dragged deeply on the cigarette, started to cough.

Arturo nodded, and Vlad released the jack, brought it crashing down. It sounded like someone stepping on a baby chick with a heavy boot.

35

"Still nothing?" Arturo stood in the middle of the media room, arms crossed. He was still wearing the green Kevlar three-piece suit he had on yesterday afternoon.

"Nobody is reporting anything at the grove," said Clark, the recliner tilted back almost horizontal as he flipped channels on the big-screen TV. "No blood, no body, no reports of gunshots. Say what you want, Guillermo never leaves the cops anything to chew on. Man is tidy."

"Frank said he was tidy, too," snapped Missy, cinching her red bathrobe tighter. "That didn't count for much, did it?"

"Frank lied to us, just like Arturo said." Vlad sat on the floor, knobby knees pressed against his chest. His socks drooped around his ankles. "I'm sad about it, too, but Pinto was the one who killed our cookers. Pinto and some guy named Mellon, not Guillermo."

"Maybe Guillermo lied to *Frank*," Cecil said from the edge of the sunken media room, perched uncomfortably on the steps. "I agree with Missy: You should have gone ahead and killed Guillermo."

They ignored him.

Clark kept switching channels. The coffee table in front of him was strewn with half-eaten bowls of cereal, congealed eggs, and coffee cups. Sugar granules were scattered across the shiny black surface from where Clark had loaded up his Frosted Flakes.

"You fucked up, Arturo, no two ways about it." Missy sat on the couch, her legs tucked up, twisting her blond hair back and forth as if trying to start a fire. "Driving off the way you did, to interrogate a grease monkey, no less . . . no wonder Guillermo thinks we're weak."

"Guillermo thinks we're not dumb enough to fall into a trap—*that's* what he's thinking now," Arturo said to her, his voice wound as tightly as one of the watches Vlad wanted to take apart someday. "You should be *thanking* me and Vlad, instead of insulting us. You should be grateful for what we did last night, and what we did a hundred other nights."

"Arturo . . . dude, maybe you *should* have brought Frank here, so we could talk to him." Clark tapped the remote control on the arm of the chair as he spoke, sleepy-eyed and slack. "See, now we're not sure if he was hired by Guillermo or the Yellow Magic boys or maybe even—"

"How could we trust anything he said?" asked Arturo.

"You *make* him tell us the truth," said Missy. "Isn't that what you and Vlad do?"

"We do a lot more than that," said Arturo.

"Too late to argue about now, so let's kiss and make up." Clark yawned, pulled a vial of pills from the pocket of his pajamas. "Who wants to get high?"

"*I* do," called Cecil.

"Anybody?"

"Me!" said Cecil.

Clark looked around, shrugged, and shoved the vial back into his pocket.

"You should have brought Frank back here and forced the truth out of him," Missy said to Arturo. "That's all I intend to say on the matter."

"Let me tell you something." Arturo stepped toward her, but she just kept on twisting her hair. "*Some* people, it don't matter what you do to them, they're going to lie to you with their dying breath. Just like Pinto last night. Raising the car up, giving him room, letting him think there's a chance . . . that's when they break. Not Pinto. He was hard-core to the bone. Guys like him, they're going to lie just so they can feel like they got the last laugh. That's what Frank is like, too. Exact same."

Vlad tugged at his socks. "You said you had a lot of respect for Pinto."

"*Lot* of respect," said Arturo. "After the way he handled himself last night . . . yeah, he died like a man."

"Then that must mean you have a lot of respect for Thorpe, too," said Vlad.

Arturo's face got red.

"I think he's got you there, Arturo," said Clark. "That's what they call a logical syllogism."

"I'm going to get another ice tea." Arturo stalked toward the kitchen. If Cecil hadn't scooted out of the way, he would have been kicked aside.

There was a beeping from the couch. Missy pulled out her PDA, checked the screen. She opened the e-mail, curious, then closed it, slipped the PDA back between the cushions.

"Who was it, babe?"

"Nobody," said Missy. "Just more junk."

"I'm *in,*" said Warren, clapping his hands together like a Vegas dealer making a shift change. "How long, Billy?"

Billy looked out over the beach, impassive and untouchable. The morning light gleamed on his shaved head, his skin so black that it was purple, the color of kings. He was large and powerfully built, but graceful, oddly dapper in ocher slacks, a loose cotton shirt, and a yellow paisley ascot. Sometimes Thorpe thought Billy chose his wardrobe to see if anyone would laugh. No one ever did.

"Billy?"

"Four minutes, fifty-eight seconds," said Thorpe.

Warren's blue-tipped hair was spiked like a cockatoo. "You fucking with me?"

"Not even a remote possibility," said Thorpe.

"Under five minutes . . ." Warren nodded, flipped Missy's business card back to Thorpe, and went back to the wireless laptop balanced on his knees. "That's acceptable." He sat on a bench just off the beach bike path, wearing a black mesh tank top, Lycra bike shorts, and customized silver-flecked Rollerblades. Without his black leather jacket, he looked scrawny and vulnerable, but his sneer was still in place.

A few minutes ago, Warren had sent Missy spam. She had spiked the free offer without downloading it, but just opening the e-mail had inserted a worm into her operating system, a keystroke-sniffing program that Warren had created himself. Four minutes and fifty-eight seconds later, he had her password and files at his disposal.

"Off-the-shelf encryption . . . why do people even bother?" Warren sat hunched over, immobile except for his fingers dancing over the keys.

"Can you do it?" asked Thorpe.

"Don't insult me," said Warren.

"In the interest of fair play, I think Warren and I deserve to know what you're up to," said Billy. "The last time I saw you, your little wake-up had gone awry. It doesn't seem like you've made much progress since then."

"Not much."

"If you want our help, if you're exposing us to potential harm, I think it only appropriate that you tell us what you're planning." Billy sat down beside Warren, smoothed his ascot, playful now. "Of course, my own curiosity does factor in, too."

Thorpe hated to admit it, but Billy was right. If Thorpe had leveled with Bishop, he might still be alive. He casually checked the area, but there were only joggers, bicyclists, and skaters, all with their headsets on, moving to their own private beat.

Billy didn't say a word while Thorpe filled him in on what had happened since they had breakfast at the Harbor House Café. It had been only eight days since they had sat on the outdoor patio reading Betty B's column, Billy asking Thorpe if it was his doing. Everything had changed at that moment, and Thorpe hadn't even realized it. He told Billy everything that had happened in the last eight days. He left out only Danny Hathaway's involvement and the convenient departure of Gina and Douglas Meachum.

"I'm very sorry to hear about the death of your friend," said Billy when Thorpe was finished.

"We only knew each other for a few days. . . ."

"It's not really a matter of time, is it? It's what you share, the decisions you make."

"He was my friend, Billy."

Billy patted Thorpe's arm, and for a change it wasn't an attempt to be proprietary or intimidating. It was oddly tender. "Don't beat up on yourself, Frank. Mistakes happen. The problem with being a lone wolf is that your mistakes magnify because you have no one to bounce your ideas off of, no one you trust to tell you no. I'm not telling you this to persuade you to work with me; I know you have to carry this wake-up of yours to its conclusion." His eyes were warm. "When you're finished, though, I hope you'll reconsider what we've discussed."

"Thanks, Billy." Thorpe meant it. "I just can't . . . I just can't quit. Not now."

"That's why you're the best at what you do," said Billy.

"What happened to the businessman who smacked the kid at the airport?" Warren crossed his legs, spun the wheels of his skate. "The art dealer. What happened to him?"

"He's in Hawaii," said Thorpe. "He's drinking mai tais with his wife."

Warren shook his head. "What's the name you want me to hack from her address book?" he asked, fingers poised over the laptop.

"Arturo . . . I don't know his last name," said Thorpe.

"No big deal," said Warren, tapping away. "I'll just run through her recent e-mail exchanges."

"Don't crash his PDA until I call," said Thorpe. "I don't know when I'll catch up with Missy. You're sure you can do it on a moment's notice?"

"Spare me your doubts, okay?" said Warren. "I'll toast him."

Billy gazed off into the distance, past the Boogie boarders and the building waves, past the curve of the earth, for all Thorpe knew. "You haven't mentioned the Engineer. Was that deliberate?"

"I'm meeting him next week," said Thorpe. "We're going to talk about old times."

Billy raised an eyebrow. "Really? I had no idea your contact had progressed to that stage. Are you sure it's wise?"

"I'm sure."

"You've been on-line with the Engineer?" Warren looked from one to the other. "You should have told me, Billy."

Billy ran a hand across his bare scalp. "Frank knows what he's doing."

"How long do these on-line chats last?" Warren asked Thorpe.

"No more than five or ten minutes," said Thorpe. "I use a cell phone to make my connection. No landline. That's safe, right?"

"Depends on how good the Engineer is," said Warren. "Five or ten minutes isn't enough time to snag your address, but if the hacker is good, really good, he could narrow your location. He could get within a few miles of you."

"A few *miles*?" said Billy. "No harm done."

Warren glared at Billy. "You should have told me he was talking with the Engineer. That's what I'm here for."

"I apologize," said Billy. "I'm truly sorry."

"Dump your cell phones, Frank, every one of them. Dump them *now*," said Warren. "I have a box of cloned phones in the car. Take as many as you want. Use them."

"Why are you doing all this?" asked Thorpe. "I appreciate it, but—"

"The Engineer made initial contact with you because of my mistake," said Warren, blue-crested, even more birdlike as he hunched over the laptop. "He backtracked on my own search for him; he *used* me." His lip curled. "You think you're the only one with a sense of responsibility? The only one who cleans up after himself? Just do me a favor—stay off the Net for a while."

"Scout's honor," said Thorpe.

36

Thorpe waited for Missy to get out of her car before he called Warren and told him to go ahead and crash Arturo's system. Warren snapped his fingers into the receiver, said, "You're welcome," and broke the connection.

He followed her through the Fashion Island mall for over an hour before making his move, tracked her through Prada and Chanel and Versace, Missy striding along in her sleek forest green skirt and top, snapping her fingers from the dressing rooms, barking at saleswomen. The clothes that didn't meet with her approval were tossed aside, diaphanous dresses thrown onto the floor; those she liked were packaged for delivery later. Fashion Island was four stories of platinum AmEx finery and hauteur, nymphets practicing their sneers as they window-shopped, their mothers proud of their own washboard midriffs, looking like their daughters' older, harder sisters.

In a tapered blue-black suit and with a newly cropped haircut, Thorpe fit right in—"the New Militarism," the stylist had called it. Thorpe checked himself in the mirror. His face reminded him of an ax blade, but there was something off about his eyes. He had glimpsed Claire only once or twice through his window since they had made love. Neither of them made any effort to contact the other, their fleeting intimacy fractured, sending them in opposite directions. That didn't mean he didn't think about her.

Missy headed for the elevator to valet parking, and Thorpe closed in. "I would have passed on that last outfit you bought, the silvery one," he said, the words barely out of his mouth before she turned. "It made you look like a Martian hooker."

Missy stared at him. "Arturo is going to be disappointed, but I'm not. You look dangerous enough to eat, Frank. Did you kill Guillermo?"

"No, but I took his bulletproof car away from him."

Her mouth twitched. "I almost believe you."

"Ask around. I'm sure someone has heard Guillermo lost his wheels."

She watched him, then nodded to the small round tables outside the French-themed café. The waiter ambled over a few minutes later, a skinny kid with scimitar sideburns, leaving just as slowly with their café au lait orders. Missy crossed her legs, showed just enough thigh to get the attention of every passing male. "How *did* you get away from Guillermo?"

"Smoke and mirrors."

She showed the tip of her pink tongue. "Whoever hired you to cause trouble between Guillermo and us chose the right man." She waved at someone behind Thorpe's back. A woman—he could see her in the reflection of the café's window. "Alison Peabody," she said, looking past him, still waving. "Last time I ran into her, she asked me if it was true I was collecting decorative ceramic thimbles. *Cunt.*" She turned back to Thorpe. "Who *was* it who hired you, by the way?"

"Guillermo hired me, just like I told you. He wants you and Clark dead. That hasn't changed. He just doesn't think he needs me anymore."

The waiter interrupted them, set their drinks on the table, one cup wobbling, spilling a few drops of café au lait into the saucer. He backed away without a word.

"Vlad and Arturo were supposed to back me up at the orange grove. We could have ended both of our problems." Thorpe sipped his coffee. It was weak and barely warm. "I thought we had a deal."

"You lied about Guillermo's taking down our cookers. That ended the deal."

"I didn't lie. That's what he told me."

"That's what Cecil said." Missy tossed her blond mane. "When Cecil starts agreeing with you, Frank, you're in big trouble."

Thorpe pushed aside his coffee cup. "When I was sitting in Guillermo's Town Car, just before his *pistoleros* made their play, Guillermo said he was officially canceling my contract. He said he had somebody

205

on the inside working for him. They were more expensive than me . . . but Guillermo said he could be more certain of the outcome."

A pencil mustache of foam curved across Missy's upper lip. She slowly licked it off. "Of course, Guillermo didn't tell you the name of this *someone*."

"No."

"I bet you could find out, though, if I deposited money in your off-shore account. Where is it, the Caymans?"

"Isle of Wight. Tighter bank security laws than the Caymans."

Missy laughed. "What *ever* are you up to?"

"Same as ever . . . I'm up for telling the truth and having fun telling it. I'm up for doing unto others before they do it to me. I'm up for giving you a hard ride and making some money, too. The all-American dream. *You* up for that, Missy?"

Missy's eyes flashed, and he knew that look, pure blood lust masquerading as eroticism. She stirred her coffee, the spoon clinking against the side of the cup. "Someone *inside* our operation. There's probably a dozen people who qualify. Dealers, cookers . . . our accountant, our contacts at various chemical supply houses. You *must* have some idea who Guillermo was talking about." She spooned the foam into her mouth. "Otherwise, what do you have to sell?"

Thorpe smiled. She was fast. "I don't know, but we can find out."

"*We?*"

"That's right."

"Now I am intrigued. Why don't we go back to the house and see if Clark wants to play."

"Clark doesn't get to play. Arturo wouldn't have hung me out to dry if Clark hadn't okayed it."

"Arturo made that decision on his own."

Thorpe shook his head. "This is between you and me."

"I'm flattered."

"I thought you would be."

Missy had a small laugh that dirtied everything it touched. "I can't get a handle on you, Frank. I love the way you talk . . . but I wonder what I've done to deserve you." She crossed her legs again, treated him to the rustle of silk. "I'm a married woman, a happily married woman, but I know what men are like. I think you show yourself movies in your head when you're all alone. Sweaty movies with lots of grunting and groaning, and I think I'm the star, aren't I, Frank?"

Thorpe allowed himself to fall into her eyes, and he wondered what Clark would have been like if he hadn't met her. A man could drown in those cold blue eyes; a man could lose himself and never find the bottom.

"I think we could have some fun, Frank."

"I think we've already started." She didn't work on him, but Thorpe was impressed. She used everything she had to claw her way up the food chain. So did he. "Do you have a PDA? Vlad and Arturo were always checking their PDAs."

A little confused, Missy dipped a hand into her purse, brought out her wireless PDA. "Do you *really* think Guillermo has an inside man?"

Thorpe took his time answering, waited until she inclined her head toward him, an inadvertent sign of vulnerability, but enough. "I'm not sure. He might have been just fucking with me. Maybe he *let* me get away, thinking I'd come to you with the story, and set you worrying about who was about to betray you. No better way to ruin an operation than from within." He shrugged. "I don't know if Guillermo was lying, but I know how to find out the truth. It will cost you one hundred thousand dollars." He slid the number of his offshore account across the table to her.

"Do you expect me to trust you?"

"No, I'll trust you instead." Thorpe smiled. "Just before I came here today, I contacted Guillermo and made him an offer. I said unless he paid the balance due on my contract, I was going to tell you that he had compromised your organization."

Missy looked down her nose at him, waiting. "*Well?* What did Guillermo say?"

"He said he wanted to think about it. He also asked for his car back."

"So all I have is your word that—"

"Log on to your PDA. Send an e-mail to everyone in your operation. Everyone in your address book. Tell them it's a test, that you want to make sure they're monitoring their messages, and that they should send you an e-mail response immediately." Thorpe stood up. "I'm going to take a stroll, give you some privacy. I'll be back in ten minutes. That should be enough time."

"For what?"

Thorpe started walking. He didn't need to look behind him to know she was already sending out the e-mail. He took twenty minutes to return. Never let anyone be able to clock you—that was one of the first things Billy had told him when he signed on. Returning in five minutes would have been just as effective.

"You're late," said Missy. The PDA was on the table.

Thorpe sat back down. "Has anyone gotten back to you?"

"What do you think? I said I wanted a response *immediately.*"

"Then you'll know soon enough who's the inside man." Thorpe looked just past her, watched the reflection of the passing shoppers in the café window, all the pretty people on parade. "After I spoke with Guillermo, I sent him an e-mail with my offshore account number. Inside the e-mail was a doomsday virus that bypassed his fire wall and corrupted the hard drive. Anyone Guillermo sent an e-mail to in the last hour had their computer infected. Anyone he contacted had their system fried." He tapped Missy's PDA. "I figured that after I spoke to Guillermo, the first thing he would do is contact his inside man. So, anybody who doesn't answer your e-mail . . . that's the guilty party."

Missy stared at her PDA.

The waiter appeared. "Hi. Can I—"

Missy waved him away.

"How many of your people still haven't responded?" asked Thorpe.

"Three."

"Kind of exciting, isn't it?" Thorpe stood up. "You owe me one hundred thousand dollars. Send it to my account as soon as you're down to one no-show. I work on the honor system." He kissed her hand. "Strangely enough, no one ever stiffs me."

37

"I can't do it." Vlad ran a hand across a rack of brightly colored shirts, the hangers going *clickety-clack* under his fingers. "I *can't*."

"Come on, it's not like you haven't done this kind of thing before," said Clark. "This is your function, man, the fucking prime directive."

"Arturo is my friend."

"Your *friend* sold us out," said Missy. It was the day after Thorpe had surprised her at Fashion Island, and *she* was ready to get started, but all Vlad wanted to do was make excuses, and Cecil giving her that "I told you so" face, which made her want to kick him. As soon as this thing with Arturo was settled, she was going to ship Cecil back to live with their uncle. He could see how well that attitude worked at the filling station.

They were standing in the salesroom of the Huntington Beach Camp Riddenhauer, the smallest store in the CR chain, ostensibly managed by Vlad. Located in a failing minimall on Warner Boulevard, it'd had almost no foot traffic since the used-CD shop next door had closed five months ago, but it still maintained an air of imminent success. The shelves were fully stocked, carrying the complete CR line of jackets, shorts, shirts, sandals, tanks, and tees. Surf posters covered the interior walls—tiny surfers riding mountainous blue waves, and black-and-white blowups of classic Hawaiian postcards from the 1930s and 1940s, beefy kahunas staring into the camera, their longboards planted in the sand behind them. Reggae music pounded out of the speakers, but they were the only ones there to hear it. Only 5:00 p.m., but, as usual, Vlad had sent the staff home for the day. Every few weeks, a step van would come and take most of the merchandise away to an incinerator, then come back and refill the store with fresh designs. It wasn't Clark's fault if the public had no taste.

"*Arturo* was the one who decided not to go after Guillermo," Clark explained to Vlad. "*He* sold Frank down the river, and he didn't ask for my okay. You don't think that's suspicious?"

"Arturo hates Frank," said Vlad. "I don't understand it, but he does."

"Don't forget, Arturo needs money big-time," Cecil piped up. "I heard him bitching to Vlad about all the cash he lost in the stock market, going on and on about how he wasn't never going to be able to retire now. Bitch, bitch, bitch. Arturo probably didn't even know I was in the room. Nobody pays any attention to Cecil. Cecil is just part of the furniture. Put your foot up on Cecil's face and get comfortable."

"Talking about yourself in the third person is the first sign of insanity," Clark said to him. "One word, dude . . . *lithium.* Make the molecule your friend."

Cecil had a nasty answer, but he kept it to himself. Instead, he held a geometric Aborigine-print shirt against his chest for Missy to see. "How do I look?"

"Go jiggle the handle of the toilet," said Missy. "Somebody left it running."

Cecil threw the shirt down, stomped off to the rest room.

"It was *Arturo* didn't think I was doing my job," Clark said to Vlad. " 'Too much surf, not enough turf,' that's what he said." He glanced at Missy. "He's not the only one who thought I was backing off, but he was the only one who tried to fuck us over."

There was a wind roaring through Vlad's head, a static storm, but he could hear every word they said.

"Arturo was the only one who didn't respond to my e-mail yesterday," said Missy. "The *only* one. When I finally got him on the phone, he said his PDA was shot. No idea how it happened." She jabbed a finger at Vlad. "*You* know what happened. We all know what happened. Frank talked to Guillermo, then Guillermo tried to send Arturo an e-mail and crashed his PDA. Arturo is the inside man. What more do you need?"

Vlad didn't move. No one could tell that he was even breathing. "I believe you," he said at last. It sounded soft as a surrender. "What Arturo did was wrong, very wrong . . . but I can't take his life."

"What, you expect *me* to do it?" said Clark.

"*I'll* do it," said Cecil, back from the rest room.

Missy and Clark laughed, and even Vlad smiled.

"What's so funny?" demanded Cecil.

"Seriously, man, thanks for the offer," said Clark, "but killing Arturo . . . it's not like running down a little old lady."

Cecil just stood there. His red hair looked like it was about to catch on fire.

Vlad stared at his hands, turning them over as though they didn't belong to him. He wiggled his fingers. In just the last day, his cuticles had turned black. He hadn't noticed until now.

"I can call Frank," Missy said to Vlad. "*He'll* do it if you won't. He's not scared."

"Fuck Frank," said Clark. "Arturo's got that coyote radar—Frank gets anywhere near him, Arturo is going to come out guns blazing. But *you* . . . he trusts you, Vlad."

"Frank is very focused, very well trained. You can tell just by looking at him," said Vlad. "That's why he was able to get away from Guillermo. A man like Frank—"

"Damn it, Vlad, will you just shut up?" said Clark. "I'm trying to give you a compliment."

"Arturo always lets me talk," said Vlad. "He doesn't yell at me, except sometimes when I eat fatty foods that he would like to eat himself. I don't blame Arturo for being angry. My metabolism isn't fair. It's not my fault, but it's not fair."

"You understand what the *hell* he's talking about?" Clark said to Missy.

Missy smiled at Vlad. "I know you and Arturo are friends, but we're your friends, too, aren't we?"

Vlad shook his head. "Not really."

"We pay you plenty, don't we?" said Clark. "Arturo ever give you a dime?"

"I don't need a dime."

"You're missing the fucking point," shouted Clark.

"I'm here," said Cecil, talking to himself. "I'm ready, willing, and able, but does anybody ask Cecil to do the job? No way, José."

"I told Arturo we're having our weekly meeting here tomorrow," Clark said to Vlad, "so get yourself prepared. Six o'clock. While Missy goes over the financials, Cecil will bring in Diet Coke or Diet Pepsi, or whatever diet crap Arturo is drinking these days, and when he reaches for the glass, you sidle over and put a bullet in his head. One shot should do it. We'll double-bag Arturo, then stuff him into one of the containers of excess clothes. Next morning, the truck comes and takes the load to the incinerator." He grinned. "No muss, no fuss, no bother."

"Sure, let Cecil bring the drinks like Jeeves the butler," muttered Cecil.

"Why don't you give Arturo another chance?" asked Vlad.

"You got to be shitting me," said Clark.

"Maybe if you give him a chance, Arturo will turn on Guillermo," said Vlad, looking around. "Arturo just needs to be appreciated more. Told that he's doing a good job. He worries all the time. Maybe if you were nicer to him, he wouldn't worry so much."

Missy stared at him, wondering what she would have to do, how high they would have to rise, before she and Clark would be dealing with a better-quality person. The loyal ones, like Vlad and Cecil, were pea brains. Arturo was smart, but greedy, and untrustworthy. All of the time she and Clark had put into the business, all their talent and hard work, and here they were, surrounded by weaklings and Benedict Arnolds. She had to ask herself, Really, what would it *take*? "Vlad, honey," she said evenly, "I don't think Arturo sold us out because he was worried."

"If you were nicer to him, Arturo might switch back," said Vlad. "Then, instead of Guillermo having Arturo on the inside of *us,* we would have Arturo on the inside of *him.* Please, Clark? Arturo deserves another chance."

"He deserves to be burned up and have his ashes dumped in a land-fill." Clark scowled. "Maybe I *have* been too easygoing, but that's about to change. Just be here tomorrow, Vlad, and be ready to do your job. Smile, dude. Tomorrow's the first day of the rest of your life."

38

"Excuse me, miss?" The Engineer put on his earnest but weary expression. It wasn't hard. It was barely 9:00 a.m., but he was already tired. For the last three days, ever since the checker at Ralphs gave him the heads-up on Thorpe, he had been knocking on doors within walking distance of the Belmont Shore pier. His feet were sore and his face ached from smiling. "Could you help me, please?"

The woman stopped, eyed him as the security gate closed behind her with a rusty squeak. She shifted her briefcase. "I'm in a hurry."

The Engineer put his hands up. "I just need a moment of your time. I'm not selling anything. You have my word on that."

"Just a minute." She walked to a car parked in front of the small apartment complex, popped the trunk.

No slack from this one. She was all business. A lot of them said they were in a hurry, but she meant it. Nice-looking woman, but a real stick up her ass. Give him ten minutes, and she'd loosen up. A California State University, Fullerton, staff parking sticker was on her rear window, right next to one from Cal State, Long Beach, and another one from Golden West College. What was that old song—"Hot for Teacher"? He watched her stow her briefcase, admired her figure in the tailored trousers and jacket. Some women looked like dykes when they dressed like men; others became even more feminine. The Engineer would bet that half the college boys in her class sported a woody when she wrote on the blackboard.

"What do you want?"

The Engineer gave up on the smile. "I was hoping you could help me find someone. I think he lives in the Shore, but I don't have an address on him." He fumbled in his notebook, a practiced clumsiness, designed to reinforce his nonthreatening aspect. The Engineer, with his high-water pants and white short-sleeved dress shirt, his pocket protector stuffed with ballpoints, was a nerd out of water in the Shore, a doofus lost in the cool zone. "State . . . State of California owes him an inheritance from his late uncle, but he moved without leaving a forwarding address." He handed her the photo of Thorpe. "Have you ever seen him around here?"

She stared at the photo.

It was a lousy photo, eight years out of date, taken when Thorpe was discharged from the military, all steely-eyed and with that knowing grin that the Engineer wanted to burn away with a blowtorch. He dabbed his moist forehead with his clip-on necktie. It was a lousy photo, but it was the only one he had.

"He looks kind of familiar."

"It's an old picture." She held on to the photo, which was a good sign. The Engineer looked at her directly. "I'll be honest with you. I represent a company that tracks down dead accounts in the state Department of Revenue." He pulled a business card from his pocket, handed it over. "That's me, Earl Johnson. The uncle died over six years ago, but I just got the file last week. If the account isn't paid out in three months, it reverts to the state." He tugged at his pants.

"What's his name?"

"I'm embarrassed to tell you, but we don't know what name he's going under right now. That's what makes this job so tough. He's kind of an . . . underground type, you know? Real name is Frank Stanford, but your guess is as good as mine as to what the name is on his driver's license. No matter to me. We aren't connected in any way, shape, or form with law enforcement, so you won't be getting anyone in trouble. All I want to do is find him and have him collect his money. I'll be honest with—"

"You said that already."

The Engineer smiled. It hurt, but if he'd had barbed wire through his gums, he would have smiled for her. Lousy bitch interrupting his flow, seeing if she could trip him up. Too smart for her own good, just like he thought. "Well, Miss . . ." She didn't give up her name. Fine, see where that gets you. She was lucky he was focused on finding Thorpe and wasn't about to let anything distract him. Business before pleasure. "I guess I do repeat myself, and I apologize. . . ." He hitched up his pants again. "I just wanted to let you know that when I locate him, I get a ten percent finder's fee, which is a nice chunk of change. Any help you give me, I won't forget when I get paid."

She handed back the photo. "That's very nice of you, Mr. Johnson."

"That's the way I was raised, ma'am."

She flicked his business card with her thumbnail. "I *do* remember him. Frank somebody, just like you said."

The Engineer kept his distance, not wanting to scare her off, the tips of his fingers tingling with anticipation.

"I used to see him running along the beach. He lived on Claremont. Last time I talked to him, he said he was moving. He said he had a new apartment in . . . Los Alamitos, I believe."

"Los Alamitos? You're sure?"

She flicked his business card again. "Frank said Los Alamitos had better freeway access. He was always complaining about the traffic."

"Thank you very much. Could I have your name, just in case I find him?"

She walked around to the driver's side of her car. "That's all right, Mr. Johnson, you work hard enough for your money. I hope you find him. He didn't seem like a bad person. Maybe the inheritance will help him straighten his life out."

"Thank you, miss. I wish everyone I met was as kind as you." The Engineer watched her drive away, then headed toward his car at the end of the street, trying to restrain his excitement, his heart fluttering in his chest as if it were going to burst free. He unlocked his car, got behind the wheel. Little Miss Teacher maintained perfect eye contact and kept her voice casual, but she was lying. There was a little park down the street, just a patch of brown grass, a couple of graffiti-etched benches, and swarms of pigeons. The Engineer was going to pick up a loaf of bread and stake out the park. Pigeons were filthy, disease-ridden scavengers that shit indiscriminately, but people opened up to a man feeding birds. What did *that* say about humanity?

Claire kept her eyes on the road as she pulled her phone out of her purse. She crossed Studebaker, took the entrance ramp to the 22 freeway, speeding now, driving aggressively, which she rarely did. Her class at Cal State, Fullerton, started at ten o'clock, but she didn't need to speed. The conversation with Earl Johnson was bothering her. That strange, creepy man had put her on guard immediately, and the more he talked, the more defensive she'd become. She forced herself to drive at the legal limit.

She was still angry at Frank, hurt and humiliated by his erratic behavior, but there was no way in the world that she would have told Earl Johnson where he lived. She had gone beyond mere denial, however; she had actively *lied* to the man. She didn't feel guilty about it, either.

There was a connection between her and Frank, a mutual attraction, try as they might to deny it. The good ones, the interesting ones, they were always trouble, but she was bored with the worm boys in the department, assistant professors desperate for approval, eager to please. No thanks. Then there was Frank, who sent out conflicting signals, forced her to make the first move, but was great fun in bed. There was no way Frank sold insurance. She had known that for a long time, imagining all kinds of interesting reasons why he would make up something like that. Maybe he had a trust fund, or an ex-wife who paid him alimony. He didn't seem to be involved with anything illegal. She dialed Frank's number. Earl Johnson had given her the perfect excuse to call him.

The number rang and rang, then finally went dead. She tried it again, with the same result. No message. No voice mail. She was half-tempted to turn around and go back to his apartment and wake him, or leave a message taped to his door, in case he was still incommunicado. She kept driving. She hated being late for class, and she *had* sent

Earl Johnson off chasing his tail. Today was a full day, two Elementary Psych classes at Fullerton, and an Adolescent Behavior class way up at Cal State, Northridge. She wouldn't get home until late this evening. Time to tell Frank about Earl Johnson then. She was going to beat on his door until he answered, make a complete ass of herself if she had to. Frank would probably laugh, tell her she had just turned away his big windfall. She smiled, dialed his number again with one hand.

39

"Krino says he can move all the Viagra-crank combo we can deliver," said Arturo, seated at the table in the back room of the Huntington Beach store. "Jason is late again, second time this month." He shut his new PDA, looked across at Clark. "Business is slow, according to him, but I think Vlad and I should pay Jason a visit tomorrow."

Vlad fidgeted beside him.

Arturo pulled a manila envelope out of his suit jacket, tossed it to Missy. "Forty-seven thousand. Everybody except Jason is up-to-date."

Missy slipped the envelope into her purse without opening it.

"I've been asking around about Guillermo, but he's gone completely underground," said Arturo. "I've heard some rumors that don't make a lot of sense. I'll keep checking."

"You do that, dude," said Clark.

"We can handle whatever Guillermo is up to, right, Vlad?" said Arturo.

Vlad didn't answer.

Arturo reached into the box of powdered doughnuts on the table. "I shouldn't do this."

"Then don't," said Vlad. It felt like wires inside him were sparking.

Arturo looked at him. "Easy for you to say. I'd kill for your metabolism." He put the doughnut back, licked his fingers.

Cecil grabbed one of the doughnuts, took a big bite, powdered sugar drifting onto his pants. He had a new haircut, a flattop with the front waxed up. It made him look even more like a pig, a bristly red boar with nasty eyes.

Clark laid four Baggies on the table, pushed half of them to Arturo, half to Vlad. "Here's the latest product line. A new batch of neo-X, which should give a longer high, and a Vicodin analogue that's cheaper to make than the real thing. Tell them we want feedback by next week."

Arturo picked up the Baggies, looked at Vlad. "You sick again, *mi hermano?*"

Vlad had closed the store early, turned off the lights in front, and waited for Arturo to arrive. Missy and Clark were quiet, but Cecil was making jokes and doing karate moves like the fat Elvis. Vlad had begged them to give Arturo another chance, but Clark just shook his head, said for him to be ready for when Cecil brought Arturo his diet cola. "Cecil's going to shake up the can, so when Arturo pops the top, it foams all over," Clark said. "*That's* when you make your move. Arturo will be yelling and brushing soda off himself, and you just stand up, like you're going to help, and you shoot him. One bullet to the back of the head and we can move on. I can count on you, can't I, Vlad?"

"Why don't you come home with me when we're done here?" Arturo said to Vlad. "I'll have Fortuna make you some soup."

"Fetch us some cold drinks, Cecil," said Missy. "Maybe that will perk Vlad up."

"How's that new PDA working out for you?" asked Clark.

"They didn't want to exchange the old one," said Arturo, "but I made it clear that the customer is always right." He waved the PDA. "I spent half the morning inputting information: diet and workout program, calendar—"

"It's never too late," blurted Vlad.

They all stared at him; then Missy laughed, her voice hurting Vlad's ears.

"You talking about me and the stock market?" asked Arturo. "Trust me, it's too late to make it back. I'm into bonds now, strictly investment-grade corporates and T-bills. No risk for me. I got enough stress in my life."

"Everybody makes mistakes." Vlad tried to stand, to hustle Arturo out of the store, but his legs weren't working. It was if they belonged to someone else, someone he didn't know, someone who wanted to stay sitting. "What's important is to admit it."

"I admitted it." Arturo plucked a doughnut from the box. "That's why I'm in bonds. I'm no stock picker. You ask me, brokers are the biggest crooks there is. They ought to make dope legal and buying stocks a felony."

"Don't say that," Clark joked. "You're going to put us all out of business."

Cecil walked over from the refrigerator, his arms full of cans and bottles. He set an Évian in front of Missy, a Pepsi for Clark, Cherry Coke for Vlad, and a Diet Pepsi for Arturo.

"I don't drink Diet Pepsi, you idiot." Arturo tossed the can back to him. "Diet Coke. It's been Diet Coke since the first time you asked me. What's that been—two years, and you still can't remember? Doesn't *anything* penetrate that brain of yours?"

Missy laughed again, louder now, as Cecil sulked back to the refrigerator. She took a long drink from her bottled water, watching Vlad.

Clark's eyes were too bright. Arturo was going to know something was wrong.

"I hate that redheaded bastard," Arturo said to Missy. "I know he's your brother, but I can't stand him." He took a tiny bite of the doughnut, glanced at Vlad. "I'm only going to eat half of this, so don't give me that look."

"Have you ever seen *The Lion King*?" Vlad said to Arturo.

Arturo pushed the rest of the doughnut into his mouth.

"*The Lion King,*" said Vlad. "It's a cartoon movie. Haven't you ever watched it with your kids?"

"Diet *Coke.*" Cecil banged the can onto the table.

"I guess so," Arturo said to Vlad. He licked powdered sugar off his fingers.

"Remember how in *The Lion King* everybody blames Simba for killing his father in the stampede, even though it wasn't really his fault?" Vlad glanced at Clark. "See, it was *really* his bad uncle Scar who was responsible, but everyone blamed Simba. . . ."

"If you say so." Arturo picked up the can of Diet Coke, snapped it open. Diet Coke sprayed the table. "Son of a *bitch*." He jumped up, soda dripping off his chin, and backhanded Cecil, sent him flying. "You did that on purpose."

Vlad tried to stand, but his legs still wouldn't work. "Even though everyone thought Simba was guilty, they didn't kill him." He braced his hands against the tabletop, pushed himself upright. "I mean . . . Scar *wanted* to kill him, but the pride rules called for Simba to be exiled. . . ."

Arturo wiped soda off his jacket with angry sweeps of his hands.

"Simba was part of the pride," Vlad pleaded with Clark and Missy. "You don't kill a member of the pride just because they make a mistake, even if it's a big mistake. . . ."

Arturo shook out his handkerchief, dabbed at his face.

"You *exile* him, and then after a while, he gets to come back, and everybody is happy again." Vlad looked around the table. "That's how it works."

"This isn't *The Lion King*," said Clark.

"Yeah, Vlad, what are you talking about?" asked Arturo.

Cecil stepped behind Arturo, shoved a gun in his ear, a tiny gun, a lady's .22, and pulled the trigger.

It made such a small sound that Vlad thought at first that the gun had misfired. Then Arturo twisted away, took a step toward Vlad, and fell. Vlad pushed off from the table, slid onto the floor beside Arturo.

"Yes!" Cecil jabbed the gun at Arturo. "How's that feel, fucker? That penetrate *your* brain?"

Clark winced at the blood dripping from Arturo's ear. "Whoa."

Missy backed away from the table.

"Didn't think I could do it, did you?" Cecil said to Clark, waving the gun in the air. "Give the job to Vlad, give the job to Frank, but never even *think* about giving it to Cecil. Shit, I'm just *family*, right, so what do I know?"

Vlad cradled Arturo in his arms, singing to him, trying to revive him, but all the weight in Arturo's body was gone.

"Lookee here at your big tough hombre," crowed Cecil. "He don't look so tough now, does he, Clark? Pow. One shot, just like you asked for. So much for his fucking bulletproof clothes. Hey, man, anytime you want, you feel free to thank me."

Clark looked at Missy. "Who *knew*?"

"That's my gun," Missy said to Cecil. "You didn't ask if you could take it."

"You *always* underestimated me," Cecil said to Missy. "Vlad's standing around jabbering about cartoons, and *I'm* the go-to guy." He pretended to fan the little semiauto. "Fucking stone killer, right under your noses, but you never even noticed."

Vlad rocked Arturo. In movies, men always talked before they died. They told their true feelings, and gave messages for their families. In movies, men said it didn't hurt, or sometimes that they felt cold, but Arturo had died without saying a word. Vlad hung his head, feeling the life drain out of him, too.

"Things are going to be different *now*," Cecil said, out of breath, pointing the gun from one to the other. "I want . . . I want my *own* damn car, and my own credit card, too. I want . . . I want a plasma-screen TV in my room, and . . . and . . . I want a *big* fucking gun."

"Bag Arturo up before he bleeds all over the place," Missy said. "We're going to have to scrub the floor down. There's ammonia in the bathroom for the floor and—"

"Don't look at me," said Cecil. "*Vlad* gets the shit job for a change."

Missy rubbed her temples as if she had a headache. "Vlad, bag Arturo up. *Please?*"

Vlad shook his head.

Clark took another sip of Pepsi. "Here we go. Nothing is ever simple."

Cecil sauntered over to Vlad, looked down at him. "My sister told you to do something, *bitch*." He poked Vlad in the forehead with the .22. It looked like a toy gun, but it left a red ring on Vlad's white skin. "You hear me?"

"Back off, Cecil," said Clark.

Vlad looked past Cecil. "What am I going to tell Arturo's wife and children?"

"Don't tell them anything," said Missy. "The plan stays the same. We pack Arturo in with the clothes, and then take him to the incinerator tomorrow morning. His wife knows better than to check up on him for a few days. By then . . . he's just smoke."

"You said we were going to talk to him," said Vlad.

"You talked to him," said Cecil, moving on the balls of his feet, as if he were onstage. "You talked to him *your* way, and I talked to him *mine.*" He aimed the gun at Vlad. "Now do what my sister told you, before I fucking talk to you, too."

"You're not going to turn Arturo into smoke," Vlad said to Missy.

"Put the gun down, Cecil," said Clark. "We're all friends here."

"Bull*shit,*" said Cecil.

"Cecil, you do what Clark says," said Missy. "Go on, give me my gun back."

"No fucking way," said Cecil. "I told you before. Everything is different now. Cecil don't fetch and carry no more. Get used to it."

"I'll take care of Arturo," said Vlad. "I'll give him a proper funeral."

"Vlad . . . dude, it's got to be done like we planned," said Clark.

"Get your ass up. I don't want to tell you again." Cecil posed with the gun, pointing it out vertically and horizontally at Vlad, making gunshot sounds. "You want me to pop *him,* too, Clark? I'll fucking do it. This killing thing is no big deal. You get used to it real fast, that's the God's honest truth. I think I got me a natural aptitude."

"Give me my *gun,* Cecil," ordered Missy.

Cecil whirled on her. "I *told* you. Everything is—" The gun went off, and Missy gave a little cry, sat down in the chair.

"Missy?" said Clark. "Missy!"

"I didn't do anything," said Cecil.

Pink liquid ran out of Missy's right eye and down her cheek.

"Look what you done," Cecil said to Vlad. "You distracted me."

Clark clutched at Missy, but she flopped onto the floor. He stood over her, calling her name, howling like he had been the one shot, but she didn't move. Just like Arturo: One minute they were alive, and then next minute they were gone, and all the shouting didn't make a bit of difference.

"This is *your* fault," Cecil said to Vlad, so angry that he was sweating. "*You* did it." He shot Vlad. Shot him again. And again.

Vlad barely felt it. He brushed powdered sugar from the doughnut off Arturo's lips.

40

Thorpe watched from an outside table at the Los Flores Taqueteria as Paulo Rodriguez made a loop through the park across the street. Every minute or so, Paulo would pass into view, bent low over the handlebars like a fighter pilot, his teeth bared in delight. He had customized the bike Thorpe had left for him, adding streamers from the handlebars and about a dozen reflectors interspersed among the front and back spokes. A tiny Mexican flag hung from the seat, flapping as he sped away.

At the side of the path, his mother sat on a bench, chatting with two other women, string bags of fruit and snacks in their laps. It was early evening, still light, and they moved unhurriedly, nodding their heads in agreement, occasionally waving away the hovering insects. As Paulo sped toward her, his mother chided him to slow down, and he slammed on the brakes, locked the back wheel, and skidded to a stop in front of her. She wagged a finger, and he hung his head, more to hide his grin than from shame. She slipped a section of orange into his mouth and sent him on his way.

Thorpe crunched into his second pork taco, adding more hot sauce in between bites, juice dribbling at the corner of his mouth. The lemonade was fresh and ultrasweet. He watched Paulo and his mother and tried not to think. His wake-up had gotten Betty B and Ray Bishop killed. . . . He had to take small pleasures where he found them.

A trio of languid homeboys sat at an adjoining table, slender teenagers with lupine faces, their skinny arms wrapped with tattoos. They glanced at him from time to time, not hostile, but not friendly, either, just keeping track of him. He listened to them discuss him in Spanish, their voices high and musical. One thought he was a narc. One thought he was *la Migra*. The third, the smallest, an overgrown child with a sunken chest and—from the way he regularly touched his pocket, reassuring himself—the only one strapped, thought they should take him down and find out.

Good time to be driving an armored car. Thorpe called Danny Hathaway. He answered on the second ring. It was noisy, wherever he was. "It's me," said Thorpe.

"Frankie!"

"Where are you?"

"Vegas, land of milk and honey. I'm at the Bellagio, jackpots going off around me like the Fourth of July. I drove straight out here after I left you. The Town Car gets lousy mileage, but it's one sweet ride."

"I wanted to give you my new cell phone number."

"I haven't got any paper." The clanging of slot machines interrupted Hathaway. "My first night in town, I hit the blackjack tables, hit them *hard,* man. I ended up with a stack of thousand-dollar chips bigger than Ron Jeremy's dick. You got to visit, Frank. They comped me a suite."

Thorpe smiled. "I'll call you soon."

"Everything work out with Clark and Missy? You got them tearing at each other's throats?"

That was a hard one to answer. He must have convinced Missy that Arturo had sold them out, because this morning she had transferred the hundred thousand dollars to his offshore account. Thorpe had already wired the money to Ray Bishop's wife in Pennsylvania. Right after he had called the Laguna PD and told them there was a body in the kitchen of the house on Pearl Street. Thorpe might have convinced Missy, but that was no guarantee.

Thorpe watched Paulo's mother eat fish crackers from a Ziploc bag, eat them one at a time, daintily. Her head was covered with a yellow scarf dotted with red roses. She kept turning slightly, following Paulo's progress through the park, keeping up her end of the conversation with her companions the whole time.

"Frank? Did it work out?"

"I'm going to call and make sure. I've got a date with the Engineer in a few days, and I want to have my mind clear."

"Kill him for me, will you?"

"Roger that." Thorpe hung up, then called Missy. The phone rang for a long time, and when it was finally answered, it wasn't Missy. "Cecil?"

"Just the man I was hoping to talk to," said Cecil, oddly chipper.

"Let me talk to Missy."

"Lose the attitude, Frank. I'm a professional myself now."

Thorpe rolled his eyes. "Can I speak to her?"

Cecil sniffed. "Missy's dead."

Thorpe stared at the phone.

"It was an accident. Vlad distracted me."

Distracted? Thorpe watched Paulo taking another lap. "You killed your sister?"

"I told you already. It wasn't my fault."

"Is Arturo there?"

Cecil cackled. "DOA. That was one uppity Mexican, but I put him down like a bag of warm shit. You *got* to get over here and see what I done, Frank. It's pretty impressive, if I do say so myself."

Thorpe couldn't speak. He had expected Vlad to get the assignment, but never Cecil.

"Practice makes perfect, Frank. It's true. You wouldn't believe the trouble I had running down that old bitch, but tonight, facing off against Arturo and Vlad, I was in the *zone*. Come over and see for yourself. I'm the real deal now. We got a lot to talk about, you and me. I'm at the Huntington Beach store."

Cecil had killed Betty B. Thorpe looked past the homeboys at the nearby table, still trying to picture Cecil as the angel of death. Arturo was dead, and Missy, and maybe Clark and Vlad, for all he knew. That should be enough. Enough to make up for Ray Bishop getting his head hammered in. More than enough. Thorpe watched Paulo make another pass through the park, standing on the pedals, hollering.

"Come on by, Frank. I don't know what I'm going to do if you don't."

Thorpe clicked off the phone and started for his car.

Paulo drove past, making his loop-de-loop, racing with another boy about his age, the two of them barking like dogs as they pedaled. Paulo glanced at Thorpe but didn't react, didn't recognize him. Thorpe smiled. That was as close to a happy ending as he could expect.

41

"Welcome to the scene of the crime." Cecil grinned as he waved Thorpe inside. "Check it out."

Thorpe stepped into the back room of the surf shop, closed the alley door. A folding cot was set up in the far corner of the room, Vlad's clothes strewn on the floor. Missy sprawled beside a table, her elegant black dress hiked, one of her high heels snapped off. There was a hole through her eye. Vlad sat on the floor, his back against the sofa. Arturo lay on his back beside him, hands neatly folded across his suit jacket. Other than the fact that one ear was caked with dried blood, he looked as if he were resting. The room smelled like molten copper.

"*That's* the only downside of the evening." Cecil pointed at Missy's body. He had two guns shoved into the front of his pants like Billy the Kid, Arturo's machine pistol and a small .22 semiauto. "Damn Vlad got me all upset and threw off my rhythm. Pissed me off, I'll tell you that much."

Vlad's complexion was even whiter now, waxy and translucent, a road map of fine blue veins visible under the skin. Thorpe realized that the dark spots on Vlad's shirt weren't part of the tie-dyed pattern. "You've been shot."

Vlad nodded.

"I told you, Frank, he pissed me off," said Cecil. "I won't stand for that kind of thing. Not anymore. What we got here is a fucking new day for Cecil. You and me going to work together. You best understand that."

Thorpe laughed.

"What's so funny?" asked Cecil.

Thorpe made eye contact with Vlad. "Do you remember the art dealer Missy used? The one who sold her—"

"Douglas Meachum," said Vlad. "He was at the party. He saw me standing in the corner, shaking . . . but Meachum just walked past. You were the only one who stopped to help."

"I asked you a question, Frank," said Cecil.

Thorpe ignored him but kept track of him with his peripheral vision. Any sudden moves . . . "Arturo went to Meachum's house a few days ago," he said to Vlad. "He went there and killed a man. Were you with him?"

Vlad's face was blank. "Arturo didn't kill anyone at Meachum's house."

"The man's name was Ray Bishop," said Thorpe. "Arturo beat him to death with a claw hammer. Were you there when he did it?"

Vlad scratched his head, and tufts of white-blond hair drifted down. "I wasn't there. Neither was Arturo. He would have told me if he had done that."

Thorpe stared at him. Vlad was a lot of things, but he wasn't a liar. "You're sure?"

Vlad nodded. "We were partners."

Thorpe turned as Cecil reached for the machine pistol in his belt. "Don't do that."

Cecil gripped the butt of the gun but didn't draw it. His face was incandescent. "I don't take orders anymore."

"Okay," said Thorpe. Vlad coughed, and Thorpe glanced over, saw blood bubbling from his lips. Thorpe took his eyes off Cecil for only an instant, but it was long enough.

"I'm willing to forgive you for putting my head through the wall that time at the house," said Cecil, the pistol steady on Thorpe's chest. His knuckles were raw. "I'm willing to forgive and forget, because I'm a little shorthanded now, and I'm going to need some help when I take over the operation."

"Clark might have something to say about that."

"I'm not worried," sneered Cecil. "You should have seen him, blubbering like a baby, talking to Missy like he expected her to answer. When he left, he told me he was going to grab his board and paddle out until it didn't hurt no more." He shook his head. "Hey, she was my sister, but you don't see me dying about it. You got to move on, right, Frank?"

"Easier said than done."

"Well, I said it and I done it." Cecil's finger curled around the trigger of the machine pistol. It was all he could do to hold himself back. "You going to work for me or not?"

"I don't even want to be near you."

Cecil grinned, pulled the trigger. Nothing happened, of course.

Thorpe stepped closer, pulled the pistol away, and swatted him across the head with it. "You have to flip off the safety."

Cecil groaned, rolled across the floor, holding his head in his hands.

Thorpe turned to Vlad. "If you and Arturo didn't kill Bishop . . ." He was thinking out loud, and not liking the answer he kept coming up with.

"Frank?" Vlad nodded toward Cecil.

Thorpe flipped the safety off, pointed the pistol at Cecil. "Don't do it."

Cecil stared up at Thorpe, the .22 in his hand. "You scared? I'm not."

"Put the gun down and get out of here," said Thorpe.

"I don't think so," said Cecil.

"Go home," said Thorpe. "It's over. We can stop now. All of us."

"I don't want to stop. This ain't the old Cecil you're talking to."

"I don't want to kill you," said Thorpe.

"Look at you, all serious and concerned." Cecil showed his bad teeth. "I don't need you after all, Frank. Like I told Missy, I got an aptitude." His finger tightened on the trigger.

Thorpe shot him three times, knocked Cecil backward in a spray of blood. Ears ringing, Thorpe wiped the machine pistol clean and tossed it onto the table. He felt an overwhelming heaviness, as though the room were caving in on him. He had been wrong about everything.

"I know what Cecil meant," said Vlad. "It's hard to stop once you start."

Thorpe nodded. "Sometimes I think it's nearly impossible . . . but we have to try." He moved closer. "I should drop you off at a hospital."

Vlad smoothed the lapels of Arturo's suit. "The first time Arturo saw me, he crossed himself. I didn't understand, so I waved back. It was a silly mistake. A lucky mistake." He smiled. "We bumped into each other at Los Angeles Airport, and when I waved, he thought I was a courier from the Bucharest syndicate. I had worked for the syndicate before, done some *cold* work for them, but I had left to come to America. I wanted to see cowboys. Arturo and I stood in the airport, talking and watching the luggage circling round and round, and by the time my bag arrived, Arturo said he didn't care if the syndicate hadn't sent me, he had work for me." He glanced at Thorpe. "What's wrong?"

"Just . . . coincidence." Thorpe shook his head. "All of our planning and calculation and research, but ultimately our lives pivot on a missed signal or a man in too much of a hurry."

"Have you ever seen *The Lion King,* Frank?"

"Ah . . . yeah, sure. I like that movie."

"I told Clark and Missy that they didn't have to kill Arturo. They could have *exiled* him instead."

"Like Simba?"

"I *knew* you would understand." Vlad sighed. "I wish Arturo had just asked me for money, instead of going to work for Guillermo. I have over three million dollars in my closet, I would have given it to him."

"You have three million dollars in cash and you're living in the back of a store?"

"Arturo used to say that, too." Vlad patted Arturo's shoulder. "He told me to buy myself some clothes, a sports car, a house, a woman . . . but I never wanted any of those things. I never wanted anything at all. If I had found something I really wanted, I would have spent every penny . . . but I never did." He trembled. "I just wished Arturo had asked me. I would have given him all the money he needed." His shirt was soaked now. "Arturo was too proud to ask for help."

"Arturo didn't betray you. He wasn't working for Guillermo."

"Clark and Missy said he was. They had proof."

"I set Arturo up." Strange the relief Thorpe felt telling the truth. "I was the one who betrayed you all."

Vlad peered at him. "Why?"

Thorpe shook his head.

"*Why,* Frank? What did we ever do to you?"

"Ray Bishop was a friend of mine, and I thought . . . I thought Arturo had killed him. I thought I was protecting the Meachums." Thorpe looked around the room, taking in the dead. "I knew the kinds of things you and Arturo had done. Somebody had to step in . . . and that was me."

"I see." Vlad stared at him with those pale blue eyes. "Some of the things Arturo and I did . . . they made me sick. They gave me nightmares. Arturo and I, we did bad things, terrible things, but we didn't kill your friend, and Clark told us not to touch the Meachums." One eye was rimmed with blood. "Are you going to kill me now, Frank?"

"No."

"Arturo is dead. There's no one for me now."

"I'm not going to kill you."

Vlad's hands twitched in his lap. "The scientists used to talk about these *things* they created . . . these cellular catalysts. They said their best work was sleeping inside us, just waiting until we needed it, but the scientists . . ." He looked at Thorpe, forced his hands to be still. "The scientists, they didn't really know what we needed."

"Let me take you to a hospital."

A red tear slid down Vlad's cheek. "I've seen enough doctors."

42

Thorpe was halfway through the front gate before he spotted the man sitting on his front stoop reading a newspaper. The paper hid his face, but Thorpe recognized the posture, legs splayed, the same way he had sat when they were crouched in the underbrush, hiding from Lazurus's men. It was the Engineer.

"You coming in, Frank?" the Engineer said from behind the newspaper. The same voice that Thorpe had heard while lying in the plastic surgeon's office, flat and uninflected, not a trace of the European accent from the running track. "If you're going to rabbit, there's no need to sprint. I'm too out of shape to chase you."

Thorpe checked the street, checked the windows of the other apartments. He shut the gate behind him, heard it lock, then crossed toward his front door.

The Engineer folded the paper, stood up, fleshier than Thorpe remembered, his face newly sunburned. He wore dark pants, a short-sleeved dress shirt, and a clip-on necktie. Good camouflage. "I don't know if you're a comics fan," he said, tucking the paper under one arm, "but that *Dilbert* still cracks me up. Nice to see—"

Thorpe drove the heel of his hand under the Engineer's chin, snapped his head back, and knocked him onto the grass. The newspaper fluttered in the breeze. Thorpe waited, but there was no sign of Gregor, or anyone else the Engineer might have brought along.

The Engineer groaned, tried to sit up, then lay back down again.

Thorpe patted him down for weapons. Nothing.

"You . . . you *still* mad about that bit of fun at the safe house?" gasped the Engineer. "I thought we were past that." He rolled over onto his belly, got to his hands and knees. "You going to hit me again? If you are, do it now, so I won't have so far to fall."

Thorpe watched him.

The Engineer got slowly to his feet. He spit, his tongue sliding across his mouth. "You chipped my front tooth." He straightened his necktie. "I got back a few days early and wanted to surprise you. Black's Beach is nice, but you *really* don't want to see me naked, Frank." He stuck his hand out. "No hard feelings."

"Shut up."

"You think you're the only one with a grudge?" The Engineer pouted. "I'm the wounded party here. *You're* the one who stepped into my situation with Lazurus. I spent months setting that up, and you and Kimberly trashed it in a few weeks. If anyone is owed an apology—"

Thorpe backhanded him.

The Engineer stayed on his feet, spitting blood now. "Okay . . . okay. Let's agree to disagree. We can do business. That's all that matters."

"Where's Gregor?"

The Engineer dabbed at his mouth. "That's another sad story. Poor Gregor. I offered him a management opportunity, but, in the end, he just wasn't able to meet my exacting standards. In spite of my efforts, he was just another load of meat."

"How did you find me?"

"Secrets are the basis of any relationship, Frank. You keep yours and I'll keep mine. We should be focusing on the future. I have my contacts and suppliers; you have yours. We don't have to be friends, but it would be a terrible waste not to become partners."

Thorpe had spent months trying to find the Engineer, and now that he had him, he didn't know what to do. He had assumed there would be some sort of confrontation, with Gregor present, and plenty of the ultraviolence. Thorpe had assumed he would kill them both, or die trying, but this . . . Killing him now would be murder. Turning the Engineer over to the police was tempting. The Engineer's old shop would cover up any crimes he had committed on their watch, but maybe he had gotten careless lately. Perhaps he was wanted, fingerprints and eyewitnesses waiting to put him away. Warren could hack some police databases, see what came up. It wouldn't be as satisfying as killing the son of a bitch, but after the scene with Vlad, Thorpe had had enough of death.

"What are you thinking, Frank?"

"Trying to decide what to do with you."

The Engineer pursed his lips. "You could treasure me for the rare and unique individual that I am."

"That's not one of my options."

The Engineer laughed. "Come on, let's get rich and have some laughs. That's what it's all about, isn't it?"

Thorpe checked the front door to his apartment. The tiny bit of clear wax pressed against the upper jamb was uncracked, undisturbed. He opened the door, grabbed the Engineer by the back of the neck, and pushed him inside. Thorpe stepped in, crouched, the 9-mm sweeping from side to side.

The Engineer looked up from the floor. "You're not very trusting."

Thorpe locked the door behind him and went through the house, the gun cocked. He checked the bathroom, the closets, even looked under the bed. The windows were still locked from the inside, their own wax seals intact. They were alone.

"Can I get up now?" The Engineer fingered his necktie. *"Please?"*

Thorpe beckoned him.

The Engineer awkwardly got to his feet. "That's . . . better." He held his hands out, losing his balance.

Thorpe reached for him. It was a reaction, not a thought. As he steadied him, the Engineer snatched off his tie, jammed it under Thorpe's nose. Thorpe heard a faint crackle of breaking glass, and his knees buckled. When Thorpe awoke, he was seated in his leather chair, he had a ringing headache, and he and the Engineer weren't alone.

Gregor squinted at him, over three hundred pounds of ugly, his belly flopping out of the purple jogging suit. The Cyrillic tattoos ringing his thick neck seemed stretched, as though he had swallowed a Great Dane. His face was puffy and scabbed over, his left ear bandaged. "He is awake."

"It's a real mind fuck, isn't it, Frank?" said the Engineer.

Thorpe stared back at Gregor and knew that all the bad thoughts that had come to him while listening to Vlad were true. Arturo hadn't killed Bishop. Arturo had killed more than enough to deserve killing, but he hadn't killed Ray Bishop.

"Hey!" Gregor kicked Thorpe in the shin. "He's *talking* to you."

"Yeah, it's a real mind fuck." Thorpe was still weak from the anesthetic the Engineer had used on him, so numb that he had barely felt Gregor's kick. The only sensation he had was fear. He had been under fire, had jumped out of planes and crawled through tunnels where the darkness was thick with spiders, but now, sitting in his own living room, it was all Thorpe could do to stop his teeth from chattering. He wasn't afraid of dying. He had long since given up hope of a cozy old age, surrounded by grandchildren. It was losing to the Engineer that he was afraid of. Losing to the Engineer *again.*

"What is it, Frank?" asked the Engineer. "You look like you have something on your mind."

"I was just wondering what happened to Gregor? Did he try stopping a train with his face?"

"A few bumps and bruises, but I think it adds to his charm."

Thorpe smiled. "Looks like it must have hurt."

The Engineer pulled up another chair. They were almost knee-to-knee now. "Don't bother feeling under the cushion. We found the pistol you stashed. Found the one in the sofa, too. I like the way you plan ahead, the way you try and anticipate the worst. That's very laudable." He leaned closer.

Thorpe looked into the Engineer's eyes and thought of Vlad. Vlad had killed at least as many men as the Engineer, had gathered up lives by the handful, but his blue eyes were dim and dying, the sad eyes of a lost boy. The Engineer's eyes were dark and mature in their evil, full of a grimy eagerness for the work.

"In all your planning, though, did you ever foresee your present situation?" asked the Engineer. "Your hidden weapons found, the boogeyman inside your door, sitting right next to you, in fact, close enough to kiss." He smiled. "I guess what I'm asking, Frank, is did you ever imagine things going *this* far wrong?"

"So far so good."

"Indeed," said the Engineer. "I haven't hit you, haven't tied you up or restrained you in any way, haven't brutalized you. We're just a couple of men of the world having a talk." He smiled. "Since I quit the shop, things haven't gone as well as I'd hoped. Mistakes and miscalculations were made. I'm not complaining, but your personnel file was like an answer to a prayer. Some very interesting notations in that file, suggestions that you had been less than a loyal employee. Money-laundering takedowns that came up short, warehouses that turned up empty—you had some nice paydays."

Thorpe wiggled his toes, spread the fingers of his hands. Progress. Hope was the only antidote to fear, and he clung to that hope. He was going to get out of this. He *was.*

"You walked away with a bundle, Frank. I like a man with initiative."

Thorpe's head still throbbed, but he was breathing deeper now. "Ancient history."

The Engineer shook his head. "Not eggs-*actly,*" he said, sounding just like Arnold Schwarzenegger.

Gregor chuckled, fists clenching and unclenching.

The Engineer beamed at Thorpe. "I like to amuse Gregor with my imitations: Irish brogue, Eddie Murphy, laid-back surfer, Boston Brahmin, Valley Girl. . . . He's particularly fond of my Bill Clinton: 'Hilly Mae, put down that rollin' pin, darlin'.'"

"*Very* fond of Mr. Bill Clinton," agreed Gregor.

"Of course, you're already familiar with my Italian intellectual—"

"Are we going to work out our deal? This shit is boring me."

"Well, we can't have that," said the Engineer, sleepy eyes glittering. He walked over to the desk. Thorpe's laptop was already turned on. "What's your password?"

Thorpe thought about it. "Onyx three two three."

The Engineer tapped in the password, smiled as the operating system opened up. "I'm glad you didn't make me ask you again," he said, ripping through the files. "You'd be surprised how many people think they need to put on a show of resistance. I'm not sure if they're trying

to impress me, or ministering to some ego need of their own. . . ." He
stared at the screen. "An empty address book? How do you keep in
touch?"

"I'm a lousy correspondent."

"What I'm looking for are your business contacts, your connections—buyers and sellers, all the little people you use and abuse. That's
what *you* bring to the table."

"What are you bringing?"

"Always so flippant, so self-controlled." The Engineer whipped the
mouse, searching through Thorpe's files. "The only time I heard you
lose your cool was after you had left the safe house—you were getting
medical attention, if I remember correctly. You sounded scared. I bet
you're scared now . . . probably telling yourself to hang on, stay strong,
being a regular cheerleader for the home team." He glanced at Thorpe,
then back at the screen. "Three bank accounts. What are the pass-
words?" He typed as Thorpe told him, clucked with disappointment a
few moments later. "There's not nearly enough here to retire on, Frank.
At this rate, you're going to be collecting aluminum cans while you
lug around your prostate." He turned his head. "Where's the rest of it?"

"I had some miscalculations myself."

"I don't believe you."

Thorpe hesitated, thinking, but not taking too long, just maybe
long enough to indicate that he was arguing with himself and that the
Engineer had won. "Sorry, other than a storage locker full of cash and
bricks of cocaine, I'm flat broke."

The Engineer watched Thorpe, then finally shut the computer
down and handed it to Gregor. "I'll examine this at my leisure." He sat
down across from Thorpe again. "Where exactly is this storage locker
of yours?"

"You working for the IRS now?" Thorpe stretched, used the opportunity to glance out the window. Late evening now, the courtyard
empty, the sound of stereos and TVs playing in the distance. He hoped
Claire wasn't at home.

The Engineer smiled. "She's not here, if you're interested."

"Who?" Thorpe didn't turn away from the Engineer's smile, but he felt the blow. A light blow, a love tap, but it brought the fear back, worse than before.

"Claire. Lovely woman. A little *mature* for my tastes, but feisty."

"My neighbor?"

"Oh, more than your neighbor, much more, if my information is correct. Mrs. Kinsley and I had a nice chat this afternoon at the park. She's the one who let me in the gate. Made me some wretched tea while I waited for you. Sweet old lady, but her kitchen needs a good scrubbing. They get old, they lose their sense of smell. I was about to cancel her ticket, when she got a phone call and had to dash. Mrs. Kinsley says you and Claire have the look. You know the look, Frank. Mrs. Kinsley got all warm and fuzzy when she talked about the two of you, said she was eighty-three years old but that she still remembered that look."

"I threw a fuck into Claire once or twice. You want to make something of that, go ahead."

"That's rather unchivalrous of you. I met Claire this morning, showed her your photograph. She said you looked familiar. That's all, *familiar.* Then she told me you had moved away, moved to Los Alamitos because it had better freeway access. Wasn't that wonderful? It's the details that sell a lie. Having a woman willing to lie for you is one thing, but a woman who lies for you *well,* oh my, Frank . . . you truly are a lucky man."

Thorpe shrugged. The Engineer's indolent gaze was eating a hole in him.

"Here's my dilemma," said the Engineer. "I know you can be useful, and I dearly want your goods, but on the other hand, I'm still upset with you for that business with Kimberly. I can be petty and vindictive. I'm working on it, but I want you to be aware of my failings."

"Maybe you can get some kind of therapy."

"I did a seminar for a foreign security agency several years ago." The Engineer tugged at his socks, stood up. "I tried to impress upon them that torture, *physical* torture, as a means of extracting information is very inefficient. When the information is needed fast, it's even more so. By contrast, my methods never fail. Never, Frank, not once. The head of security listened, but I'm not sure he truly understood."

Thorpe nodded. He had no idea what Claire's teaching schedule was.

"Imagine this scenario. I want your cooperation, but you resist. Now, I can have Gregor start snapping your fingers and toes, but there's a problem with that. At a certain point, when the pain becomes too severe, you pass out." The Engineer paced back and forth. "So all you have to do is tough it out, knowing if I go too far, you're unconscious. Even if you *do* talk, how can I be sure you're telling me the truth?"

"Why don't you try a nice dinner and a movie?" Thorpe heard the front gate squeak.

The Engineer peeked through the curtains. "Oh goody, Frank. It's your little fuck toy."

Thorpe jumped up, but Gregor punched him in the solar plexus, dropped him hard. Thorpe lay on the floor, twitching. He heard Claire's footsteps on the sidewalk, heard her ring the bell. Heard her call his name.

The Engineer got down on the floor next to Thorpe. "Should I get that?"

"No," Thorpe gasped.

"Lazurus looked at the photos for a long time, then he took the blowtorch and burned them up," whispered the Engineer, mimicking the voice he had used in the park when Thorpe tried to squeeze him. "First he burned the photographs . . . then . . . then, he burned the broker." He smiled at Thorpe. "It's the catch in the voice that I was most proud of. That's what made you a believer. Do you remember what you said to me then?"

Claire knocked harder.

"You said, 'That's a sad story, and when this is over, we'll sit down with some herb tea and have a good cry.' *That's* what you told me."

"Damn it, Frank, open the door," said Claire. "I know you're in there. It's important."

The Engineer's lips brushed Thorpe's ear. "Why don't we invite her in to have some herb tea with us? It's rude not to, don't you think?"

"I'll take you . . . to the locker."

"Promise? Cross your heart and hope to die?"

"Yes." Thorpe listened to Claire's retreating footsteps.

"If you're not telling the truth, we're going to come back for her," said the Engineer, using his own voice again. "I'll make you watch the whole thing. The *whole* thing, every minute of it. You wouldn't believe what I'm capable of when I put my heart and soul into it, Frank."

Thorpe needed help to get to his feet.

43

"I missed driving." The Engineer sat behind the wheel of the big Buick sedan. "The worst part of the role I played with Lazurus was having to be chauffeured around all the time. Gregor has his uses, but he's not very good company."

Gregor grunted from the backseat.

Thorpe stared straight ahead, the passenger seat slightly sprung from regularly supporting Gregor's weight. He coughed, tried not to struggle against the leather belt around his neck, the belt binding him to the steel rails of the Buick's headrest, giving him not more than two or three inches of slack. He hooked a finger into the leather, tugged without effect. "You could loosen this thing."

"Yes, I could," said the Engineer.

Thorpe carefully turned his head as they stopped for a red light. He could see a car in the next lane, a Plymouth van with a woman talking on a cell phone, too busy to notice him. It probably wouldn't have mattered if she had, since the belt looked like a collar. He was just glad they had slipped out of his apartment without being spotted by Claire. If she had come out to greet him, she would have been in the back with Gregor.

"How much farther, Frank?" asked the Engineer.

Thorpe's mouth was dry.

Gregor jerked on the belt. "Speak, horsey."

Thorpe coughed, tore at the belt with both hands. "A few more miles."

"Gregor is a man of simple pleasures," said the Engineer. "Most of them cruel."

Thorpe wheezed.

"Comfortable?" asked the Engineer.

Gregor jerked at the belt again.

Thorpe gasped, arms flailing.

"Sit back and enjoy the ride, Gregor," said the Engineer. "Frank's not going anywhere."

The backseat upholstery groaned as Gregor settled in.

"You could learn something from this experience," said the Engineer, expansive, one hand on the wheel as he drove. "All the hard work you put in when you thought I was working for Lazurus, all the time you and Kimberly spent, just to make me cooperate willingly." He shook his head. "Yet, here we are, after just a few minutes of quiet conversation, and all you want to do is please me. You *do* want to please me, don't you?" He waited in vain for an answer. "There's no reason we both can't come away from this richer for the experience." He glanced at Thorpe with those sleepy eyes. "May I give you a bit of advice?"

"Oh, I'd welcome that."

"Your methods betray a certain . . . arrogance," said the Engineer. "Clever operators like you play a chess game with the target, following him around, moving your pieces into position. Suddenly, the man opens his eyes and he's in check. Now he has no choice but to move wherever you want him to." His mouth tightened. "Move into some safe house perhaps, with digital cameras everywhere, recording his every fart for posterity. That's not *my* way. I'm an artist, not a chess master. I simply find out what the target *loves*"—he licked his lips— "and I let my imagination soar."

"What do you love?" asked Thorpe.

"You just may find out, Frank."

"Stay on the PCH past Seal Beach." Thorpe croaked, his vocal cords bruised. "I'll tell you when to turn."

"I enjoy Southern California," said the Engineer. "I like the wealth and the women, the sunny days and the cool nights, but most of all, I like the absence of insects. No mosquitoes, no chiggers, no cockroaches. I grew up in South Florida in a home without air conditioning. The place was crawling with insects; all those little legs waving . . . you can't imagine what it was like. Roaches that fly, roaches the size of hummingbirds flying in your face when you turned on the light, and the sound of those papery wings . . . I used to check my bed every night, but there was always a surprise." He nodded at Thorpe. "What about you? Where did you grow up, Frank?"

"Is this the part where I realize that we're not really all that different, and we kind of sort of become best buddies?"

"How much farther?" snapped the Engineer.

Thorpe allowed himself a smile, pleased that he had annoyed the Engineer. Anything to knock him even slightly off balance. "I'm going to kill you. I'm going to kill the both of you."

The Engineer laughed. "How many times have we heard that before, Gregor?"

The belt jerked into Thorpe's throat, and Thorpe arched his back as Gregor slowly tightened his grip.

"It's not so easy to be brave without air, is it, Frank?" said the Engineer. "All those lofty emotions just go by the wayside."

Thorpe kicked at the dash, reached back for Gregor, and clawed at his face, dug his nails in. He heard the bodyguard howl, the belt tightening as Thorpe pulled at the leather, struggling to get a grip.

"That's enough, Gregor. I'm sure Frank has learned his lesson."

Thorpe gasped as Gregor eased off on the belt, snot running from his nose.

"You wouldn't believe the thoughts that run through my head sometimes," said the Engineer. "If I wasn't a morally strong person, they would drive me quite mad." He kept the Buick right at the legal limit. "The first time Claire got a look at me, I knew she didn't like me. It wasn't my innocuous pose she was responding to; she actually seemed to sense my true nature. Feminine intuition, Frank, it disgusts me. It allows them to take unfair advantage. Then, when I realized that she had lied to me, lied to protect you, I found myself possessed of a most extreme resentment. It almost clouded my judgment. I almost got into my car and followed her. My mental clarity prevailed, but still . . . I had such thoughts."

"We're almost there." Thorpe tried to slow his heart, but all the training in the world wouldn't have helped now.

"The storage locker is just the beginning," said the Engineer. "I want names and numbers, bank accounts and buried treasure. Search your memory. *Empty* yourself."

Gregor tightened the belt again.

"Let him breathe, Gregor," said the Engineer. "Suffocation is our most primal fear, Frank, more basic than our fear of falling. In the womb itself, we dread that slow strangulation—a kink in the soft umbilicus, and our pink spaceman's face turns blue, then black. All the interrogation equipment in the world, all the sharp instruments and sophisticated electronics . . . I find them irrelevant to the task. Just give me a plastic bag; that's all I require." He patted Thorpe's leg. "Imagine the lady Claire fighting for breath, twisting and struggling, hands flapping like a baby bird. . . . Trust me, Frank, you would tell me *anything* to bring her a single breath. You would even tell me the truth."

Thorpe stared straight ahead. It was another few blocks before he could speak without betraying his pain and frustration, without betraying his own small hopes. "At the next light, just past the water tower . . . take a left." They left the storefronts and restaurants lining the PCH. "Another left here."

They paralleled a nautical-themed housing development in Sunset Beach, the nearby marina brightly lighted, lined with small yachts and sailboats. A network of canals led out to the ocean, allowing the residents access to the open sea.

"Fancy neighborhood for a storage locker," said the Engineer.

"It's not located in a commercial storage complex—cops are always watching those for stolen goods. It's a private garage. I rent it by the year."

The Engineer nodded.

"The street comes to a T at the end of the block," said Thorpe. "Make a right at the dock and then follow the road along the canal."

As the Engineer slowed the big Buick to make the turn, Thorpe stuck out his left foot, jammed the accelerator to the floor. The engine raced, and the car shot straight ahead and over the walkway, the bottom scraping as they lurched over the seawall, briefly airborne. Thorpe lowered his window as the nose of the car hit the water, bobbed once or twice. A wave crested over the hood, and the car started sinking.

The Engineer tugged at the belt around Thorpe's neck. "You forget about *this,* Frank?"

"I haven't forgotten a thing," said Thorpe, his eyes locked on the Engineer as the water rose past their knees, seeing what he thought was just a hint of fear in the man now.

Gregor pushed at his door but couldn't budge it against the weight of the water. He tried to lower his window, got it halfway down before the electrical system shorted out. The water rose faster now, past the windows, filling the interior, splashing their feet, their knees, rising past their chests. Gregor screamed as the water rushed in, his head banging against the roof as the car slanted forward and settled onto the bottom.

The Engineer started to say something to Thorpe, but the water rushed over him.

The last of the air bubbled past Thorpe's face, tickling him as it percolated out his open window. He fought to stay calm, husbanding his last inhalation as the disturbed silt rose in a cloud. The water was clear and cold, but only fifteen or twenty feet deep. He could see the lights on the dock shimmering above them.

With the pressure equalized now, the Engineer slowly pushed his door open. He went to release his seat belt, but Thorpe laid his hand over the clip, made a fist, and the Engineer *knew,* fear blooming on that soft face like a poisonous anemone.

Gregor kicked at his door, but it was locked, and in his panic, he was jerking the handle in the wrong direction. More kicks, but he couldn't get any leverage. Buoyant as a whale, he bobbed around the backseat, struggling, using all his air. He beat his fists against the window, shattered the thick glass, and started wriggling through.

The Engineer tore at Thorpe's hand on the release buckle, mouthing something.

Thorpe hung on to the buckle as the Engineer's nails scratched him, the cold numbing the pain. There was a tiny flame in his lungs, but he could control it, keep it small. He thought of Claire, remembered the first morning he had awakened in her bed and seen her beside him.

Gregor was stuck halfway through the broken window, his vast middle too big to squeeze through, caught on the remnants of the safety glass at the bottom of the frame. The tiny chunks of glass were like baby teeth, and the more he struggled, the more the glass nibbled into him. Gouts of blood drifted through the interior of the car.

The Engineer lunged toward his own open door, gripped the jamb, strained to pull himself free, but his seat belt held him tight. Eyes wide now, he punched at Thorpe, hitting him in the face, but his blows were weak, slowed by the water.

Thorpe didn't try to defend himself—just let himself be hit, watching tiny bubbles pop out the sides of the Engineer's mouth like a broken strand of pearls. The Engineer kept beating at him, his eyes darting from side to side, but Thorpe stayed calm. Exertion used oxygen. So did fear.

The Engineer grabbed at something under his seat, pulled out a gun, but the weapon slipped out of his hands. Thorpe ignored the gun, just as he had ignored the punches, concentrating only on the buckle of the seat belt. The flame in his lungs was growing. Hard to keep it under control. The Engineer strained against him, his face contorted, thrashing wildly now, as though shot with electricity. They watched each other and Thorpe saw the light in the Engineer's eyes grow dimmer, saw the rage flare one final time and then go out. The Engineer's movements became fluid, racked with grace, his arms like seaweed on the tide.

Thorpe's chest was ablaze, head throbbing, spots dancing in front of his eyes. He didn't know what was funny, but it was all he could do to keep from laughing. He wanted to tell the joke to Claire. He fumbled at his seat belt, released it, his feet rising, his neck still affixed to the headrest. He braced himself, put both hands on the headrest, and lifted. It didn't budge. He felt sleepy. He thought maybe he should take a nap, then try again. *Bad* idea. He pushed at the rails of the headrest. It should have been easy.

Out of the corner of his eye, he could see Gregor, still lodged in the window, no longer struggling, his purple jogging suit rippling.

The cold worked its way deeper into Thorpe as he tugged at the headrest, slowly inching it up. He got his feet under him now, squatting on the seat, lifting with his hands and his legs. The headrest popped out of the seat. Free . . . free . . . free.

The Engineer watched him, dead eyes bulging.

Thorpe started out the window, felt a tug on his foot, looked back. It was shadowy in the car, paper and trash suspended in the murk, but he could see the Engineer's fingers bumping against his ankle, moving with the current, as though waving good-bye. Thorpe kicked away from him, squeezed out through the window, out and up to the light, the leather belt still around his neck, trailing the headrest.

44

Billy jerked awake, sat up in bed. He blinked at the darkness. "Hello, Frank."

"Hey, Billy."

Billy wore silk pajamas, red or black—Thorpe couldn't tell which—and he thought of Missy Riddenhauer in her silk robe the morning after the party, making snake sounds as she moved.

"You don't snore, Billy, not a bit, but you were talking to somebody in your sleep. What were you dreaming about?"

Billy forced himself to breathe.

"The things you were saying, the sound of your voice . . . was somebody chasing you?"

Billy's face was illuminated by the numerals of the digital clock beside his bed: 4:41. The bedroom was on the thirty-eighth floor, the penthouse. Billy had chosen the site for its isolation from the world below, but now it made him feel vulnerable. He smoothed the covers around his hips. "I don't know how you found me, but I'm glad to see you."

"If I didn't know better, I'd believe you."

"Be nice. I've sent you several e-mails. What's it been . . . a couple weeks since the Engineer and his bodyguard were pulled out of the water? I looked at Warren when the news came on, told him that no matter what the police determined, it was no accident. Congratulations, Frank. You must feel very gratified."

"I know it was you, Billy."

Billy traced the embroidered monogram on the pocket of his pajama top, reading it like braille in the darkness. The room smelled faintly of his cologne, some exotic blend he had personally prepared for him in Paris. "It all comes down to body chemistry, Frank," he had said when Thorpe had asked about it the first time.

"A couple days ago, I had lunch with Nell Cooper, Meachum's former assistant at the gallery," said Thorpe. "She *is* working at the Guggenheim, just like she wanted . . . but it's in the gift shop. She says it's just temporary, and I believe her."

"I've never met the woman, but I trust your judgment."

"Nell didn't feed the information about the fake Mayan art to Betty B. *You* did that, Billy."

"I saw an opportunity." Billy yawned. "I'd used Betty B in the past to float stories. The old shrew was very reliable. I had no idea she was going to get herself killed."

"No, I think you knew just what you were doing. I didn't know who Clark and Missy were when I flashed my fake ID, but you did. I have to give you credit: You did your research. It was just a wake-up, Billy. You made it something bigger. Something worse."

Billy hesitated, put off by the self-control in Thorpe's voice. He functioned best when the other party was off balance, angry or upset, but a soft voice was reason to worry. "Your wake-up was small and petty, no challenge at all for a man of your gifts."

"Yes, but it wasn't your wake-up. It was mine."

"Well, Frank, you could hardly expect me to put you back to work without first finding out if you were ready for the task. I had to put you through your paces. After what happened at the safe house . . . well, better men than you have lost their edge. I had to be certain."

"I was never going to work for you. I told you that at the bowling alley."

"People like us, Frank . . . we can't change who we are. We couldn't stop even if we wanted to."

"You should have believed me."

Billy reached toward the lamp on his nightstand.

"Leave the light off. I can see you just fine."

Billy complied, pulled the covers up, fuming.

"Hey, what's going on?" Warren stood in the doorway. Thorpe had heard him approaching down the hallway, trying to be quiet. "The hallway light's not working."

"Go away, Warren," said Billy. "We're quite all right."

"I heard voices. . . . I got worried about you."

"Warren . . . thank you for your concern, but I'm in no danger."

"That's not your decision," said Thorpe. "You *should* go back to bed, Warren."

"Frank? Is that you?" Warren peered into the darkness. "What are you doing here?" He took a step into the bedroom, stepped back out. "How did you get in? I got a gun."

"Go back to your room, Warren," said Thorpe. "Go back to your room, close the door, and put the gun back in the Tibetan nightstand."

"Say thank you to the nice man and leave, Warren," said Billy. *"Now."*

Warren hovered in the doorway, then gave up and walked quickly away.

"Are you *enjoying* yourself, Frank?"

"Not yet," said Thorpe.

"You should *thank* me for slipping Betty B the information." Billy was uneasy now, his pajamas rustling. "This pathetic crusade of yours, just to gain an apology to an injured child . . . it was beneath you. I upped the stakes. You should be grateful. I *saved* you."

"You didn't save Betty B. You didn't save Ray Bishop. They're dead." Thorpe still hadn't raised his voice.

"I don't even know who Ray Bishop is."

"Your loss, Billy."

A car horn blared in the distance, the sound mournful, echoing off the other buildings around them. Billy stirred in his bed. Thorpe seemed closer now. "Don't expect me to feel guilty. Some people pull the strings; the rest of the world have their strings pulled. You and I, Frank, we're the lucky ones. It didn't used to bother you."

"It bothers me now."

"You'll get over it."

"We're not saving the world anymore," Thorpe said gently. "We're not keeping nukes from terrorists, or separating racists from their bank accounts. We're just showing off."

Billy shivered, and he thought for a moment that Thorpe had opened a window, which was impossible, because the windows in the bedroom were sealed. "This is all quite irrelevant. You're *back;* that's all that matters. I rescued you from your doldrums and self-doubts. Perhaps it's asking too much for you to be grateful, but—"

"I can always tell when you're scared, Billy—you use the word *quite,* trying to maintain your reserve. You told Warren we were 'quite all right.' Now you tell me it's 'all quite irrelevant.' "

"Thank you for bringing it to my attention. I'll have to watch that in the future."

"Did you tell the Engineer where I lived?"

"Why would I help the Engineer? Granted, I was curious to see how the contest between the two of you played out, but if he needed my help to find you . . . well, what *value* would he be then?" Billy flinched. It felt like Thorpe was right beside him, sitting on the bed. "Sink or swim, that's the only choice any of us have."

"Oh, it's a little more complicated than that." Thorpe's voice seemed to come from a distant point in the room.

"What made you go looking for Nell Cooper? What made you suspect she wasn't the one who called Betty B?"

"Afraid you might have slipped up, Billy? Worried about any other of your loose ends?"

"My interest is purely academic. So . . . what was it?"

"You changed your brand of toothpaste. A special toothpaste for sensitive teeth. Your gums are receding and you *never* told me."

Billy glanced toward his bathroom before he could stop himself.

"Nearly a full tube. I hope you don't feel like you have to throw it away now."

Billy didn't move a muscle. "No need for that."

"I'll see you around."

"What does that mean? Frank?" Billy flipped on the light beside his bed, but he was alone. Quite alone.

EPILOGUE

Claire spotted him sitting in the back of the amphitheater about ten minutes before the end of her Intro to Psychology class and temporarily lost her place. She had been teaching this course for three years, could probably recite the syllabus from memory, but she stumbled over a description of Jung's collective unconscious. Maybe there was hope for Thorpe.

The last ten minutes, Claire was on autopilot, looking over, around, and through him. Then she passed out a study guide and dismissed the class. She rearranged her papers on the lectern as the hundred or so students closed their notebooks, chairs scraping as they filed out.

Thorpe got up, started toward her in the now-empty auditorium, nervous. He had rehearsed this moment for the last month, knowing that he was going to see her again, certain of it, but now he was standing there before her, and he didn't know what to say. "Claire . . . I know what you must be thinking—"

She slapped him across the face. "What was I thinking?"

He could feel her fingerprints on his cheek.

"You could have said good-bye," said Claire, still fuming. "I didn't even know you had moved out until a Salvation Army van started loading up your furniture."

"I didn't want to say good-bye. I just wanted to get away."

Her eyes were hot. "Then what are you doing here?"

"I was wrong. I've been wrong about almost everything lately. . . ."

"But showing up today is right? Now you've come to your senses?"

Thorpe nodded.

"Am I supposed to be grateful?"

Thorpe started to smile, but her expression changed his mind. "I just want you to give me a chance. Give *us* a chance."

"Now there's an us?"

Thorpe took her hand, but she pulled away. "I'm sorry."

"Great, that changes everything."

"At least let me thank you," said Thorpe. "You ran into a man the day I disappeared. He showed you a photo of me, and you pretended not to know who I was. That was a brave thing to do."

"It wasn't brave. I *don't* know who you are."

"Don't play games."

"*Me?*"

Thorpe heard Claire's laugh and realized how much he had missed the clean sound of it, the way it drew him in. He laughed along with her, laughed at himself and all the rules he set for himself, all the things he felt compelled to keep track of, and none of them were working anymore.

"Who are you, Frank? This is your big chance to tell me. I know you're not an insurance salesman. I know you're generous with your booze and miserly with the truth. I know you like rescuing damsels in distress—"

"I'm a guy who wants to stop what he's been doing. A guy who wants to change and doesn't know if he can." Thorpe took her hand again, and this time she let him. "I missed you. There hasn't been a day since I left . . ." He shook his head. "That night we sat on the steps, you told me that we couldn't wait for the perfect moment. That sometimes we just have to reach out for what's in front of us. I'm here, Claire. I'm *here.*"

Claire watched him, still on guard. He didn't blame her. "What happened to that horrible man who was looking for you? He acted like a bumbling accountant, but he had the eyes of a rapist. I called you as soon as I drove off. I remember being almost embarrassed that he had scared me, but I called you anyway."

"I never got the message. I had switched phones."

"What *happened* to him, Frank?"

Thorpe shook his head. "Don't worry, he won't be back."

Claire's eyes were large and fearless. "You took care of him, did you? That's the kind of person you are?"

"Yes."

"Just like that?"

"It wasn't that easy, Claire."

"No . . . I don't imagine it was. It's over now, though?"

"It's over."

"Good. I don't know what he did, but I'm glad he won't be back."

Thorpe put his arms around her, kissed her, and their bodies fit together easily, his hands resting against the small of her back as he buried his face in her hair. They stood there in the empty classroom, slow-dancing in the silence.

She turned her head. "What's your name?" she said softly. "Your *real* name."

He hesitated.

She waited, her face sad now. He wished she were angry; he could deal with that. She pushed him away, shoved papers into her briefcase, and headed up the steps, her pale green skirt swirling around her knees like a rising tide.

He watched her leave, and it was as if he was underwater again, back in the front seat of the Buick, the Engineer adrift beside him, dead fingers waving. Thorpe could see the lights on the dock shimmering above him as he tore at the headrest, the lights getting dimmer as he ran out of air, then dimmer still, his chest feeling like it was about to burst. "Thorpe," he croaked out as Claire reached the door. "My real name is Frank Thorpe."

She turned, looked back at him. "That's a good name."

He took the steps two at a time.

ALSO BY ROBERT FERRIGNO

FLINCH

Frightening, feral, and funny, *Flinch* is a fast-paced noir set amid the frenzied freak show of Southern California. Tabloid journalist Jimmy Gage and his plastic-surgeon brother, Jonathan, have long had a twisted and sometimes nearly fatal rivalry, but the ante was upped when Jonathan recently married Jimmy's ex. So when Jimmy begins to suspect that Jonathan is the serial killer known as The Eggman, he's neither surprised nor displeased. What ensues is this harried and hard-edged whodunnit that involves everyone from petty porn stars to WWF wannabes to gut-wrenchingly gruesome gangsters and gang lords. *Flinch* is an intricately plotted whirlwind of a tale that will grip you until the very last page.

Crime Fiction/1-4000-3024-2

SCAVENGER HUNT

Philip Marlowe and Lew Archer would recognize a kindred spirit in Jimmy Gage, reporter for *SLAP* magazine, troublemaker by trade and inclination, and the hero of Robert Ferrigno's sinuous crime novel. While taking part in a Hollywood scavenger hunt, Jimmy meets Garret Walsh, a bad-boy moviemaker in the truest sense: He's just been released from prison after serving seven years for the murder of a teenage girl. But Walsh claims he was framed and is writing a screenplay to prove it. He wants Jimmy to help him peddle it, sight unseen. The next time Jimmy sees the director, he's floating face-down in a koi pond and "The Most Dangerous Screenplay in Hollywood" has disappeared. Is Walsh a casualty of bad habits or has somebody crossed him off a list? And is Jimmy next? Combining nerve-shredding suspense and heat-seeking satire, *Scavenger Hunt* is an addictive read.

Crime Fiction/1-4000-3254-7

VINTAGE CRIME/BLACK LIZARD
Available at your local bookstore, or call toll-free to order:
1-800-793-2665 (credit cards only)